# MANHATTAN
# NORTH
# HOMICIDE

# MANHATTAN
# NORTH
# HOMICIDE

### Detective First Grade
# Thomas McKenna
### *NYPD*

### and

# William Harrington

St. Martin's Press ☙ New York

A Thomas Dunne Book

MANHATTAN NORTH HOMICIDE. Copyright © 1996 by Thomas McKenna
and William Harrington. All rights reserved. Printed in the United States
of America. No part of this book may be used or reproduced in any man-
ner whatsoever without written permission except in the case of brief quo-
tations embodied in critical articles or reviews. For information, address
St. Martin's Press, 175 Fifth Avenue, New York, N.Y. 10010.

Library of Congress Cataloging-in-Publication Data

McKenna, Thomas, 1941-
    Manhattan North homicide / by Thomas McKenna with William
Harrington.
        p.    cm.
    "A Thomas Dunne book."
    ISBN 0-312-14010-X
    1. McKenna, Thomas. 1941-   .   2. Detectives—New York (N.Y.)
—Biography.     I. Harrington, William. 1931-   .   II. Title.
HV7911.M358A3   1996
363.2'59523'092—dc20
[B]                                                            95–25909
                                                                  CIP

First Edition: April 1996

10 9 8 7 6 5 4 3 2 1

# CONTENTS

# PREFACE

Police work is not a job. It is a career. With this thought in mind, on February 15, 1965, I swore to uphold the Constitution of the United States and the laws of the State of New York. So far, my career has been everything I could have imagined it would be and a little more. Times of great happiness and periods of sadness have marked my thirty years of service. The good times far outweigh the bad.

As you the reader travel with me through my years of police work, please take note of the men and women with whom I have been privileged to share my experiences, for they are in fact largely responsible for my success. I dedicate this book to them.

To Bob Bratko, my first partner, who remained cool and level-headed in all circumstances.

To John McNally, who saw things that mere mortals could not see.

To Bill Muldoon, a friend and partner.

To Jim Mugan and Tom Conroy, who taught me daily the meaning of the word loyalty.

To Tom Sullivan, who brings humor and uncanny ability to work each day.

To Chris Heimgartner, who surely never fell off a turnip truck.

And finally to Bill Kelly, brother, partner, friend, and confidant. Thanks for all those years of kicking down doors. It's been fun.

I also dedicate this book to my wife, Marie. Thank you for teaching me the meaning of understanding and for sharing your love. You were so easy to come home to after seeing the misery of the streets.

To my children, Danielle, Tom, Kerry, Tara, and Kelly Ann. I am so lucky to have children such as you.

To the families of the victims whose stories we tell here. You are remembered in my prayers.

To the persons responsible for these horrendous crimes—tough shit, *do your time.*

Thomas McKenna

# MANHATTAN NORTH HOMICIDE

# 1

## THE CENTRAL PARK JOGGER

DURING THE NIGHT OF WEDNESDAY, April 19, 1989, a young woman was attacked, brutally beaten, raped, sodomized, robbed, and left bound and gagged, bleeding, naked, and unconscious in Central Park, Manhattan. Within a few days the case of the Central Park Jogger was known worldwide. She was not expected to survive. She did, but she had been permanently damaged. Some of her attackers would admit that they had committed these vicious crimes for no better reasons than that "it was fun" and "it was something to do." They had been—to use their term—"wilding."

I was at the time a second-grade detective assigned to the Manhattan North Homicide Squad. Because the Jogger was not expected to live, our squad was called in immediately to assist in the investigation. I had no idea then what demands the case ultimately would make on me and on many others.

On Monday, July 16, 1990, I met her at last.

I am not going to use her name. In fact, throughout this book I am going to omit some names and change others—though never without telling you—because some people

1

have endured enough and should not be subjected to more pain and suffering. I am going to call this young woman the Jogger. Timothy Sullivan called her Paula Harris, which is not her name, in his book *Unequal Verdicts,* perhaps because it would have been awkward to write a whole book without naming the principal character. The Jogger appears in only one or two chapters of this book, and I use the term New Yorkers—in fact, people all over the world—learned to call her. Too many people do know her name. No one is going to learn it from me.

Beginning about a month before the day I met her, three of her attackers—Yusef Salaam, Anton McCray, and Raymond Santana—had gone on trial in Manhattan Supreme Court. To say the trial was a media circus would be an understatement. Competing newspeople fought each other for access to everyone involved. On July 16 the Jogger herself was to testify. Although one or two newspapers had used her name, the great majority of newspeople had declined to print it—if they knew it. But to get a picture of her, to spread her face across newspaper pages and on television screens, was an obsession. To my way of thinking, that was sort of ghoulish, but I guess it's a fact of life.

The Jogger needed protection, not just for her face and name, but for her physical safety. Reporters and photographers jostling a young woman made fragile by her injuries would be only part of the problem. The Jogger had been threatened with violence, even death. To most people she symbolized the pathetic victim of senseless violence. To a few she represented something very different, an attack by the white establishment on a group of minority teenagers; and those who felt that way had threatened her life. I was one of the men assigned to bring her to court, to get her in without her being assaulted and to get her out safely afterward.

TARU, the Technical Assistance Resource Unit of the New York Police Department, had provided an unmarked van, which we planned to use to take the Jogger to the courthouse, on Center Street, not far from the Manhattan end of the Brooklyn Bridge. We had checked out the building in advance and secured permission to drive into the basement, where normally only judges and a few others could park. The ramp also was used for buses delivering prisoners for court appearances.

We arranged to meet at 72nd Street and Third Avenue at about six-thirty in the morning. We parked the van. Detective Joe Flynn of TARU was the driver, and I sat in front with him. In the rear were bench seats facing inward and one revolving captain's chair in the center. Bill Kelly, my partner for the last seventeen years, sat in the rear with Detective Bert Arroyo. The van had windows, but no one could see in. The windows were of smoked glass and visibility was one way— out.

The Jogger was brought to 72nd Street and Third Avenue in a long black limousine. In fact, there were three black limousines. She was employed at Salomon Brothers, the investment banking firm, which had provided twenty-four-hour security for her ever since her injury. Jim Stone was the man responsible for her safety. I had worked with him before, and we knew each other. He knew exactly how we would proceed, and so did the Jogger, in fact, since she had been briefed by the prosecutor, Elizabeth Lederer.

I had been told the Jogger was nervous about going to court this morning, and I won't deny that I was a little nervous myself. I had seen the pictures of her taken at the hospital shortly after the attack, and I wondered what she could look like now. In the fourteen months that had passed, she had undergone reconstructive surgery, but still I had doubts about how much could be done to restore a face so badly damaged that one of her closest friends had been unable to identify her. That young man had stared intently at her for ten minutes and had been unable to decide if she was the young woman he knew most intimately. Only when he was shown a ring that had been taken from her finger was he able to say, yes, that was a ring worn by his friend.

The Good Lord, or maybe something in the human spirit, had been very kind to her in one sense. She remembered nothing of the attack until seven weeks afterward. Her doctors had not pressed her to recover that part of her memory—and of course the prosecutors had not either, though her testimony would have been valuable. So far as I know, she still does not remember.

She got out of one of the limousines, accompanied by a man and a woman, her friends, and walked toward the van. She was a small, thirty-year-old woman, maybe five feet four, blond, her hair cut short. Her face was scarred but not conspicuously so. One of her scars was partially covered by the way her hair was combed across her forehead. I hadn't seen pictures taken of her before the attack, but I am told she'd been very pretty. She was still quite attractive.

She was dressed in a purple business suit. Walking toward us, at first she appeared entirely in control of herself. We were introduced all around, and she smiled and shook hands with each of us. When she moved to step up into the van, though, she lost her balance and almost fell. I took her arm to steady her. She was a pleasant girl, who didn't appear to demand sympathy. As I would see, she had difficulty sitting down and standing up and had to reach for support. She could not climb or descend stairs without clinging to the banisters. I would learn later that she had double vision and had to hold printed material far out to her left to be able to read it.

In homicide cases, detectives ordinarily don't get to know the victims. They're dead at the scene or have been taken to a hospital. A one-on-one between a detective and an intended homicide victim is a rarity. Often I do interview the family or friends of victims. I try not to become emotionally involved in cases, but here I couldn't help but be deeply moved. This young woman had been the victim of predators.

I was sympathetic. I couldn't help but be. Yet, more than anything, I admired her.

That morning in July she was facing another ordeal, this one in the courtroom. It had been said that she was a slut, that she had never been raped, that the semen found in her body had come from consensual acts with one or more boyfriends, that one of her boyfriends had beaten her out of jealousy. A vocal element of the community argued that the whole problem was that black and Hispanic youths were accused of raping a white girl. No one could guess what she would face in the courtroom. That morning she demonstrated a strength no one could have expected of her—though they might have guessed. After all, she had survived.

The limos followed us as we headed for the East River Drive and downtown to the courthouse.

I sat again in the front seat, turning to look at the Jogger and listen to her.

I saw and heard a young woman who, on April 19, 1989, probably saw nothing ahead of her but success and satisfaction. Intelligent, hardworking, dedicated, attractive, she'd had a brilliant career ahead of her. There had been probably no limit on how high she could have gone at Salomon Brothers or anywhere else.

On April 20, 1989, I was working the 4:00 P.M.–to–midnight shift. Long before I reported in, I knew what I would be working on that day. The Jogger story dominated the local news on radio and television. I had no idea what demands the case would ultimately make, but I knew my squad would be assigned to the case.

When I arrived at the office, 120 East 119th Street, that afternoon, I was told, "Sign in. We're on our way to Central Park."

Because the crime had been committed in the park, the case was primarily the responsibility of Central Park Detective Squad. As a rape case, it was within the jurisdiction of the Sex Crimes Squad. Manhattan North Homicide was called in only because the victim was not expected to live. There was a little rivalry as to who would take chief responsibility for the case, but that was never a real problem.

Every member of our squad is a specialist in homicide investigation. Manhattan North Homicide Squad has been called an elite group within NYPD. For reasons of modesty, *I* wouldn't say it—except that it has been said many times by many commentators, in the press and otherwise. We have been called "seasoned veterans," for example. Every one of us spent years as a precinct detective before being picked for Manhattan North Homicide Squad by our commanding officer, Lieutenant Jack Doyle. When I was assigned to the Jogger case, I had been on the Job twenty-four years. I'd carried the gold shield of a detective for twenty years. The junior man in our squad has twenty-one years of experience. I can't say we never fail. But we're the older guys, the pros, and we have a lot of pride at stake every time we work a case.

We carry no deadwood. Every one of our detectives brings something to the table. Everyone is megatalented. We are experienced men, and we are the best at what we do: investigate murder.

In one sense, we are our own judges. A man may step behind other men when they face a door where a gunman inside may be ready to fire. He may do it once or twice. If he does it three times, we'll know. All of us will know, and he'll have a reputation for it. We are judged also by our superiors. A detective may overlook an important fact once or twice. If he does it more often, his superiors will know. We depend on each other, and the department depends on us—and the city depends on the department.

The building housing the Central Park Precinct is tiny. That afternoon it was surrounded outside and jammed inside with people from the news media. Before the day was over the investigation was moved to the Twentieth Precinct on West 82nd Street, where there was much more room.

The facts of the Jogger case are well known, and I don't intend to go into all of them. For the purposes of this book, I want to tell only my own part. The basic facts were these.

The night before a group of youths—the number usually accepted is thirty-six, though there may have been more—decided to go "wilding" in Central Park. Roving as a gang, they would mug joggers and cyclists and anyone else they found. They would take money or radios, or whatever, but they were there more to beat people than to rob them. I don't think any of them went there intending to commit rape.

On the whole, these young men did not come from impoverished families. They had not lived in great prosperity, and most came from broken families, but generally they had had reasonably decent lives. They did not mug people for money to buy food. Nor did they do it to get money for drugs. They did it for the joy of beating people, then running on to another encounter and beating someone else. It was about power—mob power, face-in-the-crowd power, coward power. Their numbers gave them anonymity, they thought, and made it possible for them to do things they wouldn't have risked doing alone.

During the evening and night, the gang beat several people, including an addict in his fifties. They went after two men and let them go unharmed, one because a member of the gang knew him, the other because he was with his girl and some odd scruple deterred them. Some bicyclists escaped from them. Then the gang encountered the Jogger.

She was a slight young woman with the hard body of someone who ran every day. It might not be too much to say she was an obsessive jogger. She worked until early or middle evening every night, and almost every night she went out jogging in Central Park. The gang encountered her on the 102nd Street Crossdrive. They attacked her, dragged her some three hundred feet into a ravine, and there proceeded to rape her. When she resisted, they beat her.

The newspapers would report that she was beaten with a "pipe." That was her attackers' word for the weapon they used on her. It was not a pipe, however; it was a solid steel rod the thickness of a pipe. Some wanted to kill her. Some did not, fearing the consequences. In the end, they left her bound, gagged, and bleeding to death in the dark and damp of a Central Park ravine.

Then they went on to mug and beat other joggers, injuring some of them.

Word of the wilding in Central Park had reached the precinct station, and police officers spread out into the park and made arrests. They didn't know it at the time, but among the youths they arrested were some of the gang who had attacked the Jogger. Since most of them were not yet sixteen years of age, they were released with summonses for later appearances before juvenile authorities. But their names were on record.

The Jogger was found by two homeless men walking across the park. They were messengers of God. There was no reason for them to go into that ravine at that time of night—

it was a place where I, a cop carrying a gun, would not have walked at night without a reason.

When they found her and called for help, the Jogger had been lying on the ground maybe six hours.

My squad arrived just as the investigation was moved to the Twentieth Precinct. Even there, there was not enough room.

From the records of the past night's arrests, coupled with interviews we had conducted all day, we could identify about thirty youths who had been engaged in some kind of unlawful conduct in Central Park the night before. Obviously, not all of them were rapists and robbers—potentially murderers, since no one expected the Jogger to live. Our duty, then, was to interview all of them and try to sort the case out—which ones did what.

Other detectives already had interviewed several of the thirty. Some denied having been in Central Park. Some admitted being there and denied having committed any offense. Some named others as having maybe done something wrong.

This is how a case is built. One suspect denies having been in the park at all. Two or three others say he was, though they don't say he did anything wrong. Why would the suspect deny having been there at all—unless he has something to hide?

The interviews we conducted gave us the information we needed to identify the attackers.

We had a number of serious problems, one of which was particularly troubling to me. Every suspect has the right to remain silent and/or to consult with a lawyer before answering any questions. Also, under New York law, police officers must make an honest attempt to contact a parent or guardian of a person under sixteen before conducting an interview. A parent or guardian can exercise on the youth's behalf the same rights, to remain silent or to be advised by an attorney.

Yusef Salaam was in fact only fifteen years old, but he carried a student subway pass that gave his date of birth as February 27, 1973, which would have made him sixteen. On the basis of that pass, I believed he was sixteen and that I could question him without trying to find a parent or guardian.

Even so, he had been advised of his rights and could have refused to talk any more until he was advised by a lawyer. If he had said he didn't want to answer any questions or that he wanted to see an attorney, the interview would have stopped right then.

One of our challenges in interrogating any suspect is that nobody, juvenile or adult, wants to take responsibility for his actions. It's always somebody else who is responsible. Something else. "I grew up in a bad neighborhood. My mother didn't love me. All my friends do this kind of stuff, and I'd have no friends if I didn't go along."

To a detective interviewing a suspect, that last one, peer pressure, can be a great asset. It gives the suspect an out. "Oh," you can say, "I see. You wouldn't have done this except that all your friends would have laughed at you if you didn't. Right?"

It's much better to hear a suspect deny he was even in the vicinity than to hear him say "Oh, yeah, sure, I was there, but when I saw what those guys were doing I cut out." If other witnesses don't put the subject at the scene, you've got a tough case to make. If he says he wasn't there and you hear from others that he was, you've got something going. You've got to take a closer, in-depth look at that guy.

My biggest contribution to the Jogger case was my interview of Yusef Salaam.

He was picked up in his apartment building about 10:00 P.M. on April 20, about twenty-four hours after the attack on the Jogger. Some of the youths questioned earlier had said he was in Central Park when the wilding occurred. When I sat down with him in an interview room on the third floor at Twentieth Precinct, I knew he had been placed in the park, but I did not know that other youths had implicated him in the attack.

Salaam was a tall, well-put-together teenager. He was confident, even cocky, when I questioned him. He denied he had been in Central Park the night before. That made me believe he was lying, since other youths had told us he had been there. I wasn't ready yet to believe he had been a major player, since it was typical that other suspects would try to shift their own culpability to somebody else; but when he denied having been in the park at all, he made me believe he *had* been there. I told him witnesses had placed him there. That didn't shake him. He simply said they were wrong.

We continued to talk, and two or three more times Salaam denied he had been in Central Park the night the Jogger was attacked.

Then I decided to try a ruse. "I don't really care what you say," I told him. "The Jogger was wearing nylon pants. That's a smooth fabric, and we've been able to lift fingerprints off them. If your prints match those, you're going for rape."

It was not true. We could not take fingerprints off her running pants. But the word rape knocked him completely off kilter. Immediately he changed his story. "I was there," he said, "but I didn't rape her."

"Okay," I said. "Suppose you tell me what you did do."

He then admitted he had struck her twice with a pipe and that he had fondled her breasts. Four other boys, he said, had "fucked" her.

Normal procedure is to take an oral statement, as I had

just done, then to reduce the statement to writing and have the suspect sign it, and finally to have him repeat his statement before a video camera. I expected to do the same thing with this suspect, but suddenly the entire process was interrupted. Detective John Taglioni, a member of the homicide squad, came to the interview room and told me that Yusef Salaam's mother, Sharonne Salaam, was downstairs claiming that her son was only fifteen years old.

Also, a lawyer was downstairs asking about him. The lawyer, it turned out, was Salaam's "big brother" in the Big Brother program. He was a federal lawyer attached to the civil division of the U.S. District Attorney's office in Brooklyn. If he was attempting to represent Salaam his appearance at the precinct station was an impropriety. As a federal lawyer, he could not represent a defendant in a state case. What was more, he turned out to have very little knowledge of criminal law.

While this was being sorted out downstairs by Prosecutor Linda Fairstein, I stopped questioning Salaam. He had already admitted having struck the Jogger with a pipe and having fondled her. At first, Ms. Fairstein did not believe Ms. Salaam's story about her son's age. It was not unusual for parents to claim their children were under sixteen to impede an investigation. Ms. Fairstein insisted to the lawyer that his interference was improper and in violation of his obligations as a federal lawyer.

Eventually Ms. Salaam said she would get a lawyer for her son.

At this point Ms. Fairstein sent up word that Yusef Salaam apparently was under sixteen, that his mother was going to get a lawyer for him, and that I should stop questioning him. I did. I had learned a lot from him, but none of it was ever reduced to writing, and he did not give a videotaped statement. At the trial, Salaam's attorney would claim I had coerced his client into making an incriminating statement and would ask for a ruling precluding me from testifying about what the youth had told me.

Because the defendants contradicted each other and did incriminate each other, the Jogger case required two trials. The first began on June 13, 1990. The defendants in that trial were Yusef Salaam, Anton McCray, and Raymond Santana.

The Jogger testified on July 16. The defense lawyers had dreaded her appearance, even though her amnesia would prevent her from describing any of the horrors she had endured. The prosecution wanted the jury to see her. A jury always wants to see a victim. The defense had hoped she would not appear.

Her testimony went chiefly to the question of whose semen had been found on her tights. She testified that she'd had sexual intercourse with a friend earlier on Sunday, April 16, and had immediately thereafter pulled on the tights. That explained why the dried semen found in the crotch of her running tights matched her friend's DNA pattern. Other samples, taken from her body and her socks, did not.

She also told about the permanence of her injuries.

The defense lawyers chose not to cross-examine.

Everyone—judge, jurors, lawyers, and reporters—was impressed by her composure. No courtroom photographs were allowed. Even the sketch artists were ordered to obscure her features, and few of the news media used her name.

A week later, I was called to testify.

My testimony was the case against Yusef Salaam. It was all the prosecution had. There was no physical evidence. New York law does not allow confessions of coconspirators to be used as evidence. The question was: Who would the jurors believe, him or me? It was my word against Salaam's.

I think of myself as a pro, and I try not to get emotionally involved in my work. By the time I appeared in court to testify in the Jogger trial, I was emotionally involved more than I wanted—especially after the Jogger testified. On my first day, of my two days on the witness stand, I put a piece of tape around a finger. If I caught myself feeling too emotional, I'd rub that piece of tape. Several times during cross-examination I noticed Elizabeth Lederer rubbing her finger. She knew about the tape, and it was her signal to me to calm down, slow down.

Besides my word as to what Salaam told me on the night of April 20, 1989, the jurors also had to believe that I had been acting in good faith, really believing the youth was sixteen. If the jurors did not believe my account of what Salaam told me was true, or if they believed I had gone on questioning him knowing he was only fifteen, they would acquit him.

The defense attorney tried to make out that Salaam had been surrounded by detectives who had browbeaten him into making an incriminating statement. I testified that no such thing happened, that in fact he and I were alone together through most of his interview.

It was true that I had tricked him into making an incriminating statement—by saying we had taken fingerprints from the Jogger's running pants. I was asked if I had lied to Salaam. I said no, I had fibbed. The lawyer asked me to tell him the difference between a lie and a fib. I said that the difference, as I saw it, was that a lie might hurt somebody but a fib would not. I could have put it this way: my mother washed my mouth out with soap if I told a lie, but she would only frown and shake her head at a fib.

Several commentators have severely criticized Yusef Salaam's defense attorney. So far as I'm concerned, I've got my job to do, and the lawyer has got his. I do not resent tough cross-examination. I am not a lawyer and wouldn't want to tell a lawyer how to conduct his case. But to my eyes, he exercised bad judgment. My testimony was all the evidence there was against his client. It was damaging, and I think he should have listened to it and left it alone. Instead, he cross-examined me on many of the details. In effect, he asked me to *repeat* my testimony, some parts of it three or four times.

Another thing he did was ask if I really thought Salaam's incriminating statement was true. I said I did believe it. He pressed. He asked me on what basis I believed it to be true? My answer was that certain details Yusef Salaam had told me could not have been known to him unless he had been at the scene of the crime. If the lawyer hadn't asked me, I couldn't have testified as to what I believed about the case. But he not only asked me about what I believed, he asked me to explain *why* I believed it. Those questions and answers were very damaging to the defense.

Finally, the lawyer introduced my notepad into evidence. He wanted to show inconsistencies between the notes I'd written on the night of April 20, 1989 and statements in the report I filed a little later. He had copies made, so each juror could read my notes. Here are my notes about the attack on the Jogger, exactly as I wrote them in a spiral notepad during my interview with Yusef Salaam:

Hit her with pipe. She went down and hit her again. Cory grabbed her shirt. Saw pants being taken off but don't know who. Grabbed her tit while shirt was on and after Cory took it off. Kevin fucked her, Cory, couple of other guys. Got pipe from Cory's house. Bum was hit by guy with gold caps. Spanish jogger gold caps, green army jacket, gold caps. I hit him with my fists. He was crouching down. I got in three hits. It was racial according to gold caps. To me it was something to do. It was fun. Knife is in my house.

This is where the interview stopped when I was informed that an attorney was downstairs, inquiring about Yusef Salaam.

The day after I interviewed Salaam and made these notes, I took the time to write out a fuller report of what the young man had said. I used my notes and my memory of what he had said. Because he thought he could show inconsistencies between my notes and the report, and between both of them and my testimony, the lawyer also had the report copied and had given a copy to each member of the jury. Here is that report in full:

> On 4-19-89 at about 2000 hours he [Salaam] was in front of his building with a group of friends, Kevin, Rayou, Cory, Patrick, Sheron, Rahim, Denis. They were going into Central Park to have some fun. They joined with a group of people (approximately 15 in number) from the Taft Houses. He didn't know anyone by name but had seen them before. He stated that they entered the park and went to the road near the baseball fields. They were standing around waiting for someone to come by. He stated that a short time later a bum came by. [This was Antonio Diaz, an addict in his fifties.] He was eating food and carrying a bag. The guy with the gold tooth (name unknown) [Germain Robinson] from the Taft Houses group punched him and everyone beat him. Someone took his food and poured his beer on him. A little later a male jogger was passing and we were hiding in the trees. We chased

**1 6**

him but couldn't catch him. We heard a police car coming and split up. He [Salaam] went down to the baseball field and the group came together again. The group then saw a man and lady on a bike and tried to stop them but they got away. He went up on the hill and across the road. They were standing near the trees when he saw a female jogger coming. Kevin ran out and stopped her and she started to struggle. Salaam says he approached her and hit her with a pipe, she went down and he hit her again while she was on the ground. They took her off the road toward the trees and Cory grabbed her shirt. He [Salaam] says he was feeling her breasts while the shirt was on. Cory then pulled off her shirt and he [Salaam] began to feel her up. He saw her pants being taken off but doesn't know who was taking them off. Kevin then got on top of her and "fucked" her. Cory then "fucked" her. A couple of the other guys fucked her but he doesn't know them. He says he then left them and went back into the tree line. He was with the guy with the gold cap and others when he observed a male jogger in a green jacket coming, he says he didn't want to go near this guy because he might have a gun or something but when the guy passed him the guy with the gold tooth ran behind him and punched him in the head, the jogger crouched down, and Yusef ran out and gave him three hits to the head with his fists. He heard the sirens coming so he ran. He and the guy with the gold caps then went to the subway with 3 others and took the train home. He says the guy with the gold teeth said he was getting even for the time he got beat up by white guys. He further states that he took the pipe from Cory's house and described it as being about 16 inches

**1 7**

long with tape on it. He said he also had a knife which he had taken from home. He returned the knife to his house, but he dropped the pipe and someone else picked it up. I asked him if during the assault on the female he saw anyone using a brick and he said yes but he didn't know who it was.

Interview was stopped when I was informed that an attorney was inquiring about Salaam.

Salaam had not given me a written statement, but it was the same as if he had, since my notes and report were shown to the members of the jury. While they were hearsay and could have been excluded from evidence, Salaam's attorney wanted the jury to see them.

Elizabeth Lederer told me later that my testimony on cross-examination was a classic case of a detective coping with hostile cross-examination. She gave me a copy of the transcript and said she was sorry she couldn't have it bound in gold.

Yusef Salaam did not make a good witness for himself. There he sat on the stand, a teenager facing years in prison, and he showed no sign of concern or fear. He let the prosecutor drive him to displaying his temper. Worst of all for him, I think, was that the jury was comparing his testimony to that of a detective with twenty-five years of experience as a police officer. If he'd looked like a scared kid to the jury, he might have made them believe him.

But that was not what he and his handlers wanted. They had all decided, I believe, to show him to the city as a black kid who could sit and trade words with the establishment— and make them all look stupid. Well . . . he couldn't, and he didn't, and the tactic resulted in convictions for rape, robbery, assault, and riot—and a sentence of five to ten years.

Salaam's appeal has been rejected by the Court of Appeals. He was represented by William Kunstler. One of the grounds for appeal was that my testimony about Salaam's statement should have been excluded.

The Jogger case almost cost me my marriage—and I have a good marriage. It is my second marriage. My wife, Marie—I call her Mimi—and I are deeply in love, and we love and are proud of our daughter, Danielle. My wife understands the demands of the Job and has always been supportive. Still, she is a wife, not a cop, and this case was almost more than she could take.

I know of four marriages that broke up because of the Jogger case.

The initial investigation took only a couple of weeks. Then, for a long time, nothing happened as far as I was concerned. The prosecutors were working, developing their case, but beyond an occasional interview, none of our squad was called on. Then the case got more complicated, and the prosecutor, Elizabeth Lederer, asked that I and my partners, Bill Kelly and John Taglioni, be assigned to it.

Elizabeth Lederer and Arthur Clements, who worked with her, needed more evidence, witnesses on specific elements of the developing case for the prosecution. I suppose Ms. Lederer spent seven days a week for a year preparing for trial. I spent as many as eighteen hours a day, rarely less than fourteen, for six months.

The many witnesses in this case ran the gamut from socially responsible to drug addicts on maintenance programs. All of them had to be interviewed and prepared for their testimony at trial. On more than one occasion, Bill Kelly and I sat outside a methadone center at 114th Street and Broadway, waiting for a witness to show up for his medication. The center opened at 7:00 A.M. and closed at 7:00 P.M. Addicts could come in at any time during those twelve hours. Needless to say, our witnesses never came early. When one did show up, we would wait until he had received his medication and then pick him up and take him to the district attorney's office. Ms. Lederer would interview him, and we would take him back to his residence and tell him to meet us again the next day, so we could return him to the DA's office for additional interviewing. Sometimes the witness would meet us, but more often he didn't and we had to go looking for him again. This consumed an immense amount of time.

Besides helping her develop her case, we had to protect Elizabeth Lederer herself. The element in the community that had made the Jogger case a matter of the "system" persecuting black and Hispanic youths also had made Ms. Lederer a villain. They had threatened to kill her. She and the cops, lawyers, and judges might own the courts, they said, but *they* owned the streets.

One of my duties, and Taglioni's, was to pick up Ms. Lederer at home every morning. Then, after a day's work, which might end at eight in the evening, we all met and spent an hour or more planning what had to be done the next day. Afterward we often stopped somewhere for a quick bite before we went home—meaning that it was after midnight when I got home.

My wife was understanding and supportive, but this was outside her experience as the wife of a homicide detective. Normally I put in eight hours at work—came home and didn't talk about what I was doing, and went to work the next day. For six months I came home after midnight, after my family was in bed, and got up and left the house again while they were still in bed. For weeks on end, practically my only contact with Mimi and Danielle was by telephone.

Then I testified. I was called a liar. *Newsday* ran a front-page story with my picture, suggesting I had lied and quoting me—inaccurately—as saying I would have done anything to get a confession from Salaam. My wife was frightened. She called me in tears, asking if I was in trouble. I had to explain that I wasn't in any trouble at all, that this was just what went with a case like this.

The trial was an ordeal for everyone. When the case went to the jury, the ordeal intensified. The jury deliberated for eight days—at the time, a record for a jury being out in a criminal case in New York City, I believe. Today we know much about the arguments that went on in the jury room, but of course at the time we had no idea what the jurors were doing and what was going through their minds. From time to time they sent out requests to review various parts of the evidence. Those requests seemed to suggest conviction, on at least some counts. Then they would send out an inquiry that called the entire case in question. The truth was, we could only guess, only speculate, about what they were doing.

During those days, Taglioni and I never left the prosecutor's office before the jury had retired for the night. One of our responsibilities was to protect Elizabeth Lederer whenever she had to go to the courtroom—and she had to go every time the jury asked for a readback of some testimony or a look at another bit of evidence. Where she crossed the street from her office to the courtroom, she had to run a gauntlet. The newspeople surrounded her, yelling questions. Far worse were the punks who insisted this was a racist prosecution; they threatened her life constantly, yelling threats and obscenities and spitting at her. Had she not been closely guarded, I have no doubt at all she would have been attacked and severely injured if not killed.

So we had to stay in the office. We set up a video player and watched movies.

The jury returned its verdicts on Saturday evening, August 18, 1990. My wife and I had arranged to have dinner with friends that evening at Forelini's, a fine Italian restaurant within a block of the courthouse. Our friends Dave and Kathy Lohle would join us. The four of us were to met at eight.

At six-thirty a call came, saying the jury had sent out a message and that the prosecutor had to return to the court-room. Taglioni and I led Elizabeth Lederer through the usual gauntlet, ugly with shrieking obscenities.

Anyone who has ever worked around a trial knows the routine. When the jury sends out a message, all the principals have to assemble before the court can convene to hear it. The prosecutor had arrived, but the defense attorneys had yet to come to the courtroom. As I stepped out in the hall to smoke a cigarette, one of the newspeople came up to me and said, "There's a verdict." I hurried back in to tell Ms. Lederer, who spoke to a court officer and got a confirmation. After more than a year of preparation and two months of trial, we were about to learn whether the prosecution had been a success.

At this point our duty—Taglioni's and mine—was to notify the department that the jury was returning a verdict. No one knew how the city would react, and the department had to go on alert. In particular, we notified the Fifth Precinct to beef up courthouse security and to send a detail to control the streets in the area.

An hour would pass before all was ready and the court could convene to hear the verdict. During that time I called my wife to tell her what was going on. She cried. She was relieved that the ordeal was over, but she was afraid of what the verdict might be. If the jury acquitted Yusef Salaam, it could only mean they had not believed my testimony. That didn't bother me on a personal level, but it bothered her. I told her to come on in with the Lohles. I would be at the restaurant as soon as I could. We would have our dinner as planned—no matter how it came out.

When the court convened, Judge Thomas Galligan instructed the newspeople in the courtroom that they could not leave and send out their stories until all the verdicts had been read and he had adjourned the court. He also instructed those in the courtroom that no abuse of decorum would be tolerated. Much good that did.

Three detectives sat together in the back row—myself, John Taglioni, and Bert Arroyo, the precinct detective who was the case officer assigned from Central Park at the beginning.

At last the verdicts were read. The defendants were acquitted of attempted murder, but they were convicted on charges of rape, four counts of assault (which included people besides the Jogger who had been assaulted), and riot. We listened. "Guilty, guilty, guilty . . ."

The families and friends of the defendants went into angry hysterics. Reporters bolted for the doors.

When we could, Taglioni, Arroyo, and I went up to the prosecutor's table. For the first time in months, Elizabeth Lederer was able to smile. She hugged me.

"Great job, kid," I said to her.

During the year I worked with her, Elizabeth Lederer and I developed about as close a friendship as two people can have. It was and is a friendship based strictly on being coworkers who learned to respect each other. I continue to hold Liz in the very highest personal regard.

The first chance she had, she got on the telephone and called the Jogger.

We went back to the prosecutor's office, where District Attorney Robert Morgenthau had called a news conference. During that press conference one of the reporters who had been interviewing jurors told us that one had said, "No one on the jury ever doubted the word of Detective Thomas McKenna. He is the best detective in the City of New York, and his credibility is beyond reproach." That got into the news reports.

I was asked to speak during the news conference. I said I was glad we had achieved convictions, because I believed justice had been done. Nobody had won; we had all been losers. The Jogger had lost because her life had been ruined. Yusef Salaam was a loser because his life had been ruined. I felt that way then, and I do now. This kind of tragedy is not like a baseball game with a winning team and a losing one. Everybody loses, including the community.

After the news conference we went at last to Forelini's. Mimi and our friends had been waiting an hour and a half or more. Of course, they knew the verdicts and were very happy for me. In fact, Mimi had seen news reports before she left home.

We sat down at a table. Elizabeth Lederer came into the restaurant. John Taglioni, Bert Arroyo, my partner Bill Kelly, and Mike Sheehan were there too. Sheehan was the lead detective in the Preppie Murder case, as we will see. In fact, most of the prosecutor's staff and most of the detectives involved in the case were there.

Then District Attorney Morgenthau came in. He had reserved a private room in back, where he intended to assemble the prosecutorial staff for dinner. When he saw the detectives, he invited us all to join him—including our friends the Lohles.

Andy Warhol once said that every man has fifteen minutes of fame. I'll be honest with you. I had three months, and you can stick it.

I've testified in I don't know how many homicide trials, but the Jogger case was the only time I had artists in the courtroom sketching me. I was not comfortable in the spotlight. I didn't mind it, okay, but it is not me. I'm a detective, not an actor. I don't want to be a public figure.

I understand why it was that way. Central Park is world famous. People everywhere know about it. It's supposed to be a safe place. Crime in Central Park is crime against New York. When you commit a dastardly crime there, you can plan on concentrated attention by the media and the full attention of the police. So the Jogger case was tried under hot lights. I'd just as soon do my job away from those lights.

Today the Jogger is back at her job as an executive at Salomon Brothers. She has a good job and is well thought of. Although she still has trouble with her balance and difficulty with reading, she is a success by anyone's standards. But how much more success, what greater contribution to the community, what greater satisfaction in a life well lived were beaten out of her by young men who had no better motive for what they did than that "it was fun" and "it was something to do"?

# ■● 2

## NO TWO MURDERS ARE ALIKE

WHAT IS A TYPICAL DAY for a New York homicide detective? Here are the stories of a few rather ordinary cases, the kind of thing we do every day—except for the last case described in this chapter. That one was far from typical.

Sunday, March 23, 1986, is as good a place to start as any.

On that day, coming to work, I was handed a report of a shooting that had just occurred at 163rd Street and Amsterdam Avenue. The report was that two men had been shot. One was dead on the street. The other had been taken to Columbia Presbyterian Hospital in Washington Heights. It was not a particularly unusual case, but it shows what you have to expect when you come to work. This investigation had little or no emotional content for me. Catching this killer was my job, and I went about doing it in the usual way, using the experience I'd gained over the years.

My partner that day was Joe Montuori. We went to the scene first, and at about five-forty we arrived at Columbia Presbyterian. There I attempted to interview a man named Glen Allen, a black male, thirty-six years of age, who had a gunshot wound on his arm and was waiting for treatment.

His home address was on Courtland Avenue in Yonkers. He said that he and a friend known to him only as Bee had been at 116th and Amsterdam. Suddenly Bee yelled, "Oh, shit!" and someone began to shoot at them. Bee went down. Allen ran but was hit in the arm.

Allen insisted he had no idea who the shooters were or why they shot at him and Bee. He described the shooters as two male blacks with dark skin, about five feet ten, maybe 150 pounds.

The case did not look like a drug shooting because Bee and Allen were middle-age men. Drug shootings usually involve very young people.

Joe and I returned to the scene. The usual procedure would be to try to question people who were on the street, people in the neighborhood. Unfortunately, often no one will admit to having seen anything, even though four hundred people may have been on the street at the time of a shooting. That's just the way it is. Many people don't want to testify. If you've ever been a witness, maybe you can understand. There are all kinds of reasons, ranging from the fact that you can be tied up in court for days on end to the suffering Julia had to endure when she became a witness against Arturo Garcia—of which much more later.

Glen Allen had said he had run into the office of a private car service to hide, so I went to the office of a private car service called Night Rider, at 165th Street and Amsterdam Avenue. I interviewed the dispatcher, a woman named Bowden, and she said that about five-ten, she had been sitting behind the desk and a male black had run in and had hidden behind a pinball machine. She noticed that he was bleeding, and she asked him what had happened. He said he'd been shot. She dialed 911 and asked for the police. She had not seen the shooting. All she could tell us was that a man who had been shot had come in and ducked behind the pinball machine.

I next interviewed a man by the name of Lorenzo "Peanut" Corbett. He said he'd been standing outside the car service office and someone told him a man had been shot. He went inside and saw a black man lying on the floor behind the pinball machine, who said that he and his friend had just been walking along the street when two men had started shooting at them. That was all Corbett knew. The witness hadn't asked why anybody would shoot at this particular pair of men.

Obviously this investigation was going absolutely nowhere, so at about six-thirty I decided to return to Columbia Presbyterian. At that time Glen Allen was still in the crash room. The crash room is where critical patients are stabilized and prepared for surgery—though sometimes an emergency arises and surgery is performed right there. Many lives are saved in the crash room. Because Allen was wounded in the arm and not in the head or chest, he had been bandaged and was waiting for surgery. I asked the nurse if I could talk to him for five minutes, and she said sure and left.

When I questioned Allen again, he stuck with his story. He didn't know who Bee was, had never heard him called anything but Bee, and he had no idea who had shot him. At this point I asked him just how good a friend of his Bee was. He said he was his best friend—his best friend, whose name he didn't know. I said, "Well, I've got to find out who he was, because we've got to notify his next of kin. He's dead."

Until this point Glen Allen hadn't been told that Bee was dead. That got to him, all the way. He began to cry, and he said, "Lonnie did it."

I asked him where I could find Lonnie, and he said at 160 Walberton Avenue in Yonkers. Lonnie lived on the tenth floor but Allen didn't know the apartment number. He said he'd known Lonnie for a long time and that Lonnie did crack.

I asked him why Lonnie would shoot Bee. He said, "Well, maybe Bee did something."

So, okay. Only an hour and a half after we got the first report of the shootings, I had the name and address of a suspect, which wasn't bad progress. I got back to my office about eight o'clock and called the Yonkers police department. I told detectives there that we had the name of a suspect who was said to live at 160 Walberton Avenue. I explained the facts of the investigation to a Detective Wyka. Wyka said he would contact the narcotics division supervisor and have him call me.

A little later Sergeant Josh Landres of the Yonkers police department called and informed me that Lonnie was in fact Ralph Norman of 211B Walberton Avenue, where he lived with a girlfriend, name unknown, on the tenth floor. He was well known to the Yonkers police.

At nine-thirty my partner Joe Montuori and I went to the Yonkers PD and met with Detective Vinnie Catalano of the narcotics division. During this conversation Catalano left the office for a couple of minutes. When he came back he said a CI—confidential informant—had told him that on Friday night two men had robbed Lonnie at gunpoint, taking his money, his jewelry, and some crack. The two men were known to the informant as Majestic and Bernard. Bernard was Bee—full name Bernard Wade—and Majestic was Glen Allen.

Now we had the motive. Majestic and Bee had ripped off Lonnie, Lonnie had caught up with them and opened fire. Bee was dead. Majestic was lucky to be alive.

The CI had no idea that Bernard was dead. His information had come from the street. It was what he had heard.

Now the story was around—Bernard was dead.

At about ten o'clock I obtained a picture of Ralph Norman, aka Lonnie, from Yonkers PD. I took the picture to the hospital and showed it to Glen Allen. He said yes, the man in the picture was the man he knew as Lonnie. Okay. Progress. Within six hours after the shooting, I had one dead, one wounded, and positive identification of the shooter.

The question now was: Should we go after Lonnie or ask Yonkers PD to pick him up? I decided to do both. As a New York City police officer, I can arrest anywhere in the state— as a Yonkers officer can arrest in the city.

I got home about 4:00 A.M., dead-tired. Even so, by eleven the next morning I was back at my office. I've said investigation of homicides is just business. That isn't exactly so, of course. When you're really on the track of a murderer, its more than just business.

At this time my regular partners in the Thirty-fourth Precinct were Joe Montuori and Philip Torres. We three went up to Yonkers.

Should we go to the apartment where Lonnie might be, or should we just patrol the streets looking for him? The call was mine, and I opted not to go to the apartment. If we had gone there and missed him, he would likely find out we were looking for him and make himself scarce.

We patrolled the streets where we knew he hung out. The Yonkers narcotics squad was looking for him too.

We looked for him all afternoon. About five-forty we went back to the city. The Yonkers guys said they would continue to look for Lonnie. A little after nine o'clock, Sergeant Landres called me at home and said they had Lonnie in custody in their station house. They had grabbed him on the street. He'd had a gun in his pocket, and they were holding him on a weapons-possession charge.

I left home and went up to Yonkers, where I confronted Ralph Norman, aka Lonnie, read him his rights, and proceeded to interview him. The way we do that is we read a subject's rights off a card. We date that card, write the time on it, and initial it. Then we write the time and date on the back and ask the subject to sign it. Most of them do sign it.

How did he come to be called Lonnie? I asked. He said his middle name was Alonzo, and he'd shortened it to Lonnie. He also said his first name, Ralph, was "a dog's name." He was cool to the ladies, and he just couldn't imagine them calling him Ralph.

I asked him about the shootings. He said he knew nothing about any shootings. Oh, he'd heard about them, but what he'd heard on the street was all he knew. Did he know the two men? I asked. He said he knew Bernard—Bee. He said he'd heard on the street that Bernard had been killed downtown and that Majestic had been with him. He said he'd heard they had been ripping off the crack spots in Manhattan and had gotten shot. He said he'd never heard of a man named Glen Allen. He did know Majestic, and Majestic had ripped him off on Friday night.

At that point I asked him to give me a written statement, which he did.

What had he done on Sunday, the day of the shootings? He said he always got up early. He'd hung out on the block, then had gone to see his girlfriend. He said he'd watched a boxing match on TV in his girlfriend's apartment, and he told me the name of one of the fighters he had seen. He said his girlfriend had been with him all the time he was watching the fight.

He admitted to dealing crack but asked that his mother not be told.

I told him then that ballistics tests had matched the gun he was carrying when he was arrested to the one that had killed Bernard Wade—a fib. He said he'd had the gun for six months but that it had never been used to kill anyone. I told him ballistics didn't lie, but he insisted the gun had not been used to kill anyone. I told him Majestic had identified him as the shooter, and he said Majestic was lying.

At this time he said he thought he'd better get a lawyer. That of course concluded the interview.

It was now about ten-thirty on the evening after the shooting. I went back to get an arrest warrant. Actually, I didn't really need one. The Yonkers police department was holding Lonnie on the gun charge, and I could have taken him back to Manhattan without a warrant. Crossing from Westchester County into the city is not like extradition.

But I did get an arrest warrant. I swore an affidavit and appeared before a judge. There is always a judge available twenty-four hours a day, 365 days a year. He issued the warrant. I presented that warrant to a Westchester County judge, who transferred Lonnie into my custody. I took him back into the city, where he was charged with murder. He was convicted and is doing twenty-five years to life.

This was a smooth investigation. Everything went right. It was typical of the cases I handled in the Thirty-fourth Precinct. That's "a day in the life of." Some cases are very difficult and take months to resolve, but many cases work like this one. You have to know what you're doing, but the investigation goes from point A to point B, and you follow the trail to the end.

On Tuesday, May 20, 1980, a group of friends—eight young Hispanics, five males and three females—were in Edgecombe Park. This park is bounded on the west by Edgecombe Avenue and on the east by Harlem River Drive, which runs parallel to the Harlem River. A little farther north it is called

High Bridge Park, but it is all the same park. Young people in the area go to Edgecombe Park to play or to hang out.

These friends were teenagers, with an average age of about fifteen. They were in an area of the park called the Swing, so called because it is equipped with swings, seesaws, slides, and the like. They were not there for any particular purpose, just to mingle and socialize.

About 12:30 P.M. a group of nine older black males came into the park looking for a confrontation. They were after members of a street gang called the Aztecs, and they took this group of eight to be Aztecs. The fact is, they were wrong. None of these kids was a member of the Aztecs or even had any association with that gang.

The blacks were members of a gang that called itself the BJs. In the forefront of this group was a male, twenty-one years old, named Kelvin Strong. The night before, Kelvin's eighteen-year-old girlfriend—we'll call her Rose—had been harassed and pushed around by members of the Aztecs. She had not been beaten or robbed, but she had been taunted, jostled, and generally humiliated. Kelvin was looking for Aztecs so he could save face for himself and Rose and take revenge.

Besides the nine young men who had come into the park, four or five other members of the BJs stood out on Edgecombe Avenue and watched. To get from there down into the park, you have to go down about fifteen steps, so these others were well above and looking down.

Among the group up on the sidewalk was Calvin Strong, Kelvin's identical twin. Both these young men were exceptionally well built; they looked as if they might have been bodybuilders. They were not very tall, but they were built like fireplugs, with broad shoulders and thick chests, no waists, and very muscular arms and legs.

The BJs had come to have it out with some Aztecs. They

expected a fight. None of them, though, expected to kill any-body—with the possible exception of Kelvin Strong.

Kelvin and his group corraled the eight Hispanic kids and began to ask them questions: "Are you Aztecs?" "Are any of your brothers Aztecs?" "Are any of your friends Aztecs?" The answers to all these questions were no.

Kelvin Strong was not satisfied with the answers he was getting, so he took out a gun and began to pistol-whip the kids. The more he did that without getting the answers he wanted, the more furious he got—until eventually he decided he was going to make his point by shooting somebody.

He took a young man named Ramon Ariga, sixteen years old, and had him sit on a swing. He told Ramon to swing. Ramon did; he began to swing back and forth, terrified and shaking. Kelvin aimed his gun at Ramon from about six feet away and fired one shot. His bullet hit Ramon in the head, killing him.

The Hispanic girls began to scream. The BJs broke and ran, up the steps and out of the park.

The first police unit that responded took the names of as many as possible of the people who were there. One who had remained was Calvin Strong! Well, Calvin knew he hadn't done anything, so he didn't figure he had to run.

We interviewed all these people, including Calvin Strong. He denied any knowledge of anything that had happened. He denied seeing anything. Of course, he did not say his brother was involved.

He did admit he had heard of a group called the BJs. They came from an area around 135th Street and Broadway. They were one of many street gangs in the city at that time who made a practice of setting up players and amplifiers and play-ing music—loud. They called themselves DJs—disk jockeys. They weren't on the radio. They just set up their equipment on the street or in the middle of a project and blared music, to which some people danced. This gang did that. How it got from DJs to BJs, I don't know.

We went to the Youth Gang Task Force. A detective there by the name of Ivan Guinall supplied us with the names of some members of the BJs. The names included the Strong brothers, Kelvin and Calvin.

That made a good place to start. We had a description of the shooter that included the information that he'd been wearing a black hat, black jacket, black pants, and sneakers. We went to 201 West 112th Street, the residence of the Strong family, arriving there about six hours after the shooting.

Kelvin answered the door. He was still wearing the black jacket, black pants, and sneakers. He'd seen no reason to change his clothes. We asked him to step outside the apartment, and we placed him under arrest. We had there a prima facie case. He matched the description of the shooter, was wearing the described clothes, and was a member of the named gang, the BJs.

Kelvin denied he was the shooter. He said his brother had shot Ramon Ariga.

Do I need to say we had a problem? If we put these identical twins in a lineup facing the witnesses to the shooting, who can say which one is fish and which one is fowl? As we were to discover, some of their closest friends were not always sure which one they were talking to.

Calvin had given us the names of the young men who had been standing on the sidewalk with him. We brought them in for interviews. All four of them said Calvin had been up on the sidewalk with them. Problem was, how could they be sure the one who had been standing beside them was Calvin and not Kelvin?

We dressed the two brothers identically and put them in a lineup. I must say frankly that I couldn't tell them apart. Then we let these four friends look at them. Two of the friends could not tell which was which. The other two could.

We called their mother in. Initially she denied either of her sons had anything to do with the murder of Ramon Ariga. At that time she had not spoken with her sons. When she did talk with Kelvin, he admitted to her that he was the shooter.

After that, Kelvin admitted to us that he had shot the kid and said his brother had had nothing to do with it. Maybe his mother had persuaded him to confess.

Bill Harrington had a couple of questions. "First, what became of the gun?"

"We recovered it."

"Well then, wouldn't the fingerprints have identified Kelvin from Calvin?"

"My friend, you are obsessed with fingerprints. You almost never get fingerprints off a gun. *Almost never.* The surfaces are too rough. Sometimes you get them off a bullet."

"Okay, next question. What happened to Kelvin Strong?"

"He got twenty-five years to life."

"My final question is, what did the other BJs think of what Kelvin had done? I mean, they stood and watched their friend and fellow gang member commit a senseless, brutal murder. How did they react to that?"

"It didn't bother *them* any. They didn't care. All they cared was that they hadn't done it and they wouldn't do the time for it."

Ironically, the next case I caught in the Three-four Squad was six months later. (Probably I should explain that in the police department we call the Thirty-fourth Precinct the Three-four. The Twentieth is called Two-oh, but the Twenty-fourth is the Two-four. And so on.) How could it happen that I went six months without catching another case? Certainly we had many more homicides in that period. The answer is that the cases came in when I wasn't catching. I've already explained that we work in teams, and during any shift one of us is catching cases—meaning, receiving new cases as they come in. By coincidence, when new cases came in during those six months, I was off duty, working outside the office, in court, or whatever.

In any event, the next one I caught came in on November 15, 1980. That was a Saturday night.

The victim of the homicide was a man I am going to call George Agostino, a male white, sixty-three years of age. Agostino was a semiretired Mafia soldier, affiliated with one of the Five Families. He worked in a numbers location on Nagle Avenue in the Three-four Precinct. He took numbers bets. He worked nights, usually from about five o'clock until a little after midnight.

On the night of November 15 he was in the store—it was a storefront operation—a sparsely furnished room where people could come in and bet on a number. It was Agostino's practice to stay in the store until the last number came in.

The winning numbers would be determined by the results at some racetrack. The simplest way was to use the last three numbers of the total handle at some track. For example, suppose Aqueduct reported on the tote board that the total bet there that evening was $3,854,101—the handle. That made the winning number 101. The guy who's got 102 slaps his forehead and complains, "Jeez, if some son of a bitch had just bet one more dollar, I'd have won!" For the most part this is nickel-and-dime business. People bet fifty cents and collect $300 if they win. The odds are bad, and it's a highly profitable business.

Anyway, Agostino had just made his last payoffs and was

alone counting his bucks, when the door opened and a young man entered. The young man produced a gun and demanded the night's receipts. Agostino gave him the money. He wasn't happy about it, because he was an Italian and this damaged his respect.

Now the robber demanded Agostino's ring. It was a ring given him by his deceased wife, and George Agostino refused to give it up. He told the guy, "You can have anything in the store that belongs to *them,* but you can't have anything that belongs to me."

The robber raised the muzzle of the gun and shot Agostino in the chest. Then he ran outside, jumped into a vehicle, and drove away. A witness got the license number of the car.

When we arrived at the scene, Agostino was in an ambulance on his way to a hospital. It looked as if he might survive. But in New York City an emergency room can close down and refuse to receive more patients when it considers itself at capacity. The ambulance driver knew from his radio that the nearest hospitals were not taking more emergency-room patients. Consequently Agostino had to be hauled a long distance in the ambulance, and he died.

The witnesses had given us a New Jersey license plate number. We traced that number to an auto-leasing agency in Ridgefield Park. With that information, Bill Kelly, my partner on this case, and I had a scent. We went directly from the scene to the agency.

The owner of the auto leasing agency invited us in, he pulled out a bottle of Chivas Regal, and offered us a drink. We said we were there on business and declined. Looking around, though, we got the impression that the whole operation was illegal. It was just instinct, I suppose, but this leasing agency for stretch limousines somehow looked like a high-class pimping operation.

We told him we wanted to know who had rented the car carrying license number so-and-so. He told us the car had been leased to a young woman I am going to call Samantha Rogers. Samantha, he said, kept company with "a black Oriental."

Bill Kelly and I went looking for Samantha. We found her. She said she had lent the leased car to her boyfriend, Donnie Anderson. Anderson, she said, lived in the Riverdale section of the Bronx. She too described him as a black Oriental and gave us his address.

Bill and I decided not to go after him that night. We weren't sufficiently prepared. We didn't know the layout of the building where he lived. We needed more bodies. Before dawn of the night when George Agostino was murdered, we knew who had done it and where to find him.

The next day we went to his house looking for Anderson. He wasn't there. After that he knew we were looking for him. He was a bad guy and a strange duck. Knowing we were looking for him for murder, he might have taken off. But he didn't. The only reason I have ever been able to think of was that he loved his mother.

The case came to the attention of Detective Tom Halinan of the Major Case Unit—a unit that handles kidnappings, unarmed bank robberies and other sensitive investigations. He took the time to camp out on Kappock Street and watch the Anderson address. A few days later he called us and told us he thought he had spotted Donnie Anderson. Bill Kelly and I jumped in a car and hurried up there.

We waited from about noon to about a quarter to seven in the evening. At that time he came out, and we moved on him. The three of us—Bill Kelly, Tom Halinan, and I—were all over him in an instant. We cuffed him and put him under arrest before he knew what had happened.

Donnie Anderson, as it turned out, was the black Oriental Samantha and the man at the auto leasing agency had described. His father had been a sergeant in the army, and his mother was Japanese. His father had met and married her during the Korean War. Anderson was twenty-three years old, a tall, handsome fellow. It was easy to see why Samantha had fallen for him.

So far as we were ever able to find out, Donnie Anderson had been robbing numbers operations to make money to give to his mother. His father was dead, and his mother received a pension from the army, but Donnie seemed to feel an obligation to contribute something to his mother's support.

He was charged with the murder of George Agostino and went to jail.

Then an odd thing happened: Donnie Anderson got out. Pending trial, he was released, apparently on bail. Or maybe somehow he slipped through the cracks. Nobody has ever been able to explain to me why he was released. He had been properly arrested, charged, identified in a lineup, and indicted, but still he got out.

As soon as he was on the streets again, he went back to his old tricks. One night he strolled into a numbers operation on Jerome Avenue in the Bronx and announced a holdup. He pulled his gun, and the proprietor pulled his. Donnie Anderson got what we call a .38 caliber migraine headache.

I have no evidence for what I am about to say, but I have always had it in the back of my mind that Anderson might have been set up to be shot in the place on Jerome Avenue. When he murdered George Agostino, he may have murdered the wrong man. I certainly don't know if what I've suggested is true, but I've always wondered about it.

Another case I want to tell about happened on August 15, 1988, on First Avenue, at about 119th Street, in the Two-five

Precinct. It involved a crack location in an abandoned building—a "hole in the wall."

Crack dealers often break into the back of an abandoned building and set up operations. The windows on the front ordinarily are sealed with cinder block. They punch a small hole in the cinder block and deal crack through that hole.

This particular hole-in-the-wall operation was what was known as a "blue cap." Crack is sold in vials with different colored caps: blue, red, yellow, pink, orange, and so on. The color of the cap usually tells you whose operation it is. The blue cap usually—though not invariably—identified a major crack dealer by the name of George Fluellen.

Fluellen had been twice tried for homicide and acquitted. He was one of the biggest dealers in Harlem and was known for his rough enforcement tactics. Basically, it was understood in Harlem that you didn't mess with George Fluellen and you didn't mess with his operations. If you were the kind of guy who wanted to rip off a crack operation, you didn't do it to Fluellen. In any neighborhood, it was understood what operations belonged to him. Nobody played games with him.

At about two in the afternoon on August 15, 1988, two men broke in at the rear of the building at the First Avenue address, went through the building, and stuck up the crack dealers. We were told they took about 1,500 vials of crack and about $4,000 in cash.

Fluellen found out about this about half an hour later. Now, the stupid thing about this was that the guys who stuck up this operation were themselves addicts—which meant that the dealers they stuck up knew who they were. If you're a neighborhood user, every dealer in the area knows you by face and probably by name. This meant that Fluellen's guys could tell him immediately that one of the stickup men had been Valentino Colon.

Colon was thirty-three years old and lived on 118th Street.

Fluellen was furious, and decided he would find Colon and get back his crack and money. The thing was, George Fluellen never just got back his property.

About four-thirty that afternoon Fluellen found Colon on the roof of his apartment building. He forced him to return to 2336 First Avenue. In a sense, probably in his own mind, Fluellen acted like a cop, a judge, and a jury—plus an executioner. He showed Colon to his dealers so they could identify him—like a lineup. He found Colon guilty of robbing his operation. Then he took him to the roof.

On the roof, he demanded that Colon return his property. Colon continued to deny he'd had anything to do with it. George Fluellen drew a gun and shot Colon twice in the head.

Unknown to George Fluellen, a young man nicknamed Green Eyes was on a nearby roof flying his pigeons. Green Eyes was a local who knew Fluellen very well. He also knew Colon very well—and he was a witness to the murder.

I was at that time a member of Manhattan North Homicide, and Chris Heimgartner and I came to help the detectives of the Two-five catch their murderer. We began to question people on the street and soon heard that a young man named Green Eyes had information. It was not difficult to find Green Eyes. Not many African Americans have green eyes.

Naturally, Green Eyes denied he had seen anything. Witnesses are afraid. Witnesses don't want to get involved. And so on.

I have a step procedure I use in these cases. The first step is to get the witness to admit he heard the shot. If you can get him that far along, you have a live witness. Why? Because we know that any person on the street, or anywhere, who hears a shot instinctively does two things: He ducks and he looks.

Duck and look. To duck is the first instinct. The next is to make sure whoever is shooting is not shooting at you—so you look. Another instinct is to get away, get out of the way. The witness looks to see where the shooting is coming from, so as not to run right at the shooter while trying to get away from him.

So you say to your witness, "Okay, you heard the shot, so you looked. You *had* to look. You wanted to get away from the shooter, whether he was shooting at you or not, so you had to look. You couldn't get away from the shooter if you didn't know where he was. You looked, pal. So tell us what you saw."

The next thing you say is "I suppose you didn't see the guy fire the shot. No. You looked after you heard the shot. What you saw was the guy standing there with the gun in his hand. You can't testify that you saw the guy shoot the gun, and I'm not asking you to testify to that. Hey, I'm your friend. I wouldn't ask you to testify you saw the guy shoot the gun when you didn't. All I want you to say is what you saw, that the guy had the gun in his hand."

This is the way you work on a witness, step by step. It's not a quick process. Sometimes it takes hours. In the case of Green Eyes I did something else. He said he was thirsty and wanted a Coke. I got him a Coke. Then he wanted another one. I got him another one. Over the hours he drank about six Cokes. By the by he wanted to go to the bathroom. I said no, not until we get this settled.

Obviously I couldn't have used that tactic on a suspect. It would have violated his rights, coerced a statement. But Green Eyes wasn't a suspect; he was a witness.

Of course he got very uncomfortable. What I was saying to him at this point was "Look, we know you didn't do anything wrong. You're not accused of anything. So give us this statement we need, and then you can go to the bathroom." Finally he told us he had seen George Fluellen kill Colon. He also told us that Fluellen had left the First Avenue address in a silver-color station wagon, one of those with a chrome-plated rack on top.

At 1:30 A.M.—that is, within twelve hours after the killing—we had a good idea where to look. Danny Rodriguez, a homicide detective, knew Fluellen to be a big drug dealer, and he told us that the Fluellen brothers often visited their mother, who lived in a project on First Avenue.

In my car were Lieutenant Jack Doyle and Detective Pat Heaney, both from the Homicide Squad, and myself driving. I always drive. I never get in a car that somebody else is driving. Following in a trail car were Detectives Rodriguez and Johnny Schlagler, plus Green Eyes. The plan was that if we spotted Fluellen's car, we'd have the trail car bring up Green Eyes to make a positive identification. After that the guys in the trail car would take him to the precinct station, and they'd come back so we all could watch the station wagon.

We located the car at 101st Street and First Avenue. Green Eyes was positive it was the car. We ran a plate check, and sure enough, the car was Fluellen's. We sent Green Eyes back to the station house.

About 3:30 A.M. the man we would later identify as George Fluellen came out of the apartment building. He was looking all around, doing what we call "a turkey"—that is, jerking his head around, looking on all sides. It's second nature for these guys to be looking over their shoulders all the time.

His car was the third car parked in the block, between First Avenue and the East River. Ours was the first car, facing east on the corner of 101st Street and First, and it was obviously a police car with three men in it.

He walked south about half a block, then suddenly turned

and came back and went to a public phone. He picked up the phone with his right hand and punched in numbers with his left. Although he seemed to be talking intently with someone on the phone, what he really was doing was staring at us. Then he hung up the phone and walked south again, then he went back and picked up the phone again. He did the same thing, picked up the phone with his right hand and punched in numbers with his left.

He was in the light from the phone booth, and I could see him plainly. He was looking at me, and I was looking at him. I remember thinking Isn't this ironic? There you are looking at me, and I'm looking at you, and if you're who I think you are, you're mine, you son of a bitch.

This time he put down the phone and walked directly to the station wagon. He got in the car and pulled out. Jack Doyle now radioed the unit that was shadowing us. Fluellen turned right to go north on First Avenue. I followed him and switched on the lights and siren. He pulled to the curb, and we were all over him. He immediately admitted who he was.

I pulled him out of the car and got him down on the pavement. I turned to the lieutenant and said, "Lou, give me your cuffs." He didn't have any. I asked Pat for his. He didn't have any. And of course I didn't have any.

I said to Fluellen, "Listen, my friend, these three professional detectives from the homicide squad don't have any cuffs. But I have a gun at your head, and if you try any shit I'll blow your head off,"

At this point I looked across the street, and here's a square badge, which is what we call a uniformed guard who is not a member of the NYPD. We wear shields. They wear square badges. But he had a pair of handcuffs, and we borrowed them.

Inside the station wagon we found several weapons, including what was later identified as the murder weapon.

At the trial, I testified to the above facts. I didn't realize it, but for some reason the question of whether George Fluellen was right-handed or left-handed became a key issue. For that reason, my description of him as picking up a telephone in his right hand and punching in numbers with his left became very important. I hadn't thought of it, but of course a right-handed person would have picked up the phone with his left hand and hit the number buttons with his right.

George Fluellen was convicted and sentenced to twenty-five years to life.

There was a personal irony for me in that case. The day after we made the arrest, we had search warrants to serve. Before we went out to do that, one of the detectives in our office made a joke. He pulled out his revolver, opened it, and ejected the shells, and blew down the barrel—"To blow the dust out," he said. I went along with the joke and tried to do the same, but I couldn't. My gun was so corroded that I couldn't pull the trigger and the cylinder wouldn't revolve. When I told Fluellen I would blow his head off, I couldn't have. If he had gone for a gun, I couldn't have shot him.

What had happened was, I had been carrying my revolver in an inside holster. That kind of holster attracts sweat. It had been a hot month. I have never used that kind of holster again; and, needless to say, I check my gun every day.

A homicide occurred on March 11, 1983, just a little after midnight, at 541 West 158th Street, which is in Washington Heights. At the time I was assigned to the Three-four Precinct detective squad and was working with Bill Kelly.

We had a phone call from uniformed officers at about 1:15 A.M. Bill and I went to the address. A male Hispanic lay on the landing between the first and second floors. He had a gun in his hand and was dead of multiple gunshot wounds to the chest. He was identified as José Bonnelly, about twenty-two years of age.

A blood trail ran up the stairs to the fifth floor, to the door of Apartment 5-E. It looked as if Bonnelly had left that apartment bleeding heavily, had stumbled down the stairs and collapsed and died on the landing. The sergeant at the scene had decided not to force his way into the apartment, thinking it would be an illegal entry.

I am outranked by a sergeant except at a crime scene. There the ranking detective runs the show. It was my decision to make, and I decided to break in. I kicked the door in and entered the apartment.

The apartment was lit only by candles burning on a little altar dedicated to some saint or other. This is characteristic of drug spots. The dealers and addicts often stop for a moment at these little shrines and drop a few coins in the dish.

The blood trail led down the hall. It was a scary situation. You never know what you are going into. We knew somebody had been shot in the apartment. We didn't know if the shooter had bailed out or was still there.

Bill Kelly and I followed the blood trail along the hall to the door of a rear bedroom. We could hear a clicking, as if maybe somebody was cocking a gun. As we got closer it sounded as if somebody was dry firing.

We kicked the door open and threw the beam of a flashlight into the room. On the floor was another male Hispanic with a gun in his right hand. He was aiming it at the door and shooting—*click, click, click.* He too suffered from multiple gunshot wounds, including one to the head, and was bleeding heavily. He was in fact dead—or was for all practical purposes—but some kind of reaction kept him pulling the trig-

**4 7**

ger of his gun. Even after I kicked the gun out of his hand, his finger kept pulling the trigger.

His name was Rafael Martinez, thirty-eight years old. What had happened, as we learned in the course of the investigation, was that Bonnelly had come to the apartment to do a drug deal. They'd had an angry dispute over price or something else, and Bonnelly had decided simply to pull his gun and take what he wanted. But Martinez had a gun too, and they wound up shooting each other. Ballistics tests proved that the gun found on Bonnelly had killed Martinez and the gun found on Martinez had killed Bonnelly.

I went to the front of the apartment and looked down at the street from the window. There was a crime-scene station wagon there, plus two blue-and-white police cars, and two ambulances—all flashing their lights. Besides that, there were three detective cars on the scene. And at this point, with all that police presence so obvious, two men had decided to have a gun battle on the street!

There had to be twenty cops on the scene, but even so these two idiots were shooting at each other from opposite sides of the street. As I looked down on this, I was in absolute shock, watching these two guys attempting to kill each other.

Bill Kelly and I went downstairs and managed to arrest this pair. We questioned them. Why did they do this?

They were trying to kill each other because one of them had called the other one's sister a whore *thirteen years ago* in the Dominican Republic! This was the first time the men had seen each other in thirteen years. The one whose sister had been called a whore didn't care how many police would see what he did, or if he got caught. He was going to avenge his sister, defend her honor, no matter what. The other guy shot back simply to protect himself.

Maybe it's not funny, but to us as police officers it was

funny. It was like looking at the shooting at the O.K. Corral. In the very middle of all that police manpower, these two jerks decided to shoot it out. In police work you see things you just can't believe.

A case not so typical of ones I handled while I was a detective in the Three-four involved my own father. My dad called me to tell me his paycheck had been stolen from his mailbox. This had happened a couple of months earlier. He had not reported this to the police, only to his employer. His company replaced his check, so Dad wasn't out the money, but he asked that the company send him a copy of the stolen check. When he got the copy he saw that his check had been cashed by the B & B Candy Company in the South Bronx.

Now, two months after the theft, my father called me. He thought I was a great detective and that I would find out who had broken into his mailbox. He figured that by telling me he had planted a seed and that I would follow up. From my point of view, why should I spend off-duty time trying to track down a mailbox thief? I had enough cases to work on.

But I decided I'd give it a try. Working on my own time, I made some inquiries in the Bronx, where my father lived, where the theft had happened.

The candy company, it turned out, did not exist. Even so, it did have a checking account. When the thief cashed the check, he had endorsed it to the B & B Candy Company, which had deposited it in an account in Chemical Bank. I went to the bank and asked for the address on the account. They gave it to me, and that turned out to be a nonexistent address.

I visited some bodegas—Spanish grocery stores—and asked them if they ever did business with B & B Candy Company. They said yes, the man came in often to deliver candy.

So I waited on Willis Avenue for three days, looking for the truck from this candy company. And, sure enough, it showed up. I spoke to the driver of the truck, and he said he was the owner of B & B Candy Company. I will call him Willis Foster. We walked back in an alley, and I showed him the check, He said sure, he had cashed that check and deposited it. He said, though, he couldn't remember where the check came from.

At that point, the guy from the candy company was out the amount of money represented by the stolen check. My father's employer had notified the bank that the check had been stolen and the endorsement forged, so the bank was taking the money out of the candy company account.

I decided to let the matter go. I took note of the man and of B & B Candy Company but I took no action.

About eight months later a detective named Danny Strauss of the Three-four Squad had a case involving stolen checks. Green boxes had been broken open and the mail stolen. A green box is a postal service drop box, where a mail truck deposits mail to be picked up by the route carrier, who opens it with a key and takes out the mail that he delivers to homes and businesses. This kind of box has no slot, and you can't put your mail into it.

Included in the stolen mail were tax refund checks, pension checks, Social Security checks, and so on. This had come to the attention of detectives in the Three-four because people were coming in to complain that their checks were missing. They didn't claim, though, that their personal mailboxes had been broken into.

Danny Strauss took a personal interest in these complaints. He didn't like the idea of people's mail being stolen.

A month and a half later a Secret Service agent came to the precinct office. Besides protecting the president of the United

States, the Secret Service has a number of other duties. One of those duties is investigation of forged checks—which is logical, since the Secret Service is part of the Treasury Department. The Service also works closely with the postal inspectors. Opening of green boxes—or any other mail boxes, for that matter—was within the jurisdiction of the Secret Service and something they didn't take lightly.

The Secret Service agent told Danny Strauss that it was looking at check fraud in the million-dollar range. The green box theft we were aware of was only one of many. The thieves had somehow gotten a key, and those keys don't fit just one mailbox; they fit all those in an area.

Danny showed me one of the stolen checks bearing a forged endorsement. It had been cashed by the B & B Candy Company! The Secret Service man showed us a number of other checks, all cashed by B & B.

We went to Chemical Bank. The B & B account had been closed.

The scam was that Willis Foster had opened a bank account in the name of the candy company, depositing as much as $25,000 in cash. Then he had stolen checks from the mail, forged endorsements, and deposited the checks. He eventually deposited as much as $1,500,000 in the account. He liked government checks especially. He knew that a government check takes approximately three months to bounce. It takes that long for the government to process checks and discover a fraud.

Also, he knew that the bank would allow him to withdraw funds against the checks after the usual seven-day collection period.

So, he began to make withdrawals. Soon he had withdrawn his original cash deposit and would begin to draw against the checks. He never drew the account down to zero.

Continuing to deposit stolen checks, he always maintained a balance of as much as $200,000. He was stroking the bank, you could say. They didn't worry too much about an account that had that much money in it.

Foster went to Middletown, New York, and bought a house for $210,000, which he paid in cash. Banks are legally obligated to report the arrival of that much cash, some banks are so happy to get it that they forget the law.

We went out to look for Foster. It took us two days, but we found him, and the others gave me the pleasure of putting the cuffs on this guy. When we locked him up, he said to me, "I knew I had a problem when you found me that day. I knew I should have given you the amount of your father's check and tried to give you five hundred or a thousand on the side. But when you grabbed me in the alley, I was afraid that if I tried to give you a thousand you'd have stuffed me in the garbage can. I never guessed, though, that a two-hundred-and-ten-dollar check would bring down my scam."

I called my father that evening and told him to read the papers the next day. "Your check," I told him, "cracked a major case for the federal government."

# 3

## LIVE AND LEARN

I AM OF IRISH DESCENT, born in New York City and reared in the Highbridge Section of the Bronx. My paternal grandparents came to the States from County Monaghan. My maternal grandparents, named Brannigan, came from County Kerry.

My father, Eugene Thomas McKenna, was a short, well-built, good-looking man. He loved boxing, had been a semi-pro, and could handle himself very well. He was an above-average baseball player too. While he never graduated from high school, he was one of the smartest people I have ever known.

Dad grew up in a tough neighborhood on the West Side, just above Hell's Kitchen. My grandfather McKenna was a chauffeur; and, though he never lost his job during the Depression, his income was much diminished. As the oldest of six, my father had to go to work to supplement the family income. For my father that decision was easy—he *had* to go to work; the family needed the money. They survived the Depression intact. My father and his brothers and sisters grew up to rear their own families. I am sure that family values and a strong hand by my grandparents had much to do with it.

Grandmother Brannigan died when my mother was young. Grandfather Brannigan worked for the Transit Authority as a motorman and died shortly before I was born. His job continued, through the Depression, so my mother's family did not suffer the way my father's family did.

My father had three jobs. Days, he worked for Railway Express. Nights, he was a bartender at the American Legion hall. And on weekends, he worked at the racetrack, selling tickets. He was devoted to his family and wanted to give us the best he could.

My mother, Ellen Brannigan McKenna, was a pretty woman, with a warm smile and a pleasant word for everyone. I don't recall her ever being mad at anyone, or ever raising her voice. She too worked. She was a secretary for the Transit Authority and ultimately was promoted to a buyer in the purchasing department.

Mom was very family oriented. Though her own parents were gone, she insisted that all of us visit my dad's every Sunday. I loved my grandparents, but I remember how I hated those visits. Though my grandparents once lived in the same building with us in the Bronx, they had moved to Manhattan. Sundays, when I wanted to play stickball with my friends, I had to go to my grandparents' apartment and sit indoors. Television had not yet become the baby-sitter for bored kids.

We lived in a nice neighborhood, and I can't claim to come from "the mean streets." But I always understood the importance of being able to take care of myself. Somebody would test you, sooner or later. My father gave me boxing lessons. Important as being able to dish it out was being able to take it, and I learned to do both. I was never a street brawler, but I would not run from a fight. I might have been small, but I could handle myself.

My brother Gene and I were sent to Sacred Heart School, in the Bronx. Since it was our parish school, my family paid no tuition. I learned a very different set of morals and standards from what children do today. For example, we went to church every Sunday. You went whether you wanted to go or not. In truth, I don't remember ever *not* wanting to go. The nine-o'clock mass every Sunday morning was Children's Mass, and we went to mass by school classes. If you wanted to go to school at Sacred Heart, you went to that mass, just the same as you went to school every day.

Mom and Dad went to High Mass every Sunday morning at eleven-fifteen. They never missed.

We received communion every Sunday and confessed every other week. *Everyone* received communion. It was expected. The only excuse was that you'd had something to eat or drink since midnight. In those days you could not receive communion if you had eaten or drunk since midnight, even a glass of water. If you had gotten a headache during the night and had taken an aspirin with water, you could not receive communion—and that was the only acceptable excuse. If you had an unconfessed and unforgiven sin on your conscience, you could not receive communion, but no one ever wanted to admit to that. It would have been a scandal.

It never occurred to me not to do my religious duties, and I never found them a burden. In fact, when I graduated from grammar school—that is, from the eighth grade—I was seriously considering becoming a Christian Brother, a member of an order. Why didn't I? As I matured a little more, I learned that the life of the religious involved giving up a great many things, including an interest in girls, and that was not for me. I just didn't have a vocation to the religious communal life.

Even so, some of the religious had a major impact on my life.

I remember vividly a man named Brother Paul. Brother Paul had a bad leg and wore a brace built into a boot. Even so, what a ballplayer that man was! During the season he played football with the boys at Sacred Heart. In baseball season he played baseball. In track season he ran track with us. A handicapped man. How we looked up to him!

After grammar school at Sacred Heart, I went to Cardinal Hayes High. In those days, tuition was $10 a month, and if a family had two kids in Hayes, it was $15. My brother was already there, so our education there cost my father $15 a month.

Cardinal Hayes was a factory, graduating nine hundred students a year. Here too, much emphasis was laid on religious and moral instruction. Many of the teachers were priests or brothers. They were from a variety of orders— Franciscans, Marists, Christian Brothers . . .

Apart from the religious instruction, we studied all the subjects given in any high school, and we had to pass the same New York Regents Exams as students in public schools. There was a difference, though. We *had* to pass the Regents. If you didn't, you couldn't stay at Cardinal Hayes. Public school students get another chance. We didn't. Also, we had to maintain a certain average.

What's more, you couldn't stay at Cardinal Hayes if you were a disciplinary problem.

What happened if you were thrown out? A terrible penalty. You had to go to public school—and for us, that *was* a terrible penalty: a disgrace to your family.

Cardinal Hayes High was a fine school. In one sense I felt privileged to go there—in the sense that I would have an exceptionally fine education, an excellent credential. But in a deeper sense I did not feel privileged. I knew my parents worked hard to send me there, so I felt an obligation to do as well as I possibly could.

I always loved athletics. When I graduated from high school, I was one of the smallest in my class, only about five feet four and maybe 130 pounds. I had the body of a fly but the heart of a tiger. I was too small to play football, so I played baseball and ran track. I was a second baseman, and I was a sprinter, ran the 220. I wasn't a star, but I loved it just the same.

My father taught me that if you're good enough to participate, then you should do your best and make your contribution. The whole thing in life is, when something takes more than you yourself can give, then that's when you work as a part of a team.

When I left school, I had never thought about becoming a cop.

On graduating, I took a job in the mail room at Continental Can Company, working there until I entered the U.S. Army.

I didn't have a career in the army, but I had a useful experience that everyone should have. I went in as a nineteen-year-old kid and came out as a twenty-one-year-old . . . man? Maybe not. Maybe I was still a kid. But if so, I was a responsible kid. I had learned about taking orders and about hierarchy and structure, and above all about responsibility. It was good preparation for the police department.

More than that, I saw how people in other countries don't have what we have here in America. When I saw people who didn't have food for their table, it gave me a different understanding. I know it made me appreciate our own country more, but I think it also made me better able to understand that other people live in different circumstances.

The whole thing was a maturing experience. I didn't want a career in the army, but I'm sure glad I served the way I did. When I got home, I went to work for Railway Express, where my father worked. He got me that job. I was entitled to live on veterans' benefits for a while, but I didn't. I went right to work. I lived at home for a while. I wasn't happy with that.

In November of 1963 I got married to a neighborhood girl. We didn't marry out of the neighborhood, so I'd known her for years. I knew her family too, of course. When I came home on leave from Fort Dix, I started dating her. The relationship blossomed, you might say, and when I got out of the service we got married.

She was a pretty girl, a neighborhood girl, a good Catholic. We were married in the same church where our parents had been married—St. Vincent Ferrer. It seemed like a marriage made in heaven. Maybe it was. We had four wonderful children.

So how did I become a policeman?

I had been a booster member of the American Legion even before I went in the service. I played baseball for the American Legion team. When I came home, of course I joined the Legion. Around the Legion hall I met many policemen. Some were motorcycle policemen. The department bagpipe band practiced in the Legion hall. I was impressed. They were good people, and they had a good job.

I liked what I saw of NYPD. It offered respect in your profession, job security, good benefits, and a structured work environment. I've never had any problem with hierarchy, about calling someone else boss, about taking orders. I thought it would be great to get a job with the department.

In 1962 I took the exam. Unhappily for me, I'd been out the night before, drunk more than was good for me, and during the examination I got sick and had to get up and rush from the examination room to the bathroom before I finished. Technically, I'd failed. I couldn't take the exam again for six months.

That six months cost me two years' seniority. A friend who took the exam that same day was appointed to the force in February 1963. I took the exam again six months later and passed it with a very high score, but I wasn't appointed until February 1965.

People have asked me about that test. Mostly it was an intelligence test. There was a reading comprehension section, a math section, and a general knowledge section. Only a few questions related to police procedures, which you weren't expected to know in advance. But common sense helped answer those questions.

Having passed the test, I was on a civil service list. New appointments have to be made from that list. But the department can take only so many people at a time. So I waited.

Eventually I was called. I was sworn in on February 15, 1965. Now I was a cop. My first assignment was of course to the police academy, where a class spends five months learning the business of being a police officer. Even though I was only a recruit in the academy, I was a cop. I had a shield, and I carried a gun.

I remember my first arrest.

My wife was what my grandmother would call "a port-hole"—meaning that she was forever looking out the window, watching the neighborhood. She did this because she had difficulty sleeping when she was pregnant, and in the early years of our marriage she was always pregnant. We lived in the Bronx. She woke me up one night and told me a store downstairs had been broken into and some guys were carrying off a television set. I grabbed my gun and my badge, ran down the stairs, and charged out on the street, yelling "Stop! Police!"

The perps didn't stop. They ran faster. I chased them four blocks. The one carrying the TV dropped it on the pavement and split as fast as he could—which was the end of the television set. I caught up with the other one from behind and made a grab. The perp struggled a little, and I grabbed at the lapels of a jacket. I had two handfuls of breasts! It was a female! My first collar was a girl.

Well . . . no matter. I held her until a radio car arrived. A rookie from the academy had collared a burglar.

My first arrest. Before I moved away from that neighborhood in 1967, I had more than seventy off-duty collars, all of them felony arrests. Every time the radio call was "Policeman holding one," they knew it was me. My neighbors never called the police-emergency number. They just called me. I was never off duty. I'd run out on the street anytime.

I was nuts, is what I was.

The incident of the television set was not the only one of its kind.

One night in 1967 I came home at about three in the morning. I'd made three burglary arrests that night during a riot in Brooklyn. I had to be in court in the morning, so I went to bed and tried to get some sleep. No way. My wife was pregnant, wasn't sleeping well, and was at the window again. I had barely gotten to sleep when she woke me up and told me it looked like two men were kidnapping someone out on the street.

She was right. That was exactly what was going on, though I didn't know it yet. Two men were kidnapping the owner of Wimpy's Hamburgers. The man's girlfriend was an important witness in a white-slavery case, and these two wanted to pressure her not to testify.

I went to the window and saw what my wife saw—two guys hustling the other guy down the street. I grabbed my service revolver, my leather case that carried extra ammunition, and my shield, and I ran out of the house. All I was wearing was a pair of cut-off Bermuda shorts—no shirt, no shoes, no socks—and so dressed I chased those guys down the street.

I yelled at them to stop, but they didn't. Instead they fired at me. And I fired back.

The chase began on 165th Street between Ogden and Summit Avenues. They ran east on 165th and turned south on Ogden, then west on 163rd. They ran to Summit and turned south. When they reached 162nd Street, they turned east again and ran back to Ogden. And there, in the shadow of Yankee Stadium, one of them stopped and gave up. He was exhausted and couldn't run any farther.

In the course of the chase I had fired eighteen shots, reloading as I ran. When I caught the exhausted man and collared him, I was out of ammunition. They had fired forty-six shots at me.

Fortunately, all we'd managed to kill were several parked cars and some plate-glass windows.

Patrol cars arrived, of course. The first officers on the scene couldn't believe this shirtless, shoeless character was also on the Job. But I convinced them. Soon we picked up the second kidnapper.

I was a uniformed officer for three years, during which time I made more than three hundred arrests. I guess I was a nosy cop. I've never been the kind who could see something suspicious and just walk on. If something didn't look right, I had to look deeper. I couldn't just walk away.

Not even now. One night in the Christmas season, 1990, I was driving home after visiting with my sister-in-law. I was driving along the street after midnight when all of a sudden a guy literally runs across my car. I mean, he ran onto the hood, sort of threw himself over, and ran on as fast as he could.

He was a young man and looked clean and well dressed.

He looked me square in the face before he took off, and I could see he was badly shaken. I guessed he was either an employee of the garage or a customer. Something going on down in the garage had terrified him. It didn't take a genius to guess what.

I knew the routine. Sometimes late at night a gang will invade a parking garage, hold the employees at gunpoint, and steal a few of the most expensive cars. I guessed that was what was going on. I'd guessed right.

Maybe I should have driven on. I'm a homicide detective, and this wasn't my problem; but I'm not made up that way. I backed up and drove my little Datsun down the exit ramp. When I reached a lower level I heard yelling and saw three men running. I'd driven right into the middle of a stickup.

The thought of getting out of there fast pushed into my mind. All the wrong thoughts came in a flash—how it was the holidays and how the holidays had always been a jinx for me, how cops got killed at holiday time. I was forty-eight years old and not as fast as I used to be. I had a five-shot revolver and no backup, and I'd seen at least three men. I thought to myself, How the hell do I get myself into these things?

Even so, I did what I had to do. I backed my car up the ramp, then blocked it at the top by parking across it. I got out and waited. I could hear yelling down in the garage, then car doors slamming, then the squeal of tires. I knew they'd be coming out. All I could think of at that moment was my little '81 Datsun. It had served me well for years, and as it sat there blocking that ramp I felt I had more or less sentenced it to death. What if they rammed it? The City of New York wasn't going to pay for repairs or buy me a new car. How would I get to work?

Before long a big, expensive Mercedes comes up the ramp.

The driver had to stop. He slams on the brakes and stops inches from my Datsun. I'm behind my car, yelling that I'm a police officer. The adrenaline is pumping, which always seems to put everything in slow motion—besides focusing your attention. In other circumstances I might have said, "Sir, please step out of your car and let me see your license and registration," but in these circumstances the street in me comes out, and I yell if he doesn't get out of that fuckin' car with his fuckin' hands up, I'll blow his motherfuckin' head off!

I can see he's a lean guy with a flushed face all pitted with acne scars. He's wearing a black hat. I see him grab for a gun. I don't think now he meant to shoot me; I think he grabbed too quick and nervous and accidentally pulled the trigger. It doesn't make any difference. The gun goes off. I duck. For a minute it's a face-off. I'm behind my car, and he's behind a big glass windshield and can see my gun sighted on him.

At this point somebody opens a window in an apartment across the street and yells that if us guys don't quit making so much fucking noise he's going to call the cops. Great! That's just what I want him to do. To make him madder and make sure he does, I let him have a string of words I certainly hadn't learned at Sacred Heart or Cardinal Hayes High.

I keep yelling at the guy in the Mercedes to put his hands on the dashboard where I can see them, and he yells, "Don't shoot, don't shoot!" He decides to give up. I open the door of the Mercedes and pull him out. It's amazing how strong you are when the adrenaline gets pumping. I throw him to the pavement and rear-cuff him. Sure, I am tense, but he is actually shitting his pants.

In the meantime, two more cars came up the ramp, and the drivers discovered it was blocked. The first was another Mercedes, and the second was a Jaguar. The guy in the Jaguar threw it into reverse and started backing down the ramp. He rear-ended it into a wall, got out, and ran down into the garage. The man in the Mercedes jumped out and ran too.

At this point a patrol car, lights flashing, siren screaming, charged into the block. The man in the apartment had called the police, all right. He'd heard the shot fired and called 911, saying he'd heard shooting. A shots-fired call was on the air.

Again, my first problem was to convince the two patrolmen that I was on the Job. I kept my foot on my prisoner but put my gun on the hood of my car and turned to face the patrol car, hands up. One of the young cops recognized me. The two officers from the car walked up to me. While I was telling them what was going on, three more police cars and a sergeant arrived.

About this time a garage attendant came out. He said the other two robbers had gone down to lower levels in the garage. They couldn't get out, he said. All the doors from adjacent buildings opened into the garage. If you were in an office building, you could get into the garage. But if you were in the garage, you couldn't get into the office building.

I told the sergeant I was going down into the garage to get the other two guys. The sergeant wanted to wait for Emergency Services and a K-9 unit to arrive. I was hot and didn't want to wait, so I started down the ramp. At this time the young officer started down with me. The others then followed. One guy we found hiding under a car the third level down. The last guy was found on the fifth level down, hiding in the ceiling on top of some water pipes.

Getting back to my years in uniform, my assignment was to the Tactical Patrol Force. We were a unit that was sent wherever extra police presence was needed, always in a neighborhood being overrun by crime. We were specially trained for riot duty. If a neighborhood was in trouble, we were sent in to saturate that area and make arrests.

It sounds like tough duty, but in fact those years were some of my best years on the Job.

I was assigned to the Sixth Squad in TPF. It was a Manhattan North Squad, working out of the old Two-five Precinct on 126th Street between Lexington and Third avenues.

My first partner on the TPF was Bob "Pops" Bratko. Bob was just twenty-six years old, but because he was balding, everyone called him Pops. He had been on the Job two and a half years, which in the TPF qualified him as a senior man.

I remember my first night on patrol. Pops and I were on the 6:00 P.M. to 2:00 A.M. tour. It was a summer night in June, and I was fresh out of the academy. I was a nervous wreck. In the academy they teach you the penal law and the proper use of your firearm, but they don't teach you to walk the walk and talk the talk. That comes from watching and learning, and Pops was a great teacher. The first night I walked a post with him he told me to watch what he did and always to watch our backs. Nobody walks between us, and nobody gets behind us. The way he put it, it's a back-to-back business.

That first night we were assigned to a one-block post, 117th Street from Madison Avenue to Fifth Avenue. The first thing we did, while it was still daylight, was to go to the roofs of the buildings along the street and sweep them of bottles and rocks. The criminal element on the block didn't want us there, and during the day they would carry rocks and bottles to the roofs, so they could throw them down on us as we walked our post. We would go up on the roofs and throw their ammunition down into the alleys behind the buildings. Most of the buildings in that area share walls, so you could go up to the roof at one end of the block and walk from roof to roof to the other end. We swept the roofs at the beginning of our tour, because it was still daylight then and we could throw the rocks and bottles down into the alleys without danger of hitting somebody below. Only after we had thrown all the rocks and bottles off the roofs could we get down to work the post.

We started that night by doing car stops. Usually double-parked cars leave only one lane open on a street like 117th, and we would step out into that lane and stop a car—which would immediately block four or five, or more, cars behind. We would tell a driver that this was only a routine safety check and we wanted to see his license and registration. If he was okay, he had a license and his registration, we would wave him on and check the next car. What we were really looking for was stolen cars and other problems.

This was my first night on a tour, remember. At 7:10 P.M. we stopped a car and, looking into it, I saw what looked like the butt of a rifle sticking out from under the seat. I signaled to Pops, and we drew our guns and ordered the occupants out of the car. We handcuffed them. The butt I had seen turned out to belong to a strictly illegal weapon: a sawed-off shotgun. Each of the men in the car was carrying a handgun. They were a stickup waiting to happen.

Pops was attending college in the daytime on Mondays, Wednesdays, and Fridays and did not want to make arrests because he might have to go to court on those days. So I made the arrests. Only a little more than an hour into my first tour, I made three arrests. Pops and I worked that way. So he wouldn't have to go to court, I made the arrests. I hated to write summonses, so he wrote the summonses. A great partnership.

We processed the arrests, lodged the prisoners, and were back on the street by nine-thirty. At ten o'clock I arrested a person driving a stolen car. You might say my career in the NYPD was off to an arresting start.

Patrol in Harlem was always an adventure. The TPF was known for arrests. Narcotics possession or sale has always been the catalyst of crime. Urban blight and the decay of the inner city can be directly linked to narcotics. My early years on patrol were tuned to narcotics arrests.

Pop and I would turn out at 6:00 P.M., go to our post, and make our roof check. If we had an abandoned building on the block, we would enter it and check each apartment. As I mentioned, the front door of an abandoned building in Harlem is usually sealed with cinder block, so we would go to the roof of another building, cross the roofs, and enter the abandoned building by going down the rear fire escape and in through a broken window.

Typically, local junkies used two or three apartments in an abandoned building as shooting galleries. If we were lucky when we entered one of these apartments, we would find some people and would arrest them for possession. After we searched them, we would handcuff them to a radiator and wait for more junkies to appear.

Sooner or later more junkies would arrive, having come over the roofs and down the fire escape just as we had. As they came in the window, we would throw them to the floor and collar them for possession. They had no reason for being there other than to shoot heroin and get high, so we didn't have to worry about collaring innocent people.

We would cuff people to radiators until we ran out of handcuffs—of which we always carried three or four pairs apiece. Then we would radio for a supervisor to come and transport the prisoners.

\* \* \*

One night Pops and I were on the corner of 102nd Street and Park Avenue, on the west side of the street. That was our post. When we left the station house, we had brought his car—a nine-year-old Pontiac—along and left it between 103rd and 104th on the west side of Park.

I was looking north on Park Avenue and saw a guy trying the doors of a car. Then I saw him open the car and get in. I said to Pops, "Hey, somebody just got into your car." He didn't believe it, but when he saw the lights go on he saw it was his car.

Because of the one-way street, the thief had to drive right toward us. Another car was stopped at the light, and Pops walked over to the driver and asked him to turn off his engine and not move when the light turned green. The guy driving Pops's car came up behind that car and had to stop.

I was mad. Pops was calm. He walked up to the guy driving his car, told him this was a routine automobile safety check, and asked to see his license and registration.

"The registration is in the glove department," the guy said in heavily accented English.

Pops said, "Okay, let me see it." Then the guy said he must have left it at home, and Pops asked him to step out of the vehicle. The guy got out, but he kept up this bullshit about how if we'd just let him go home he'd come right back with the license and registration.

I was furious. I said to the guy, "I want you to ask this police officer one question. The question is 'Whose car is this?'"

The guy said, "It's my car."

I said to the guy, "Sir, you're not listening to me. Ask the officer whose car it is."

So the guy asked Pops, "Whose car is this?"

Pops said, "It's mine."

At this point the thief shit his pants. Literally.

Since we were going to take the guy to the station house in Bratko's car, we made him take off his pants and clean himself up as well as he could. He tossed his underpants away, and we let him put on his regular pants. We cuffed his hands behind his back and put him in the backseat.

On the way to the station, I asked Pops, "What are you going to charge this guy with?"

"Nothing," said Pops Bratko.

"Nothing?"

"Nothing. What I'd really like to do is kill him."

At this, the guy's bowels let go again. The smell was terrible. We pulled him out of the car, uncuffed him, and made him use his pants to clean himself up. This left him bare-ass.

Inside the station, the question came up again—what was Pops going to charge him with? Pops charged him with attempted larceny/auto. And we had a little argument about whether he should be charged with indecent exposure for coming in the station house with no pants.

It was a rule at the time that if a TPF officer made 150 arrests in three years, he would be interviewed for the Detective Bureau. I made three hundred, which qualified me to be transferred.

I was assigned to the Night Neighborhood Detective Task Force for about a year, then to the Fourth District Robbery Squad. Then I was assigned as a precinct detective in the Three-four Squad. I had the gold shield. I was assigned to a squad. Now all I had to do was learn to be a detective.

On January 1, 1971, the New York City Police Department went into a phase called specialization. During this period detectives would no longer work at the precinct level, handling all types of cases, but would become specialists in investigating a particular type of crime.

I opted for the robbery squad. One of my reasons was that the boss of the Fifth Detective District Robbery Squad was going to be Lieutenant Gene McDermott. His reputation in the police department was beyond reproach. If he had looked like his reputation, he should have been a six-foot-five giant of a man. In fact, Lieutenant McDermott was a small man with an infectious smile. In any case, he commanded respect for his knowledge of the Job and the Detective Bureau and his unique ability to be fair.

Here is an example of how fair the man was.

While I was serving under him, I was assigned to attend a training class at the academy for a week. One morning I walked into the office on my way there. I noticed there were very few detectives working that morning, so I figured it would be okay if I drove an unmarked police car to the training session.

About one o'clock I was called to the phone at the academy. On the other end of the line was Lieutenant McDermott, who read me the riot act about taking the car and ordered me to bring it back to the office immediately. Arriving at the office, I was directed into the lieutenant's office, where he reamed me out some more. He told me that in spite of my title of detective and my assignment to the prestigious robbery squad, I was a rookie on the Job, having only six years, and a baby in the Detective Bureau, having only three years. Now that you understand your status around here, he said, the matter of the car will be forgotten.

I was crushed. I couldn't believe he would ever forget my offense. My career in the police department was probably over. I went to my desk and occupied myself with some busywork, just hoping I wouldn't see Lieutenant McDermott again that day.

One hour later a call came in that a police officer had been shot at 99th Street and Riverside Avenue. Two uniformed officers had responded to a call about a disorderly man in an apartment on Riverside. They had gone to the door and knocked. The man inside had opened the door, immediately shot one of the officers, and then slammed the door.

A radio call for assistance had gone out. An Emergency Services unit had arrived and secured the area outside the door. The situation was now "barricaded felon."

I found myself driving a car, taking Lieutenant McDermott and Captain Richard Nicastro, later chief of detectives, to the crime scene. So much for avoiding the lieutenant.

Captain Nicastro was the ranking detective on the scene and called the shots. He ordered the Emergency Services unit to break down the door, which they did. Looking into the apartment, we could see that the man had overturned a couch to block the hallway that led to the rear. Someone told us his mother was in the apartment and that he was threatening to harm her.

The man was emotionally disturbed. From time to time he would come out to the couch and stand there ranting and raving for a minute or so, after which he would turn his back on us and return to the rear of the apartment.

Captain Nicastro decided to take him the next time he came out. The plan was simple. When the man turned to walk back along the hall, we would rush him. Lieutenant McDermott told me the plan.

I could see what my job was. The lieutenant was in his forties. The captain was in his late thirties. I was twenty-nine, an athlete, and a little on the nutty side. I figured I was the man who had to run into the apartment, jump over the couch, and tackle the headcase.

I figured wrong. The man came out, ranted and raved again, and turned his back on us, just like before. I jumped into the doorway. The problem was, Captain Nicastro and Lieutenant McDermott had never meant to send me in alone, and all three of us went for the door at once. It was a tight squeeze!

Even so, I managed to break through, jump over the couch, and tackle the shooter. In a second, Lieutenant McDermott landed on top of me, followed by the captain, the future chief of detectives. We subdued the man who had shot the policeman, cuffed him, and placed him under arrest.

When we got off duty that night, Gene McDermott asked me if I'd like to join him for a beer. He'd said he'd forget the incident with the car, and he had.

The worst night of all my years with the police department was Thanksgiving eve, 1971.

I had been with the Robbery Squad since it was formed, about a year before, and my partner from the beginning had been Billy "Blue Eyes" Muldoon. He was called Blue Eyes because his eyes were blue like a baby's eyes. Every woman he ever met was fascinated by his eyes—including my wife.

At first we saw we had little in common. He was in his forties; I was in my late twenties. He talked soft and slow; I talked loud and fast. He walked after bad guys; I ran after bad guys. For the first three weeks that we worked together, he hardly spoke to me. I saw the situation as a feeling-out process. He saw it as a checking-out process. He wanted to find out how much he could count on me. After a while he seemed to be satisfied, and I was, and we became good friends. We worked together in exceptional harmony.

On Thanksgiving eve I had to go to the district attorney's office to discuss a prosecution that was about to go to trial. All that week we had been trying to serve an arrest warrant at an address on 102nd Street between Central Park West and

Manhattan Avenue. The address was a basement apartment, and we had been there three times during the week. Bill told me that while I went to the DA's office, he was going to give the warrant one more try.

Bill Muldoon and detectives Jim Rushin and John Mendicino went to the basement, knocked on the apartment door, and were admitted. The fugitive named in the warrant was not present. Looking around, Bill saw something he hadn't seen when he had been in the apartment before. The tenants were black people, but this time a white female was there, with about ten pocketbooks.

The bathroom door was closed, and Bill Muldoon went over and tried to open it. It was locked. The building superintendent was in the apartment as well, and Bill asked him who was in the bathroom. The super said nobody. Bill told the super to open the door.

The super used his key and opened the door. Inside the bathroom stood a white male, arms extended at shoulder height, aiming a 9 mm automatic.

The super turned fast to his left, to get out of the line of fire, but the first shot hit him in the cheek, went through his mouth, shattering his teeth, and exited through his other cheek. Bill Muldoon was behind the super, and he too turned to the left. The second shot hit him in the right arm, shattering the bone between his shoulder and elbow. The third shot hit the white female in the center of her head, killing her instantly.

The shooter slammed the bathroom door shut again.

The shit was on. Big time. In this basement room, about twenty by thirty feet, people were lying all over the floor, shots were flying, as the other detectives fired at the bathroom door.

Bill Muldoon crawled to the door to the apartment. He

had the presence of mind to stop and give Mendicino not just his gun but his extra ammo too. On the street, he couldn't get into the police car and use the radio because Mendicino had driven, had locked the car, and had the keys in his pocket. Billy Blue Eyes, with blood streaming from his arm, ran two blocks to a bodega, where he could use the phone.

Right then, I was on my way back to the office in a radio-equipped car, and I heard the call. 10-13. Shots fired in basement apartment at 9 West 102nd Street. Detective shot.

My heart sank. I knew who was there, and I was *scared*. My foot hit the gas pedal.

When I reached the location I saw three radio cars, doors open, lights flashing. Uniformed officers, guns drawn, were yelling into the basement. Shots were being fired.

I heard Rushin yelling at the perp to give up. I heard Mendicino yelling for ammunition. I didn't hear Bill Muldoon, so I knew my partner was the one who had been shot.

I tried to get into the apartment, but the door was closed, and Rushin was holding it shut. He wouldn't let anyone in or out.

Jim Rushin was a first-grade detective and a sharp piece of work. He knew that the cops outside didn't know him. He was black, and he was not about to let excited young cops come into that apartment and see a black man in civilian clothes with a gun in his hand. He knew it was not a racial thing. It was a cop thing and a totally stressful situation. The guys in uniform knew a detective had been shot. Shots were still flying. Hearts were pumping. Jim kept that door shut.

Finally he and Mendicino rushed the bathroom door and crashed through it. They found the shooter lying on the floor with four gunshot wounds.

The shooter was not the man we had a warrant for. He was a man wanted for murder in Nassau County. He and his girlfriend had holed up in this apartment, and the detectives who had come to serve the warrant probably would not have identified him. It was the ten pocketbooks and the locked bathroom door that caused the trouble. The shooter recovered and is serving a life sentence.

The super survived and got a new set of dentures.

I talked to the ambulance people outside the apartment and was told that Bill Muldoon had been taken to Lennox Hill Hospital. Why Lennox Hill? I wanted to know. Because Muldoon insisted on it, they said. Then I knew he would be all right. Lennox Hill is one of the finest hospitals in New York. Billy Blue Eyes had figured, Why settle for hamburger when you can have filet mignon?

Jim Rushin and John Mendicino have since retired. Bill Muldoon was permanently disabled and never really came back to work. His doctor told him to play golf to strengthen his arm, so he switched from playing three times a week, which he had done for years, and started playing five times a week.

I left Lennox Hill Hospital and started home about four o'clock on Thanksgiving morning. I lived upstate at the time, in a small town in Orange County. I stopped at an overlook on the Palisades Parkway and got out of the car to clear my head.

I felt bad. I had to get my head correct about what had happened. I was sorry my partner had been shot, but I couldn't help feeling happy that it hadn't been me. Before our Thanksgiving dinner I said grace and thanked God for His bounty. But my family and I also thanked God for His protection of Jim Rushin, John Mendicino, and Bill Muldoon.

He was a great loss to the New York City Police Department. They don't make men like Billy Blue Eyes anymore. In the short time of our partnership I learned a lot. Life is a great teacher, and every day of your life you should learn something new. But with Billy Blue Eyes it was a crash course. He was some teacher!

# 4

## YOU CAN RUN BUT YOU CAN'T HIDE

IN WHAT WE MIGHT CALL my autobiographical chapter, the word "I" comes in too many times. I don't know how else you can talk about your own life, but I don't want to be construed as an "I" guy. What I want to emphasize is that successful police work is a matter of teamwork, not the work of some superstar. Sometimes one patrolman or detective makes a big breakthrough. Almost every time, he or she is able to do that because others have done their work and set up conditions that made it possible. My father, who loved sports and played on teams, taught me that whenever the job is too big for one man to handle, that's when teamwork comes in. Just about everything we do is too big for one man to handle. Police work is all teamwork.

I've already mentioned that Manhattan North Homicide Squad often has been described as something of an elite force within the department. But let's understand that we couldn't begin to function without the help and cooperation of a whole lot of other people. I never investigate by myself. At the very least, my partner works with me; and most of the time we work with a lot of other people.

A murder investigation is, first, the primary responsibility of the precinct detectives. In many cases, they've already done vital work before we get there. Also, when we arrive—the senior guys, the specialists—we don't take over from the precinct detectives. We don't give them orders. We talk things over. What have you done? What do you want us to do? What've you found out? Don't you think it would be a good idea if we did so-and-so? Almost always, the precinct detectives take the suggestion and agree it *would* be a good idea if we did so-and-so.

An investigation is a matter of a lot of hard work, canvassing a neighborhood, talking to maybe hundreds of witnesses or potential witnesses, gathering information, gathering facts.

It's a matter of little things making a big thing and making a successful prosecution.

One day during our collaboration on this book, Bill Harrington suggested that a criminal must be far more likely to get caught in a big city than in a small town. It takes a big police department with lots of well-trained people to do the kind of detective work I've been describing, he said.

Well, I did have to admit that a cold-blooded murderer who'd killed his sister and shoved her in a box once said to me, "I knew it was over when I saw it was New York City homicide detectives that got me."

"You've got the resources," Bill said. "It looks to me like a small-town police department or a rural sheriff's department would never be able to close cases the way you do."

I have to disagree with that. The small-town and rural departments don't deal with the volume we deal with. And they certainly get more cooperation from the citizenry than we get. The people of the Nineteenth Precinct and the Seventeenth Precinct—midtown Manhattan precincts—see crime and are horrified by it, and they'll come and they'll tell you, and they'll give you names, and they'll be available as witnesses. Go up to Harlem or Washington Heights and see how many people want to be witnesses. I'm not saying that Harlem or the Heights are bad places. I've worked there all my life in the police department, and I've gotten a lot of help from the people in Harlem. The problem that you have is that the criminal element does not rule the Upper East Side, but the criminal element can rule a block in Harlem. There's fear and intimidation. And it's not right. But it happens, and it's a shame.

To give you an example, there was a so-called mystery witness in the Jogger case. He was a teenager who maybe could have given the prosecution a couple more convictions. As time went by and a certain element of the press and public opinion insisted the Jogger case was only a matter of the white establishment trying to hurt a bunch of black teenagers, the "mystery witness" became afraid to testify. His mother was afraid of what might happen to him—and to her—if he was seen as the kid who testified against the others.

There's a certain element that thinks they own the streets. They've got people on the run. They don't have the police on the run.

They may think so. But they're wrong.

The first line of defense is the uniformed officers in the radio cars. Their very presence on the street *deters* crime. The guy on the street thinking about doing something criminal holds back and doesn't do it if he sees a police officer. The uniformed police are usually the first officers on the scene of a crime. The detectives have their job to do, and I think we do it very well, but the patrolman remains the backbone of the force.

One day Bill asked me, "Is there a police type, a particular kind of person who wants to be a police officer?"

In my experience, the cop is a product of society and an image of the community. He is a father, son, brother, husband; and she is a mother, daughter, sister, wife. They're your neighbors.

There is no particular "police type."

This is an important question, actually. Who wants to do this work? The stereotype TV or movie police officer is the blazing-gun, kick-down-the-door, shoot-'em-up, show-no-fear superhero. That's great show-biz hype, but it's the farthest thing from the truth.

In my thirty years in law enforcement, I've seen all types come and go. There is one constant. Men and women don't change because they've sworn an oath to uphold the law and start wearing a badge and carrying a gun. That doesn't make heroes.

Time and again I've seen the most unassuming guy step forward and take control of a situation. In some cases it's peer pressure, and in some it's training. But no amount of peer pressure or training can force a person to charge through a door when he knows that on the other side of that door there is an armed, trapped person ready to do anything to avoid a term in prison. Training at the academy and on the streets is about tactics and how-to-do-it techniques, but that doesn't push a cop through that door. The next question, of course, is, "Who goes through the door—you or your partner?"

That's pretty much cut and dried. Your case, your door; his case, his door. That's the rule, so to speak. The reality is that your partner is like a brother, sometimes closer than a brother. You spend more time each day with your partner than you do with your family. If you are lucky, as I have been throughout my career, your partner knows that the secret of a successful arrest is a coordinated effort and speed. Until the suspect is subdued and handcuffed, you have only your partner to rely on.

"What's the most dangerous kind of arrest?" Bill asked me.

"Arresting a person in his household and in front of his family. It's been my experience that kindness is too often mistaken for weakness, and if a subject suspects weakness he is more likely to make trouble. That's why we treat each incident with a businesslike attitude until it is under control.

"There's a tremendous amount of stress in police work, and it's especially great when making entries.

"Ideally we learn the physical layout of an apartment by visiting the apartment above or below. At the door the first to enter stands at the side opposite the door handle, so that when the door is opened your foot goes right into the opening and your body is pushing the door. At this point, the adrenaline rush is unbelievable, the pump is going like crazy, eyes dart all around, and your mind is going a mile a minute.

"Each step is calculated. Each room is searched independently, one at a time, so that nobody is left to your rear. Each closet door is opened and the closet searched. I have found individuals in closets behind hanging clothes and under bags of laundry. The old under-the-bed trick is tried more times than even I can believe. Sometimes we've found them trying to hide between the box springs and the mattress."

"Scared to death, I imagine." Bill laughed.

"I can tell you, when I find a guy, many times it scares me more than him.

"Let me tell you about an incident that happened in 1970. Detective John Hagan and I were working the Three-four Squad, and we were told that a man named Robinson, wanted by Hagan for robbery, was in an apartment in the

Bronx, on Anderson Avenue in the Four-four Precinct. John Hagan and I went there and knocked on the door. A woman came to the door, and we told her we were looking for John Robinson. She stepped out in the hall and told us he was in the apartment.

"We entered and searched without success. We noticed that a window opening on the fire escape was ajar, so we supposed he had gone out that way. We were standing in a bedroom, and Hagan suggested I check behind a dresser that was sitting catty-corner. I went over to the dresser and gave it a tug. To my shock, not six inches from my face was Robinson, staring at me. I jumped back, pulling the dresser with me, and I fell on my back.

"Hagan, who had been a longshoreman before joining the department, could hit like a mule. He gave Robinson one shot right on the button. Robinson fell down beside me, shaking from the punch. I was shaking from the scare."

"Okay, Tom. What you're telling me is that the police officer really *is* different and special."

"The average officer works eight hours a day. Seven hours and fifty-nine minutes he spends serving the community one way or another. Sometimes in that one other minute he looks fear in the face. If he does his job in spite of fear, that makes the guy with the badge different and special. That one minute binds him and his partner in a brotherhood that forms when two men meet danger and survive. The adventure of the job is that you never know when danger will come or how often. It's just a reality you have to deal with. You don't ponder on it."

The case I am now going to describe demonstrates, I think, how the various members of the team work together.

The case was a triple murder. It happened in 1973, when I

was assigned as a precinct detective in the Three-four Precinct. The Three-four is bounded on the south by 155th Street, on the west by the Hudson River, and on the east and north by the Harlem River. It includes the neighborhood known as Washington Heights.

Washington Heights is an area rarely visited by most New Yorkers. Out-of-towners drive through it all the time but are hardly aware of it. They drive on Interstate 95 and cross the George Washington Bridge. They think of the highway on the east side of the bridge as the Cross Bronx Expressway, and many of them don't even realize that between the Harlem River and the bridge they drive about half a mile across the northern tip of Manhattan—Washington Heights.

Twenty years ago, Washington Heights was a Latino community, populated chiefly by Puerto Ricans. Today the Latino community there is made up chiefly of people from the Dominican Republic. Very many of them are illegal aliens and so are suspicious and untrusting of the police.

In this case, a man in a bar called Casablanca on Saint Nicholas Avenue at 198th Street had killed two men in the bar and one on the street outside, about three-twenty in the morning.

What had happened was that one of the three victims, Ricardo Pinero, had come on pretty hard with the barmaid, who was an exceptionally pretty girl. We'll call her Rosa, which was not her name. Pinero didn't know two things. Make that three. He didn't know that Rosa's boyfriend, Arturo Garcia, was drinking at the bar. He didn't know that the boyfriend was one of the biggest narcotics dealers in Washington Heights—probably *the* biggest. And he didn't know that Garcia was carrying a gun.

He might have guessed about the gun. There were about forty people in the Casablanca that night, and I would guess the majority of them, including some of the women, had guns. They called their guns their "shit"—like "I'm packin' my shit." Another word for the guns was "nines," referring to the fact that most of them were 9 mm automatics. In fact, one of Pinero's companions was carrying a gun.

Garcia got tired of Pinero hitting on his girlfriend, so he came off his barstool and told Pinero to lay off. Pinero was in no mood to lay off. He didn't know who Garcia was and had no intention of taking orders from him. He got up, and there was a shoving match. That was the end of Pinero. Garcia yanked out his "shit" and fired three times. Pinero fell down dead.

At the same time, one of Pinero's friends made a lunge at Garcia. He took one shot in the head, and he too was dead.

The third man broke for the door. But he couldn't get out. Too many people were trying to get out that door. Finally he pushed his way through. Then Garcia fought his way through the crowd and reached the street. The third man, seeing Garcia coming with his gun, drew his own gun and fired. He missed Garcia, but Garcia did not miss him.

When the radio cars arrived, one man lay dead on the street and two lay on the floor of the Casablanca. About twenty people had not yet gotten away and were in the bar.

All of them were witnesses.

A funny thing, though. As they were questioned, each one, men and women, insisted they had been in the toilet when the shooting happened and had seen nothing. The men's room in the Casablanca would have been crammed tight if three men tried to get in there at once. At least ten men swore they had been in that men's room when the shooting happened.

Nothing surprising. We've all heard that one many times. People don't want to be witnesses. They are afraid to be witnesses. I've heard twenty or twenty-five men solemnly declare they were in a men's room and so saw nothing—when the men's room wouldn't hold four of them at the same time.

The patrolmen questioned all the people who were still in the bar. They took their names and let them go, which was a mistake. They should have demanded identification. When the next day we began to look for those people to talk to them, we learned something else that was not surprising— that out of twenty, only one had given a correct name and address.

I was on a shift that began at eight in the morning. When my partner and I arrived, the body had been removed from the sidewalk, but the two inside still lay on the floor. The Crime Scene Unit was on the job.

The Crime Scene Unit is a group of specialists who photograph and measure the scenes of crimes, take hair samples, body-fluids samples . . . anything that might become evidence. They also lift fingerprints. A great many glasses were on the bar, left there by men and women who had bolted for the door. Included among those glasses was the one from which the as-yet-unidentified shooter had been drinking. I asked the CSU to take fingerprints off all the glasses. That was a big job for them, but of course they did it.

Fingerprint evidence can be very important. It has been suggested that fingerprints are only rarely important, because any smart criminal will wear gloves and not leave fingerprints. Well, that's not true. Take this case. Garcia didn't know as he stood drinking at the bar that soon he was going to commit three murders, so he had no problem about leaving his fingerprints on his glass. A defense he might have liked to use—that he was nowhere near the Casablanca that night—was lost to him, because his fingerprints were on one of the glasses on the bar. His fingerprints did not help us identify him as a suspect, but once we had identified him as a suspect by other means and took him into custody and took his fingerprints, we had proof positive that he had been in the Casablanca when the shootings happened.

We began a canvass of the neighborhood. Many people lived in apartments across the street, with windows facing the scene of the crime. We went from building to building, apartment to apartment, questioning people who had been asleep and had maybe been wakened by the gunfire. These potential witnesses too were afraid to talk. Maybe it was true that none of them had heard or seen anything. In any case, they did not help us.

Except one. In one of the apartments lived a young man I will give the name Jésus. When I spoke with him, he said, "You once did me a favor, so I'll do you one. Yes, I did see something."

I made it a practice during my years in the Three-four Precinct to fill out an index card every time I responded to a call, writing down the address and the names of people I talked to. When you come to somebody's apartment in response to a burglary call or some other call, you are seen as the policeman who came to help. And they remember. More readily than other people, they will help you if they can. There were very few blocks in the precinct where I didn't know somebody I could call on.

I have to confess that I didn't then and don't now remember what I had done for Jésus. It made no difference. *He* remembered. He thought of me as a friend. And that's what counted.

Jésus had been on his way home at three-twenty that morning and had been on the sidewalk across the street from the Casablanca when the shootings happened. He saw people running in panic from the bar, and he ducked into a doorway. He saw Pinero's friend run out, saw him draw his gun and fire a shot, and saw another man fire two shots. He saw the survivor—which was Garcia, of course—run down the street and jump into a car. He wasn't sure what kind of car it was, only that it was red.

So we had one eyewitness. Unfortunately, he had not had a real look at Garcia's face and could not identify him. He was telling the truth. He couldn't have made an identification at that distance.

Later that day I tried to question Rosa, the barmaid. Like everybody else, she insisted she had not really seen what happened; but she did point to one end of the bar and told us the shooter had been standing there. Later, another witness would tell us that the shooter had been at the middle of the bar. When we matched fingerprints, it turned out that Garcia's glass had been found at the middle of the bar where the other witness said he was. Rosa had been trying to confuse us.

She also insisted she did not know who owned or managed the bar. This was not an unusual story. Often bar employees will try to protect the boss by saying they don't know who owns it or who manages it. It would seem like a simple matter to find out. All you have to do is look at the liquor license, right? Not right. Very often the license is in the name of a front, not in the name of the person who actually owns or manages the bar.

Over the years we've developed a method of flushing these characters out, and I used that method then and there. I walked over to the window, where by law the liquor license must be posted. There is a heavy fine for selling liquor without the license on display in the window. I reached down and picked up the license. "Well," I said to Rosa, "if you don't know who the boss is, I guess I'd better take this license over to the precinct station for safekeeping. It's valuable property, and somebody might steal it. When the boss calls in, tell him I'm keeping his license at the station. He can pick it up there. Okay? Oh, uh . . . you're closed of course until he comes in and gets his license."

Usually you don't get back to the station house before the owner is on the phone, wanting his license. This owner showed up fast, identified himself, and recovered his license. It turned out, though, that he really didn't know what had happened.

Rosa worked the day and night after the shooting. The next day she disappeared. We would later learn that she and Garcia had gone to Florida.

The only person who had been in the bar and had given the patrolmen her correct name and address was one of the most courageous people I have ever known. I am going to conceal her name for reasons that will become apparent. I'll call her Julia.

Julia was a pretty Hispanic girl, a single parent, living in a flat several blocks away from Casablanca. Because she had given her correct name and address, we were able to interview her. Yes, she had seen the shootings in the bar. Yes, she could identify the shooter if she saw him again, though she did not know who he was. He had been standing at the middle of the bar, not where Rosa had said he was—and, as I've said, the fingerprint evidence would prove Julia was right.

So, we had two witnesses: Jésus, who had been across the street, and Julia, who had been inside Casablanca and saw everything. Jésus had seen someone shoot the man on the street, but he had not been close enough to identify Garcia. Julia had seen Garcia kill two men in the bar, but she didn't know who he was.

We learned his identity through a police informant.

Informers are often important. Obviously, we always keep

their identities secret—though I am going to tell you who this one was. They can be all kinds of people. Some of them are paid. Some inform because of real or imagined favors done them by police officers. Occasionally we can put in a good word with the prosecutors on behalf of somebody who has helped us with information. Sometimes we put in a good word in favor of somebody else, a relative or friend of the informer. Though I've never done this—never was in any situation where I *could* have done it—in some cities it is not unusual for the police to allow a prostitute to work the streets unhindered in return for bits of information she picks up from her clients. Johns love to brag about the great things they've done, and they never guess the golden-hearted hooker carries their stories directly to the police.

The informant in this case had the best of all possible motives for telling us everything he knew. He was Garcia's number-two man. If we put Garcia away on a murder rap, he would take over the gang.

When we did in fact put Garcia away, this man took over and called himself El Diablo (The Devil). He was a murderous criminal, responsible for at least twenty homicides. Eventually he was shot dead at 163rd Street and St. Nicholas Avenue during an exchange of gunfire with a member of the Manhattan North Narcotics Squad.

For now, he came to us with the story of the shootings in the Casablanca. He had not been there, he insisted. He had not witnessed anything. But he knew the whole story, and in time he even told us where Garcia was hiding.

It was not enough for El Diablo that Garcia had run away to Florida, taking Rosa with him. So long as Garcia was alive and out of prison, he might come back and claim leadership of the gang. What was more, the gang remained loyal to Garcia. If he had come back, they might well have put El

Diablo aside. In fact, all the time Garcia was gone, the gang sent him money to live on.

The gang, about twenty men, was a tight-knit organization. They were wholesalers. Heroin was the drug of choice in 1973, but you couldn't buy a deck of heroin—that is, a glassine envelope selling for $5 or so and containing enough for one shot, one high—from them. You had to buy your deck from a street seller. Garcia dealt only kilos.

How much money passed through their hands in a month, I couldn't guess. You can be sure it was a lot, and El Diablo had a powerful motive for putting Garcia behind bars.

We knew the gang hung out in a social club. My partner and I went there, smashed the window by throwing a garbage can at it, and jumped into the place with guns drawn, yelling "Police." We heard a clatter. There were fifteen guys in there, some of them playing pool, and they had just dropped fifteen guns on the floor. They weren't going to get caught on a weapons charge.

None of them, of course, had witnessed the shooting. None of them knew where Garcia was. None of them knew anything. El Diablo was there. We questioned him, the same as we questioned the others, not letting the others see that we knew him. Talking in the presence of his friends, he knew nothing. Nothing at all.

We gathered up and confiscated fifteen guns.

El Diablo had told us not just that Garcia was in Miami Beach, but in what motel and in what room. We called Dade County Homicide and asked for assistance. I took a package of information on the case, including a photo of Garcia, to LaGuardia Airport. I identified a flight going to Miami and asked the pilot of that flight to carry the package. He agreed. Then I called Dade County and told them the package was on the flight, in possession of the pilot. Within five hours,

Dade County had the package—NYPD's answer to overnight mail!

The Dade County detectives checked the motel and put it under surveillance for a few hours, until they could be sure Garcia was in his room. Then they broke down the door. Garcia and Rosa were naked on the bed, in the midst of a most intimate activity.

The Dade County guys turned the couple over to us, and we brought them back to New York. Rosa was released on the condition that she would be a witness at Garcia's trial.

Now hell began for Julia. Garcia and his family knew who the witness was. We had not used El Diablo—we couldn't use him. Jésus was a witness to the sidewalk shooting but could not identify Garcia. Julia was a witness to the inside shootings and *could* identify Garcia.

Members of Garcia's family began to visit Julia. Each time they came, they abused her unmercifully. Holding guns to her head, they forced her to strip naked and remain naked while they swaggered around her apartment, calling her names and threatening to kill her unless she promised not to testify. More than once they raped her, in front of her children. Why they didn't kill her, I will never understand.

New York has no witness protection program, and the NYPD simply did not have the resources to give her twenty-four-hour protection. She had no relatives or friends to whose homes she could have retreated.

We arrested Garcia's brother and got a rape conviction—for raping Julia. We made several other arrests and got other convictions. But that did not help Julia. Every time these people found her at home, they stripped her and then abused her both verbally and physically—and raped her again and again.

For six months we tried to get her a new apartment, away

from the neighborhood. That ran us up against the stonewall bureaucracy of the City of New York. Because Julia didn't live in a subsidized housing unit, she couldn't be transferred to another subsidized housing unit. She had to apply for housing assistance, and the bureaucracy took *months* to process her case. The fact that she was a vital witness in an important case cut no ice. The fact that she was being repeatedly abused and violated meant nothing. The housing people opened a file and worked it through all their usual procedures, in no particular hurry. In a sense, Julia was as much a victim of the city bureaucracy as she was a victim of Garcia's family.

When, just before the case went to trial, the housing bureaucrats finally found her an apartment in south Manhattan, two other detectives and I rented a truck and moved her ourselves, to be sure her abusers wouldn't interfere with the move or follow her and see where she would be living.

I said she was one of the most courageous people I've ever known. The more they abused and hurt her, the more stubborn she became. She was determined to appear and testify. And she did.

On her testimony, Garcia was convicted on two counts of murder. Because ballistics tests proved that the same gun that killed the two men in the bar also killed the man on the sidewalk, and because we had Jésus's testimony, Garcia was also convicted of the third murder

He was sentenced on all three, and today remains in prison doing life. El Diablo is dead, as I mentioned. I don't know where Julia is. I hope she's found a good life.

During one of our talks I found out that Bill Harrington, like many readers of crime stories and TV watchers, had an exaggerated idea of the importance of fingerprints. "Of how much value is fingerprint evidence, really?" he asked.

"Oh, it's great. We're always getting guys that tell us, 'I was never there, I was never in that apartment, I was never at such-and-such a place . . .' and we got fingerprints!"

"I suppose you'd never get a burglar that way."

"Why not? Sure we do."

"You mean they don't have enough sense to put gloves on?"

"You kiddin'? Of course not. Hell, no. Safe-crackers, big-time guys. *They* wear gloves. Burglars? All they want to do is get in, grab what they can, and get out."

"And leave their fingerprints behind so they get picked up?"

*"They* don't care."

"Well, that raises another point I wanted to ask you about. As a lawyer, I had some experience with criminals. Besides, I worked on a committee to revise the Ohio criminal code and so interviewed all kinds of people: criminals, cops, wardens, and so on. The general impression I got is that, though there are some smart criminals, the great majority of the people who commit crimes do it because they're too damned dumb to do anything else."

"I can tell you, the average burglar is dumb as shit. The average murderer . . . Why do they always still have the gun on them when they get caught? If they had any brains, they'd throw the gun away. But no. 'Why throw away a perfectly good gun? I know it works. I killed that son of a bitch with it, so I know it works.' That gun convicts them, and they've still got it."

"Well, if they tossed the gun in the East River, you proba-bly never would find it."

"Sure we do. Sometimes a witness says, 'Right there is

where he threw it.' We call in Harbor Scuba Unit, and they find it."

"Scuba Unit. Tell me it's not an advantage to be working with a big police force!"

# ● 5

## THE PREPPIE MURDER

TUESDAY MORNING, AUGUST 26, 1986. Pat Reilly, a mutual funds trader, was riding her racing bicycle in Central Park. She worked long hours, and if she didn't ride early she got no exercise that day. So she was in Central Park by 6:00 A.M. As she passed Cleopatra's Needle just behind the Metropolitan Museum of Art, she saw someone lying on the ground. A bag lady sleeping, she supposed. Then she took a second look and realized it was no bag lady. The young woman lying there was naked except for some clothes pulled up around her neck. She was silent, probably dead.

Pat Reilly rode to the nearest working telephone she could find and called 911.

The call reached a patrol car in the Park at 6:21. Two officers sped to the scene. The call was "Woman down," meaning a woman who needed assistance. Helped by Pat Reilly, the two officers found the young woman. In a moment they realized she was dead. Nothing could be done for her. They called for detectives.

When the patrol car pulled off the road and onto the grass, a crowd began to gather. They were joggers, mostly, and they kept back a respectful distance, near a stone wall. One member of the crowd sat on the stone wall, watching intently. His name was Robert Chambers. Several of the people around him noticed that his face was marked with deep scratches. Independent video cameramen were working the area, trying to get tape they could sell to the New York news stations, and he was clearly visible on their tapes. Robert Chambers sat on the wall, calmly watching police investigate the murder of Jennifer Levin.

The first detectives on the scene decided that what they were looking at was a dump job—that is, a case where someone dumps the body of a murder victim, probably far from the scene of the death. Central Park and the rivers are favorite places for dumping bodies. The initial responding officers had driven their car right onto the crime scene, leaving tire tracks in the soft grass. When detectives arrived, the patrol car had been moved; and the detectives, seeing the tire tracks, assumed incorrectly that the body had been thrown from a car. Some supposed the victim was a hooker, killed and dumped. There are lots of cases like that. Dump jobs are too common.

Detective Mickey McEntee didn't think this was a dump job. He was a Central Park Precinct detective, newly transferred from Bronx Narcotics. This slender, tanned, neatly groomed girl did not look like a hooker to him. While the Crime Scene Unit worked around her, looking for anything they could find—hair samples, body fluids, anything—McEntee explored the area. He found a lipstick case, a handkerchief, and a pair of panties, all some distance from the body.

When CSU was finished, detectives could check the pockets of the victim's clothes and look for identification. About the same time, a team of detectives from Manhattan North Homicide arrived—not my own team; I came on duty later in the day. It would be my role to question some of the many witnesses who were contacted.

My part in this case illustrates the way we work as a team. One of the things we knew was that Central Park would have had some joggers, some bike riders, and some dog walkers on the roads and paths very early in the morning. We knew also that many of these would be the same people every day. So we went out in the park and stopped joggers, bike riders, and dog walkers the next morning. Some of us had to run along beside joggers while we talked, because they were not willing to break their pace. We identified a number of people who had in fact seen a couple apparently having sex about the place where Jennifer died.

The girl had been carrying identification. She was Jennifer Dawn Levin.

The medical examiner inspected the body. She concluded that Jennifer Levin had been strangled.

The investigation was pretty much routine for a case of this kind. Having identified Jennifer Levin, it was necessary to notify her parents—a tough duty, incidentally. Her father said she had been out with her friends the night before her death, and he named some. Detectives contacted those friends. Friends identified other friends. At first we did not tell her friends that she was dead, only that she was missing.

An investigation of this kind is a matter of accumulating every little shred of information we can get, then putting it together and making a case. The park joggers, for example, couldn't have identified Robert or Jennifer, but they told us about the videotapers, which led us to view the tapes that showed Chambers sitting on the wall.

Soon the detectives knew that Jennifer had left a bar the night before with a young man named Robert Chambers. It seemed likely that he was the last person who had seen her alive. Detectives went to the apartment where Chambers lived with his mother and asked him to come to the Central Park precinct station to help them investigate the matter of a missing girl. They did not tell him she was dead.

But he knew she was. If he hadn't killed her, in any case he had been sitting on the wall watching the investigation—as the videotapes proved. He knew. He had seen the police remove her body.

Robert Chambers was a handsome young man, twenty years old, charming, personable, persuasive. His mother was an immigrant from Ireland, a nurse. For a short time she'd been nurse for John-John Kennedy. The family was prosperous but not rich. Robert was educated in prep schools, including Choate (where he didn't do well and soon left)—hence the name "the preppie murder." His chief problem in life was that most of his friends were securely wealthy. His mother and father gave him a good life, but he was not in the same class with the people he most wanted to associate with.

He was a wannabe. What he wanted to be was rich. He wanted to live like the rich people he associated with. He didn't want them to know he couldn't.

He coped in two ways. One, he lied. He described big important jobs his father held. Two, he stole. Some of his friends became aware that Robert would go through coats in closets, through bureau drawers, carrying off what he found. Some of them saw through him and simply stopped inviting him to their parties. He was expelled from one school for stealing, or helping a friend to steal, a teacher's purse and credit cards.

The summer after he graduated from prep school, his

mother got him a job working on a yacht owned by a wealthy friend. The yacht was moored in the East River, and the woman who owned it gave parties aboard. Robert worked there for a short time as a sort of steward, helping to stock the yacht with wines and expensive foods. After the owner discovered bottles of champagne and cases of liquor were missing, she fired him.

He enrolled in the Boston University School of Basic Studies. He was an indifferent student and soon fell behind— maybe because he was doing a lot of drinking and snorting coke. By midterm of his first semester he was under warning that he would be dismissed if he didn't make up his work. He was dismissed, all right, but not for that reason. He was expelled because he stole a credit card and used it to buy dinners.

In the fall of 1985, Robert enrolled at Hunter College in New York. But he showed up for classes only occasionally. One of his chief problems now was using more and more coke. He was stealing to get money to buy drugs. He also used stolen credit cards to buy clothes and dinners for his friends.

His mother knew something of this—not all of it. With a mother's optimism, she talked to her friends about Robert finishing his education at Oxford, even though she knew he had been asked to leave BU. One of his problems, she said, was that he was irresistibly enticing to young women.

That he was. There was a dramatic contrast between him and most of the preppie boys. He was taller, better built, more mature, and he had about him a particular charm that debutante types couldn't resist. Girls clung to him.

Jennifer Dawn Levin was born in 1968, a year after Robert Chambers. She was the daughter of a Jewish couple who separated early in her life. Her mother took her to live in California for some years, but they came back and settled again on Long Island. From early childhood, Jennifer was known as a showoff, a kid who tried to win acceptance and affection by putting on a show.

She was an attractive young woman by anyone's standards. In fact, Jennifer Levin was beautiful.

Her father remarried and made money in Manhattan real estate. He and his second wife lived in a renovated SoHo loft, a huge amount of space expensively furnished and decorated with art. When she was fourteen, Jennifer moved from her mother's Long Island home to her father's loft apartment. He and her stepmother set her up in a big area of her own, which she decorated to her own tastes. They gave her a telephone of her own and an answering machine. They enrolled her in a private high school. It's not an exaggeration to say she was a privileged kid.

She found what she thought was a wonderful way of life. By 1985 or so, people her age were welcome at Studio 54. Once the trendy home of "beautiful people," it had fallen on hard times and became an attraction for teenagers with fake IDs. She learned to drink. She fantasized about sex, and after a year or so gave away her virginity. Her father imposed some strict rules on her, but she moved in what was to her a heady circle, populated with "celebrities."

She dressed to suit her new life, in tiny miniskirts, sometimes in ripped jeans, often with a big cross hanging on a necklace—to which her Jewish father and stepmother objected. She bleached streaks into her brown hair. Like Robert Chambers, Jennifer was a wannabe. What Jennifer Levin wanted to be was like Madonna. The difference was, he lied, cheated, and stole. She only pretended.

In 1985, when she was seventeen, she began going to a bar called Dorrian's Red Hand, on Second Avenue. This was something new for her. The juvenile shenanigans that went over at Studio 54 did not work at Dorrian's. The place and crowd were more sophisticated, she thought. In fact, it was just a bar where bored kids hung out, drank, and did coke. Jennifer didn't see it that way. It became her favorite hangout.

When she was in her senior year of high school, she experimented with cocaine and LSD. She began having sex with more boys. She scored badly on her college admission tests and so she decided she wanted to go to an art and design school. That was her plan for the fall of 1986—the plan she would not live to fulfill.

One night in the fall of 1985 she saw Robert Chambers at the bar at Dorrian's. She didn't meet him then, but she thought he was "gorgeous." Her friends told her he had a bad reputation, for stealing. That didn't turn her off. To the contrary, it intrigued her. A beautiful man, bold and roguish. That's how she saw him.

On the night of her graduation from high school, she again encountered Robert Chambers. He told one of her friends that Jennifer Levin was "the best-looking girl in the world." The compliment blew her mind. Not long after that, she had her first sexual experience with him.

I want to say something about Jennifer Levin. Her name has been smeared. She has been called all kinds of things. It is true she lived a life very different from mine, and I'd guess it was very different from what most people live. But the way she lived was not all that different from the way other girls her age in her circumstances live. I can't approve of her lifestyle. I certainly wouldn't want my daughter to live that way. But she was not exceptional. She was not bad. I hate to see bad things said about her—when she's dead and can't defend herself.

* * *

The last summer of her life, Jennifer had sex with Robert from time to time. She worked as a hostess in a restaurant but quit to go to California and spend a week with some friends. After that she joined her father and stepmother in Montauk, then she spent some time in the Hamptons. When she returned to New York, she began to see Robert Chambers again. He was, she told him and others, the best sex she ever had.

Robert was standoffish. He made her pursue him. When she saw him at Dorrian's, sometimes he did not even speak to her. He was always the center of a circle of girls, and Jennifer knew she was not the only one he had sex with.

On the night of August 25 she decided to have it out with him. She waited in Dorrian's until nearly everybody else had left. He was still there. He had not gone out with anyone else. Finally, at about 3:45 A.M., he sat down with her. We can't know exactly what they said to each other, but witnesses reported later that their conversation was very intent and serious.

About four-thirty they left Dorrian's together. She was never again seen alive.

Two detectives, Frank Connelly and Al Genova, brought Chambers into the Central Park precinct station, the former stable that would later be the initial headquarters for the Jogger investigation. Outside, the little old building is beautiful. Inside, though, the place is tiny and decrepit.

On the way in, they had asked him no questions. In the first place, they didn't know enough about the case to begin an interrogation. Besides, it's usually a good idea to let a guy stew awhile. He was not under arrest, not handcuffed. Still, he has to be wondering, What's going on here? What kind of trouble am I in? Why don't these guys ask me something? They didn't ask because it's a technique. If a guy has nothing to hide, probably it doesn't upset him. If he does, it can very well rattle him.

It was Mickey McEntee's case. He took Chambers into a small room. First he gave him the Miranda warnings, and then he began to interrogate him.

Robert Chambers was unruffled. He said he had not left Dorrian's with Jennifer, really. They had walked out the door together, but they had parted immediately. She had gone across the street to a Korean deli to buy cigarettes, and he had gone to a doughnut shop at 86th and Lexington and then home.

How did he get the scratches on his face? Oh, he had been playing with his cat, he said, tossing it up in the air, and it had clawed him.

How did he get the wounds on his hand? He had been sanding floors for a woman upstairs, and the sanding machine had gotten loose from him and cut his fingers.

McEntee pressed, but Chambers calmly persisted in his version of events. He had not been with Jennifer Levin after they left Dorrian's, and he had been scratched by his cat.

McEntee reported that he was getting nowhere with Chambers. The young man remained calm. Two new detectives came in to question him—Lieutenant Jack Doyle, commanding officer of Manhattan North Homicide Squad, and Detective John Lafferty. They tried a different technique, chatting with Chambers about schools he'd attended, skiing, and his family's origins in Ireland—softening him up. It didn't work. When Lafferty pressed him about leaving Dorrian's with Jennifer Levin and about the scratches on his face, Chambers stuck to his original story.

No one yet had told Chambers that Jennifer was dead. Of

course, they didn't have to—he already knew; but they didn't know he knew.

Understand that Chambers was not really a suspect at this point. He'd been identified as the last person who'd talked to Jennifer. He was not yet the bad guy in the case, but he was not exactly Joe Citizen either. While he was not treated as a suspect, still, he was not treated as Joe Q. Citizen with information. Was he a little bit less than a suspect? He was a person who had to be spoken to. For all we knew they were standing on the street outside Dorrian's and some joker came along and said "Hey, Jennifer, I'll walk you home." Or maybe not. We had to know about that.

Now, Robert Chambers was a cool customer. He *wore out* detectives. He'd sit and talk about whatever they wanted to talk about, but whenever they came back to the tough questions, he gave the same answers. And he never asked for a lawyer. Oh, no. He was just the cooperative kid, trying to help us find out what happened to Jennifer. He was completely self-confident.

Eventually a Manhattan North Homicide Squad detective named Martin Gill came in to talk to Chambers. He and McEntee questioned him. And Marty Gill cracked the case.

There is an irony in this. It was Marty's last day on the Job. One day he was Detective Martin Gill, and the next day he would be Mr. Martin Gill. On the very last day, in the very last hours, of his career as a detective, he cracked an important case. I don't think he ever got the credit he should have had.

Marty was a veteran, a rugged-looking man who was as good at keeping his cool as Chambers was at keeping his. As McEntee watched and listened, Marty asked Chambers a few questions.

Chambers insisted that when he left Dorrian's with Jennifer, she had gone one way, he another. She'd gone across the street to buy a pack of cigarettes. She'd gone to buy cigarettes; he'd gone to buy doughnuts; and they hadn't been together after that.

It was the same story he'd told before repeatedly, but this time he'd made a mistake. Marty Gill knew that Jennifer Levin did not smoke.

Marty Gill had learned that fact from a witness. He confronted Chambers with it, and for the first time Chambers amended an important part of his story. Actually, he now said, he guessed he and Jennifer had walked together a little way. Just a little way, while he was on his way to buy doughnuts.

Marty pointed at the scratches. Chambers continued to insist his cat had scratched him. Other detectives had suggested that the scratches didn't look like anything a house cat could inflict, but Marty's response was something different. Well, he said, you know there are people who can tell the difference between cat scratches and people scratches.

McEntee picked up on this and said sure, the medical examiner will be able to tell.

Chambers then said Jennifer had scratched him at the corner of 86th and Lexington, where he was about to go into the doughnut shop. They'd had a little argument, and she had got mad and scratched him. Then Marty fibbed. He said he had a friend who worked in that doughnut shop. That guy'd remember any big incident on the street in front of the shop at four-thirty or five-o'clock in the morning. Hearing that, Chambers changed his story again. Actually, he said, it was the doughnut shop at 86th and Park.

Marty Gill had cracked the case. At this point Lieutenant Doyle came in. Doyle had heard that Chambers was changing his story, and he came on like an outraged father. I believed you, and you lied to me! Doyle then suggested to Chambers that he'd feel better if he got it off his chest. Marty Gill and Mike McEntee joined Doyle, saying, Yeah, you'll feel better if you tell the truth.

Chambers now admitted he had gone into Central Park with Jennifer.

Doyle and McEntee left the room, leaving Marty alone with Chambers. In the course of the next few minutes, Robert Chambers admitted he had killed Jennifer Levin.

Of course, it wasn't his fault. Nothing is ever anybody's fault. No, it was Jennifer's fault. He'd killed her, yes, but that was *her* fault, not his.

As Robert Chambers described Jennifer Levin's death, she had slipped away for a moment to urinate, then had come up behind him suddenly and tied his hands behind his back with her panties. Then she had tackled him, and when he was on the ground she had sat on his chest with her back to his face. She had opened his pants and pulled out his genitals. She had begun to stroke his penis, he said—so hard it had been very painful. She had grabbed a stick and hit his penis with it. Then, worse, she had seized his scrotum and testicles and squeezed so hard that the pain was excruciating. He couldn't take it. He had broken one hand loose from her panties and had reached up for her and thrown her off him. Having no idea he had hurt her, he told her it was time to get up and go home. That was all he'd done, just thrown her off of him. She didn't answer him. That was his story.

Bill and I talked about how this case came down. What we said on the tapes probably describes everything better than just a recital would do.

"How long had Chambers been in custody when he made the incriminating statement?"

"I don't know exactly. I wasn't on duty when he was brought in. I'd say about six hours."

"Do you think he finally just wore out?"

"Probably. What I think happened to him was that he was a smart little wannabe rich kid who got over on people all his life. He was always getting over on people. He got over on his mother, he always got over on his friends.

"He *used* people. A lot. All his life. And he was so used to getting over on people . . . Then he came up against detectives from Manhattan North Homicide . . . I mean, it sounds like an egotistical thing, but I had a serial killer tell me he knew the shit was over when he knew it was New York City detectives from the homicide squad. Chambers could have stopped the interrogation at any time by saying he wanted a lawyer, but he was so *in* himself. He thought he was better than anybody. He certainly thought he was smarter than any detective."

Marty Gill had gotten the incriminating statement. But that was his last duty on the case. His shift ended at four o'clock. It was the end of his career as a detective. Normally he would have been kept on the case, retired but called back and paid an hourly rate for his help. If anybody had rapport with Chambers, it was Marty. Chambers might decide to repudiate his statement. He might decide to clam up and talk to nobody else, to refuse to give a written statement, to refuse to talk before a video camera. But somehow—I don't know why—they thanked Marty and told him to go home. The credit for breaking the case went to others.

A lot of credit went to Mike Sheehan. I've got nothing against Mike Sheehan, who is a good friend of mine. He has since left the Job to become a professional actor. I don't in the least blame him for taking credit for this case. He made the case. I don't blame the bosses. It wasn't anybody's fault, really; it was just one of those things that happens. But it would have been a great ending for a great career, for Marty to have gotten credit for cracking the preppie murder case on his last day. Wouldn't it have been a great last hurrah for a guy leaving the police department? He's bitter about it, and I don't blame him.

I've emphasized that this is a team game. Well, Marty did an important job for the team in the preppie murder investigation, and his contribution should have been recognized more.

A lot of people think that when there's been a murder and there's been an arrest, the case is over. That's not so. The case is just beginning. Now you've got to accumulate the evidence that will convict the guy you've arrested. In this case, Mike Sheehan was just great. Without Mike, Chambers would never have pleaded guilty. Mike amassed so much evidence against Chambers that Chambers had no choice but to plead guilty. He was also a dynamite witness at the trial.

I don't want to try to go into all the elements of the case as presented by Assistant District Attorney Linda Fairstein or defense counsel Jack Litman. In my opinion, the combination of Linda Fairstein and Mike Sheehan was too much for even a lawyer like Jack Litman.

The crucial point, as it seemed to me, was that Jennifer Levin had died of strangulation and Robert Chambers had said he had only grabbed her around the neck and thrown her away from him. Common sense tells a juror that a person does not die of strangulation after only momentary compression of the throat. It takes fifteen seconds, twenty seconds, or more—probably more.

In the end, after a long trial and after the jury was about to break down and cause a mistrial, Robert Chambers was allowed to plead guilty to manslaughter in the first degree, with a sentence of five to fifteen years. He became eligible for parole in 1993 and was turned down.

Jail didn't slow Chambers down. He became sort of like a hero to some people out there. Of course, to Jennifer Levin's friends and to most normal people he was a monster. Before he was convicted he was shunned. I mean, he was the bad guy. But there was still a group out there, and there's still a group out there today, who think he got a raw deal. The bottom line is that the only person in this whole thing who got a raw deal was Jennifer Levin, because her name was smeared in death. She didn't have a voice from—the only voice from the grave she had was that of Linda Fairstein and/or Mike Sheehan and/or any detective that was called to testify as to the character of Robert Chambers. And the bottom line is that, no matter what time he does in jail, it doesn't bring back Jennifer Levin. It doesn't right the wrong. Still, some people will always say he got a raw deal. But what about Jennifer Levin? What do they say about that?

We have to wonder what she'd be if she were alive today.

 6

# "TALK TO ME": HOSTAGE NEGOTIATION

THE HOSTAGE NEGOTIATING TEAM WAS formed in 1978. That was the year in which a group of hostages were held in Frank's Sporting Goods Store in Brooklyn by a group of terrorists who went there to steal guns and ammunition. Ultimately the hostages escaped onto the roof, but not until after a police officer was shot and killed.

At that time, hostage-taking incidents were on the increase, and Lieutenant Frank Boltz had the idea that the New York Police Department should have a team of trained negotiators. He was responsible for what was originally a very small unit and now consists of about seventy negotiators.

At first, many in the department disliked the whole idea of negotiating. To a lot of men in the department, *negotiating* with criminals seemed cowardly. Better to confront them and force them to surrender, shoot them if necessary, A few even went so far as to suggest that negotiators would be betraying their fellow officers. Eventually, more rational attitudes prevailed, and hostage negotiators won the respect of the department and the public.

You may remember the name Eleanor Bumpers. Mrs.

Bumpers was a black woman, sixty-six years of age. The Housing Authority had been trying to evict her from her apartment and, on October 29, 1984, sent two men to do that. There was a confrontation between Mrs. Bumpers and a city marshal and a representative of the Housing Authority. She picked up a knife and began to threaten. Mrs. Bumpers was a strong woman, weighing nearly three hundred pounds, and the two men called Emergency Services.

Emergency Services is an elite unit, consisting of officers specially trained to act in dangerous confrontations. Officer Steve Sullivan and his partner responded. Mrs. Bumpers lunged at Steve's partner with the knife, and Steve shot her twice with a shotgun and killed her.

After a trial, Steve Sullivan was acquitted of manslaughter. United States Attorney Rudolf Guiliani found no violation of the federal civil rights laws, though some elements in the community insisted that Sullivan had fired at Mrs. Bumpers only because she was black. Sullivan was sued for $10,000,000. Eventually he was vindicated and promoted.

It was a tragedy in more ways than one. Here was Steve Sullivan, who had spent his life saving other people's lives, and he had killed an elderly woman. You can be sure Steve Sullivan didn't get up that morning saying to himself "I think today I'll go out and kill an elderly woman, maybe a black elderly woman." But before his day was over, he had done it. It was one of those situations that come up in police work. In a fraction of a second he had to decide whether to shoot Mrs. Bumpers to save his partner from her knife attack—and remember, the woman, though elderly, was not fragile, but was strong and weighed three hundred pounds—besides being emotionally disturbed. He shot her to protect his partner, and in so doing he brought down on his head the wrath of many of the citizens of New York.

It was after this tragedy that the department decided the

Hostage Negotiating Team should take on another responsibility, that of dealing with emotionally disturbed people. Mrs. Bumpers was not a criminal, and certainly she was not holding anyone. Maybe if a trained negotiator could have been there to talk with her, the tragedy could have been avoided. The department reevaluated the whole situation and decided to greatly expand the Hostage Negotiating Team. The expansion made an opening for me, and I became a negotiator.

We receive special training in the psychology of hostage negotiation, together with training in the use of the weapons we may have to employ. Today I would estimate that only about 10 percent of the negotiations we conduct involve hostages. Ninety percent involve what we call an EDP—emotionally disturbed person.

What was probably a typical situation came up in 1985. I call it typical, though it did have one very unusual, maybe even comic, aspect.

It happened on 125th Street between Broadway and Amsterdam Avenue. A man I'll call Alvin—which wasn't his name—had committed an armed robbery. The police chased him, and he ran into a laundromat. For some reason, a lot of my cases have been in laundromats. An odd coincidence. Alvin knew he couldn't get out. He might have been a user, but he wasn't then; he had his head on straight, and he understood the situation. The deal was, the police were outside. He was trapped and was going to jail for sure. But he was holding thirteen women and children hostages.

I was the first negotiator on the scene. This was about six-thirty in the evening. The second negotiator to arrive was Sergeant Pat Barry. In hostage negotiation, rank does not count, so we worked together without regard for that.

Alvin had taken his hostages into the back room of the laundromat. Pat Barry and I moved inside, into the front room, behind our steel shield. I don't think Alvin knew we were talking to him from behind a shield. He never opened the door to look out—probably thinking if he did he'd get his head blown off. Anyway, he was in the back room with his hostages, the kids screaming, while we talked to him through the closed door.

We talked to him for seven hours. The whole thing was an ordeal for him, as it was an ordeal for his hostages. But it wasn't an ordeal for me, you understand. This is my job. This is what I do. The point was to keep the dialogue going, to keep him talking, because as long as he was talking he wasn't going to kill anybody or do anything else stupid.

Over the course of the seven hours, we got all the pieces but me out of there. "Pieces" is our shorthand word for hostages. One by one he let all of them go. He'd ask for a Coke, for example. We'd say, okay, but what are you going to do for us? And he'd release one hostage for a Coke. This is part of the psychology of hostage negotiation. It often happens that for such a small thing as a Coke you can get a hostage out of danger.

One hostage got herself out. She told Alvin after a while that she simply had to go to the bathroom. If he didn't let her out of there to go to the bathroom, she'd have to defecate on the floor; she had no choice. He couldn't deal with that. He couldn't cope with it. It was something in his mind. He just couldn't accept the idea of a woman doing it on the floor. Rather than see her do what she said she'd have to do, he let her go.

Alvin couldn't face it. It says something about his mentality. In the first place, he didn't want that on the floor in the room where he was. Second, I think it said something about how he reacted to women. And third, I think he was a typical American. Europeans might not get excited about this kind of thing. But this guy just couldn't cope with the idea of a woman having to relieve herself in front of other people. He was absolutely horrified by the idea of her doing it on the floor. He just couldn't stand there and watch her do it. He couldn't.

Over the course of seven hours we negotiated all of the hostages out except one. This one was a young girl, and in the course of the hours she had developed what we call the Stockholm syndrome. That is to say, she'd fallen for her captor. She began to tell us he was ready to let her come out but she didn't want to come out, because if she did we'd hurt him. She wanted to be his protector. She hadn't fallen in love with him. It wasn't like that. She just couldn't bear to see him hurt. Stockholm syndrome.

So, we're left with Alvin still in the back room of the laundromat, with one hostage left. About this time he began to say he was hungry. He wanted a sandwich. Okay. Across the street there was a Blimpy deli. I sent a member of the hostage team to get him a sandwich, telling him to load it up, make it hot, make it oily. Make it so that it would go through him fast. If he has a problem about a hostage doing it on the floor, what about doing it himself?

It worked. He ate the sandwich. Soon he was telling us he'd give us the last hostage. Still, she didn't want to come out. What a mess! We talked and talked and finally convinced her to come out. Then Alvin came out, the main reason being that he had to go to the bathroom.

I've been asked why, in a situation like this, we don't put a laxative in a sandwich, or even a sedative.

We never do that. We don't drug or medicate any person. We don't know what his medical history might be. Give him something, it could kill him—a chance we can't take. But the spices and the salami and olive oil were enough. They loaded that sandwich up, and it loaded him up. It was beautiful. We didn't have to blow the guy away. We blew him out.

Probably the most unusual negotiation I ever took part in happened in 1989. We were in the office at Manhattan North when a call came in asking for a negotiator. The Two-eight Squad had gone to pick up a man to lock him up for robbery, and he was in a bedroom, holding a knife to his chest and threatening to kill himself.

The man who went with me on that call was Detective Scott E. Jaffer. On the way, we decided who would act as primary negotiator and who secondary. I was the senior man and it was my call, but I agreed to let Scotty be the primary man.

Emergency Services was already on the scene, working with the Two-eight Squad, and they had determined that in this typical Harlem apartment there were only two ways out of that bedroom—through the one door or onto the fire escape, both of which we had covered. The guy stood with his back to the wall and a knife to his own throat.

So, Scotty starts with the usual kind of talk: "We want you to give up. That'll be easier on you. It's not a personal thing with us. We don't want to hurt you. It's business. It's strictly a business situation here. You've been accused and, you gotta go to jail until this thing can get straightened out. So use your head, man. Make it easier for yourself."

And so on. But I was awestruck, thunderstruck to listen to Scotty Jaffer talk. He talked to that guy for an hour and a half. He never shut up. He never seemed to pause for breath. His mouth kept going and going and going.

The guy with the knife was a ghetto kid who'd been locked

up before on robbery charges. He knew he couldn't get out of there. He knew he was going to go to jail. It was just a matter of how long it would take him to decide to give up.

While Scotty talked, I was getting information. One thing we heard was that this guy had done this before. On the last occasion when he was arrested, a hostage negotiator had to talk him out. That siege had taken seven hours before this same guy dropped the knife and surrendered.

So we knew who we were dealing with. I guessed it would take a minimum of four hours, maybe as long as twenty hours, to get him out. So Scotty Jaffer talked . . . and talked and talked and talked, an unending stream of rhetoric.

Finally the kid talked to me and said, "Motherfucker, shut him up and I'll give up. I'll throw down the knife. Just tell that son of a bitch to shut his fuckin' mouth. I can't *stand* it anymore. He's drivin' me *crazy!*"

I said to Scotty, "Hey, man, take five. Let's look at this situation here."

Scotty stepped back and said nothing more.

The kid dropped the knife and said, "Get me outa here, just don't let him talk to me any more."

Scotty Jaffer literally drove the guy to sanity. We've heard about driving people insane. Scotty drove this guy sane.

Scotty is a great guy. A little story about him:

One day he bet me $10 I couldn't find out what his middle name is. I made three phone calls. The first one I made was to his mother. When she answered the telephone, I introduced myself and told her I worked with Scotty and that we were going to give him an award and wanted to have a plaque engraved with his name. So we needed to know what the E. stood for. "You're too late," she said, laughing and much amused. "He already called me and told me not to tell you."

**Left**
Detective
Tom McKenna

**Below**
The Manhattan
North Homicide
Division

**Right**
This is a picture of me and Detective Bill Kelly, apprehending a suspect later convicted of four homicides.

**Above**  Kidnap suspect Gladys Villar, arrested and charged with the kidnapping of Baby Jessica Maldonado and then selling the baby for $10,000

**Inset**  Loretto Bencumo Villar, also charged in the Baby Maldonado case

**Top**  My partner, Detective Bill Kelly

**Below**  One of my duties in the Central Park Jogger Case was to ensure the safety of Elizabeth Lederer, the assistant district attorney.

**Above**
At the scene of the crime: This picture was taken on 165th street, where I investigated the murder of Mark Britt.

**Right**
In detective work, waiting is a big part of the job. You wait on stakeouts. You wait on witnesses. Nothing ever runs on time.

**Above**
At the 35th Anniversary of the Tactical Patrol Force: (left to right)
Retired Detective Herb Wright, Detective Tom McKenna, Retired Lieutenant Mike Sheehan, Retired Sergeant Brian DeLancy, Retired Police
Officer Rich Esnard

**Below**
My wife, Marie

**Above**
My three daughters: Kelly, Tara, and Danielle

**Below left**
Having fun after the 1976 St. Patrick's Day parade: my wife Marie (center), Retired Detective Jim Mugan (right) and myself

**Above**
And my son, Tom

Detective Tom McKenna, trying out some new police equipment

Then I called the Detectives Benevolent Association. They couldn't tell me, because he had filled out his application Scott E. Jaffer. So finally I called the Sharim Society, the Jewish fraternal organization. Oh, sure, they had his application. His middle name is Eric. Why he tries to keep that a secret I'll never know.

In 1989 I became an officer in the Detectives Endowment Association. For a while I was the welfare officer for Manhattan North. We have a system where, if a detective has a problem, he can call a phone number twenty-four hours a day, seven days a week.

The way we work this is, an individual member has the duty for one week, and then it passes to another member. I had the duty the week of Christmas, 1989.

We had just gotten up, and I was enjoying Christmas morning in my home with my family. My nine-year-old daughter was opening her gifts. Suddenly my telephone beeper sounds. I look at the beeper, and it was a call from the association's answering service. I didn't want to have to get involved in something on Christmas morning, but I called the number, and the woman on the line told me a member had to talk to somebody.

I am going to call this man Detective Rob Barnes. That is very definitely not his name or anything like his name.

A million things went through my mind about why a member would call on Christmas morning. Many times it's because he has to report for duty that morning and doesn't like it. Other times he's in the office on duty and wants to complain.

Anyway, I called the number. Rob answered, and I told him who I was and asked him what I could do for him. On the other end of the line there was a slight pause, and then he said, very quietly, "I'm gonna eat my gun."

This was Christmas morning, and it was the last thing I expected. He explained. "My wife and children left me, I'm alone on Christmas morning, and I'm gonna eat my gun."

I said, "Whoa, whoa, whoa. Let's talk about this."

We talked. What had happened was that his wife had decided that Rob had become unstable, and instead of calling for help she had left the house and taken the children with her, leaving him there alone. He was a young man and he had decided his life was over, his world was gone, there was nothing left for him to look forward to, and he was going to end it all.

It didn't help that he was drinking.

I understood of course that he didn't really mean to kill himself, or he wouldn't have called the DEA number. What we really had was a cry for help. Although I think he might have done it. I mean, some guys *do* do it. I can't tell you why I think he might have killed himself.

Anyway, here's my wife, standing at the kitchen counter, asking what was going on. Christmas morning. What can be so important? Actually, she could hear the way the conversation was going and had some idea. I kept signaling her not to interrupt.

A bigger problem for me was to ask Marie to keep Danielle quiet. She was opening her Christmas presents and was very happy. For Rob, whose kids were gone, to hear that . . . Of course, it's much worse for this guy to have this happening to him on Christmas morning.

The holidays are an emotionally difficult time for many people, especially to be alone. More people tend to kill themselves around the holidays than at any other time of the year. For many people Christmas is not a happy time at all. It's melancholy, because others are happy and they're not.

And here's my daughter opening up her toys and presents. I can't tell Rob Barnes, Look, I'll have to call you back because my wife and daughter are opening up their Christmas presents. I can't even mention that I'm with my wife and my child.

After three and a half hours with Rob, I finally asked him if I could hang up for five minutes while I went to the bathroom. By this time I judged from the way he talked that I had brought him up enough that I could get away from him for five minutes. In hostage negotiation, many times you have to bring high people—that is, volatile people—down. In other cases you have to bring down people up—to stabilize them. I had to get this guy to the point where the gun was lying on the table, no longer pointed at his head.

So he agreed I could take a break and call him back.

I wanted to use my five minutes to call for help. He'd told me he had two brothers who were police officers. I had to call his brothers' command, convince the desk officer there on Christmas morning who I was—because you don't get a cop's home phone number by calling the station house. I managed to get through to Rob's brother. He said he'd pick up the other brother and be at Rob's house in fifteen minutes.

I got Rob on the line again. Now my job was to keep him on the phone for fifteen minutes until his brothers got there. I told him maybe his wife had done him a favor, breaking off the fight. She'd probably be back before long, I said. Anyway, your brothers care for you. Not only are they your brothers, they're your brothers in blue.

The brothers got there and got the gun. Now what do we do? For the next forty-five minutes I was on the phone to hospitals. We don't want Rob put in a ward with nuts. We don't want him put in with criminals, because he was a detective. Finally I found a hospital that would put him in a detox program, though strictly speaking he wasn't a drunk. He'd be cared for overnight, until psychiatrists could get to him the next day.

Next I got a call from the hospital. They were going to put Rob in a ward with criminals. I couldn't let that happen. I'd promised him he wouldn't be put in any such place. So on Christmas afternoon I had to go to the hospital and straighten that out.

The end of the story, so far as Rob Barnes was concerned, was that he got help. He was put through detox and given psychiatric assistance, and he recovered. Today he is working again as a detective—which he wouldn't be doing unless he's fully recovered.

Christmas day. My wife understood, and yet she didn't understand. She understands my job. She understands the ins and outs of the police department. Yet she doesn't understand, for example, why I never have an argument with my partners.

As in a marriage, you pick your partner. Occasionally a situation demands that you work with other people, but under normal conditions you work with your partner. You deal with work matters, not family matters. In police work you have no money problems and no problem of unfaithfulness. If you and your partner have different ideas about how a particular thing should be done, usually there is time to do it both ways. If he thinks we should search one building and I think we should search another, probably we'll search both. If a choice has to be made, the partner whose case it is makes the call. At home it's not usually that way. If a father thinks a child should go to one school and the mother thinks the child should go to another, they can't send the child to both. Can we afford a new car? Do we need a new refrigerator? Marriage partners have to make decisions, and a lot of times it's not easy.

The police department is a different world. It's a completely different world.

Bill Harrington asked me some questions about the dangers of hostage negotiation.

"Now, you're often facing a disturbed person or a desperate criminal, maybe through a thin wooden door. Do negotiators ever get shot?"

"Well, the Chinese fellow who killed his two children . . . he fired seven shots. But our men were protected by their shield."

"That's an interesting point. You work behind a shield?"

"Right. If we're just outside a door, we have a shield in front of us."

"Is that a steel shield?"

"Steel. All that kind of equipment. Sometimes you see our people up on roofs using long poles with mirrors that make it possible for us to see inside places. All that kind of equipment is made by the Emergency Services people. We've got ingenious people in Emergency Services Division. They make all that kind of stuff, and the shields."

"What about vests?"

"We have our vests. But my everyday vest isn't good enough to get me into what we call the inner circle. Only the negotiators and the Emergency Services people are allowed into the inner circle, that is, up close to the situation. When we go in there, we have to wear the Emergency Services vest, which weighs about fifty-five pounds."

"Fifty-five pounds!"

"You have hours and hours of negotiation, and sometimes you get to a point where you're ready to say 'Hey, let 'em shoot me, 'cause I can't wear this thing any more.' "

"What's it made of, steel?"

"Steel plates."

"Then your everyday vest . . . nylon?"

"Nylon or Teflon."

I had another situation in a laundry. This was on Madison Avenue between 124th and 125th streets. I'd just gotten off duty. I was in the parking lot, and I saw the lights going and heard the sirens. I asked what was going on and was told there was a hostage situation with a child involved.

When I heard there was a child, I knew I wasn't going anywhere. Manhattan North is at 119th and Park, so I was probably the closest hostage negotiator. I ran upstairs and grabbed my jacket, and I grabbed a vest out of a locker. This was a regular vest, but it wasn't mine; it belonged to another member of the homicide squad.

I went to the laundromat and got inside. The situation was that the man had had a domestic dispute with his wife and had shot his wife. He had taken his child and was in the rear room of the laundromat. As I entered the store, I could hear the child screaming. I tried to talk to the man. I talked for maybe an hour and a half, and the guy never responded.

"Were you standing right in front of the door?" Bill Harrington asked. "Couldn't he have shot at you through the door?"

"Actually, I was off to one side. I'm a guy with some smarts. I'm not just offering myself as a target. But you can't negotiate unless you're communicating, there must be dialogue. Of course, you can't see the guy, but at least you've got to look at the door. Emergency Services was there, as it always is in these cases, and what we try to do is put a loop on the doorknob. Once we've got a loop on the door, the guy inside can't open it, because we pull it tight. Almost all these doors like that one open in, which the fire laws require, and he can't open it. This means that if the guy behind the door decides to shoot, he has to shoot through the door. Since he doesn't know where you are out there, your chances of getting hit are minimal.''

"Of course, he could shoot through the wall.''

"Right. Bad guys usually shoot through doors. Cops shoot through walls. Cops also shoot down walls. See a bad guy sticking his head around the corner and jumping back. No point trying to aim. Shoot the wall. The bullet will run right down the wall and take that guy out. No problem. You have a guy hiding behind a car. Shoot at the ground. That bullet will run along the ground and take him in the ankle. Bullets don't ricochet up. They hit a flat surface, they'll run right along it.''

"Anyway, you're in the laundromat.''

"Right. And it was very frustrating, because I'm getting absolutely no response from behind the door.''

"What kind of things do you say in this kind of situation?''

"Oh, like, the baby is crying. Don't you want the baby to stop crying? I'm a father, you're a father, so say something to me. Say anything you want. If you're disturbed, tell me about it. Anything you can get them to talk to you about. . . . But you've got to get them to talk to you first. If they even say they don't want to talk to you, at least they've said something.''

I couldn't get anything out of this guy at all. I'd asked for TARU, the Technical Assistance Resources Unit, and I told them they had to get a probe through that wall so we could get a look into that room.

They got the probe through, and we looked. The guy was lying on the floor. He'd shot himself in the head. The officers who had chased him into the laundromat had heard a shot, but they hadn't known what it was. That was why he wouldn't answer. He was dead. The baby was crawling around in his blood.

I went into that room. I picked up that baby, which was covered with its father's blood, and I was devastated. I'd worked on thirty or so negotiations before, and this had never happened to me. It didn't make any difference that the man had killed himself before I got there, no difference that I'd never even had a chance to stop him. I was devastated by the sight of the baby covered with blood.

That's one thing I want to explain about this business. It's highs and lows. The high and the low, the high and the low. When you get a hostage out unharmed, you really, really feel good. When you finish a negotiation successfully, you feel a happiness you want to last, want nothing to break. That's the high.

Something else happened at that negotiation. What we were doing inside the laundromat was visible from the street, and there were lots of news cameramen there. I'd taken off my jacket, exposing the vest I had grabbed from the locker. While TARU was getting the probe through the wall, somebody taps me on the shoulder and says I'm wanted outside. I went out, and there was a chief there. "Take off that vest," the chief said. "But, Chief," I said, "I'm a negotiator. I have to wear a vest." "Take it off," he said again. "You're a disgrace." When I took it off I discovered something. I'd just grabbed that vest and ran, never really looking at it. Now I found out it had a big S on the front: the Superman logo. What was worse, on the back there was Tweety Bird perched on a bowl, and above Tweety Bird it said, "I'm so happy I could just shit!"

Negotiating with hostage-takers and emotionally disturbed people is often highly visible work, more visible than we could wish. When the hijacked Lufthansa airliner arrived from Germany in February 1993, NYPD hostage negotiators were at Kennedy Airport, ready to talk to the hijacker. As in most airport situations, the FBI was notified. Our men were there and ready, and they had developed the dialogue between the hijacker and the negotiating team. Because of this, they actually led the negotiations.

Experience has taught us some things about negotiating.

If you make any promises to the bad guy, you better keep them. Because you don't want them going into the joint and telling other bad guys, "Yeah, I dealt with them fuckin' hostage negotiators, and they *screwed* me."

When you talk this guy into coming out, to surrendering, he's coming out because he talked to *you.* He's not surrendering to them; he's surrendering to you, the negotiator. And if somebody smacks him and knocks him down, it's like you smacked him and knocked him down, because he's surrendered to you.

You've become his protector. Ten years ago, I might have knocked a hostage-taker on his ass. I can't do that now. I'm a negotiator. I can't knock him on his ass because I promised him we *wouldn't* knock him on his ass.

You don't develop a Stockholm syndrome with the guy. It's a question of credibility. You've got to have credibility. You have to be able to say to a guy "Look, if you do this or that for me, I'll do this or that for you." Then you have to do what you said. If you don't know if you can do what the guy demands, then you have to say "I'll make inquiries and see if we can do this, and I'll let you know whether we can do it or not."

The bottom line is credibility. You have to establish and maintain credibility, the same as when you're dealing with informants on the street.

In hostage negotiation, you never let them blame *you.* A

lot of them want to be able to say "If I kill this person, it's all your fault, because all I want to do is get out of here." The answer is "Hey, pal, don't lay your shit on me. If you kill that person, *you're* doing it, not me. I'm not making you do it. You're doing it. You're making that choice."

With EDPs, emotionally disturbed persons, a negotiator has to try to figure out what the EDP's state of mind is. A manic depressive is different from a paranoid psychotic. We are not doctors, but we are trained to try to recognize the subject's condition. We have to realize that words which would calm a normal person may trigger a violent reaction in an EDP. We have to be very careful about what we say. The wrong words may cause somebody to get hurt.

As I suggested before, negotiating is one of the most satisfying jobs in police work. The idea is to save lives: sometimes the lives of hostages, more often the life of a disturbed person who intends to harm himself. Or course we want to send the criminal to jail. More than that, we want to send the sick person to the hospital and the hostages home.

# ■● 7

## EVEN ANIMALS DON'T DO THIS

I WAS ON DUTY AS a precinct detective in the Three-four on the morning of April 4, 1981. Detective Mike Fletcher was catching cases that morning—receiving new cases as they came in. Because our desks were so close together, I heard the initial statement given to Mike in a case that would occupy my attention for months, a case that has never stopped troubling me.

A young man named Ramon Maldonado, a solemn, good-looking Hispanic, had come to the precinct station to report that his wife and infant daughter were missing. He was twenty-six years old. His wife, named Yudelka Maldonado, was nineteen. Their two-month-old daughter was named Jessica.

Ramon Maldonado said that the night before, at about nine-thirty, he had taken his wife and daughter to Columbia Presbyterian Hospital, which is in Washington Heights—165th and Broadway. The infant had been suffering from diarrhea and vomiting. Ramon had stayed with his wife and child at the hospital until Jessica was examined and the doctor had assured the parents that the infant did not need to be admitted to the hospital but could be treated with medication.

At this point, Ramon Maldonado had left the hospital. He worked a midnight-to-eight A.M. shift and needed to go on to his job. He advised his wife to take the baby home by subway or to telephone her brother to come and pick them up.

When Ramon Maldonado finished work the next morning, he hurried home—only to find his wife and child were not there.

Experience teaches detectives that almost always when a young woman is reported missing, one of two things has happened: she has had a quarrel with her husband and has gone to visit someone in her family, or she is with a boyfriend.

This case was unusual. Usually a young woman going to visit her family does not go after midnight, especially if her husband is working a midnight-to-eight shift. Usually also a young woman who cares enough about her child to take it to a hospital when it is sick does not take it with her while she goes out partying with a boyfriend.

We took a scratch on the case. Taking a scratch is our term for filling out an information sheet that will not immediately become an official report. In more than 90 percent of all missing-persons cases, the missing subject turns up within twenty-four hours or so. For that reason, what we generally do is hold the sheet for about twenty-four hours before putting it in as an official missing-person report. If we find out in that time that the missing person has returned, we can just rip up the sheet. We don't even give the matter a case number. If the missing person does not show up within twenty-four hours, we forward the report to the Missing Persons Squad.

We continued to talk with Mr. Maldonado, and he told us he had checked with his family and hers, and with friends, and no one had seen his wife and child.

At this point I called downtown to Missing Persons to give them the scratch.

You have to understand that in the past Missing Persons was of necessity pretty much a paper-shuffling operation. The number of people who turn up missing in the City of New York in the course of any given week is so great that Missing Persons simply does not have the personnel to send investigators out looking for people. There are certain priorities—for example, a child under ten years of age. But there are so many runaways and so many people who just decide to walk away from their lives that the police cannot spend much time looking for them. All they can do is check the morgue, check hospitals, and check the precincts, using names and descriptions, to see if anyone matching the description of a missing person is described in the reports of those agencies. Even with computerization, which they have now, it is difficult.

Anyway, I asked Missing Persons if they had any unidentified people in the hospitals or the morgue. They checked and said no.

At this point we told Ramon Maldonado to go home and get photographs of his wife and child and to bring them back, so we could send those down to Missing Persons.

While he was gone, Missing Persons called. They had a report from Brooklyn, Eight-three Precinct, that the body of an unidentified female had been found on Irving Avenue. She had been dumped in a pile of trash on the street. The clothing on the body matched the description given us by Ramon Maldonado.

I called Brooklyn and spoke to Detective John Clark, a man I had known for years, since I had served with him on the Tactical Patrol Force. He is a detective in Brooklyn

North Homicide. I asked him about the body on Irving Avenue.

I asked him first if they had found a baby with the woman, then if the woman was clothed or naked, then what was the cause of death. He told me they had found no baby. She was fully clothed, which probably ruled out a sex crime. The cause of death was strangulation.

The corpse was being transported to the morgue.

When Ramon Maldonado returned, Mike Fletcher and I took him down to the morgue to see if he could identify the body. I don't need to tell you what a horrible ordeal this was for young Mr. Maldonado—particularly when it turned out that the body was that of his wife. It was a tough thing for us too.

The corpse was lying in a pull-out drawer in the cold-storage room, covered with a sheet. We pulled the drawer out and uncovered the face. Ramon Maldonado burst into tears. He was looking at the face of his wife. The marks of strangulation were on her throat. She was the victim of a brutal murder.

Looking at that still face, we detectives were moved, too. She had been an attractive young woman, a young mother who'd had a stable home with a loving husband who worked hard to provide for her and their child. She'd had a good future ahead of her.

Now we knew that Yudelka Maldonado was dead. We knew she had been strangled. Among the many questions left open about the case was how had she gotten from Columbia Presbyterian Hospital to Irving Avenue in Brooklyn?

There was one big question that overrode all others. *Where was the baby?*

We checked with the hospital to confirm that Yudelka

Maldonado and her baby, Jessica, had in fact been there. We checked with Ramon Maldonado's workplace to be sure he had in fact been there all that night. We interviewed hospital personnel who had been in the emergency room that night. We interviewed cab drivers and drivers of gypsy cabs known to have been in the vicinity of the hospital that night. Neighbors of the Maldonados and of the Irving Avenue neighborhood were canvassed. A vast number of people had to be interviewed.

I say "we." A mini-task force of detectives from the Three-four and Eight-three Precincts was formed to conduct this investigation. It was an extended and intensive inquiry.

In any homicide case, the spouse is a natural suspect. Ramon Maldonado had impressed Mike Fletcher and me as an honest young man and the victim of a heinous crime and a horrible tragedy, and we wanted to clear him as quickly as possible. The statements of the people at his workplace that he had been at his job all night eliminated him as a suspect.

We had one possible break. A clerk at the hospital had given Yudelka Maldonado a slip authorizing the dispensing of a prescription medicine for the baby. Shortly afterward a bearded male had come in to inquire what had become of the young woman with the child suffering from diarrhea. The clerk was shown a photograph of Ramon Maldonado and photographs of a number of relatives and friends of the murdered woman. He did not identify any of them as being the man who had asked about her.

So who had that man been?

After about a week we had to close the file in the Three-four. All we had, remember, was a missing-person report, and we knew what had become of the missing person. The body had been found in Brooklyn, so the homicide case belonged to the Eight-three.

Even so, we could not forget the case. Although her body had been found in Brooklyn, we believed that Yudelka Maldonado and her baby had been kidnapped outside Columbia Presbyterian Hospital, which is in the Three-four Precinct. Because the case involved a baby and the baby was still missing, we just couldn't let go. Detectives must not get emotionally involved in the things they have to investigate, but it was hard not to have strong personal feelings about little Jessica Maldonado.

The baby remained missing. The case got a lot of media attention, particularly in the Spanish media. The Spanish-language newspaper, *El Diario,* and Spanish-language radio and television stations gave the story extensive coverage.

That would give us a major break.

About sixteen months after the murder of Yudelka Maldonado and the disappearance of her baby, a numbers runner by the name of Hugo Roman approached Detective Robert Brant, who was with the Arson Terrorist Task Force. Roman told Brant he might have some information about the baby who was kidnapped outside Columbia Presbyterian Hospital.

The case was mine now, because Mike Fletcher, who had originally caught the case, had been transferred.

I was at home and got a call from Detective Ronnie Hicks, a detective in the Robbery Unit, Three-four Precinct. Ronnie told me Brant had called to inquire into the Maldonado case. He said a man who lived in the Three-four might possibly have information about Jessica Maldonado and wanted to speak to me. I came into the precinct from my home in Queens and was introduced to Hugo Roman.

Some time before, Roman had been having problems with his common-law wife Mayra and had been thinking of leaving her. He didn't in fact live with Mayra but only stopped by her apartment when it suited him. His problem was that Mayra had gotten a little older, a little less svelte, and she had ceased to compare favorably with the younger girls who were attracted to him. Because he had money, Roman was something of a neighborhood Casanova. He was a Cuban, about forty years old, a dapper dresser. He splashed his money around. Of course, he was in an illicit business, which gave him a romantic air to waitresses, barmaids, and the like— who also got big tips from him. They found him fascinating. Mayra just didn't suit his image anymore, and he had been thinking of breaking off the relationship entirely.

Mayra, though, had told him she was pregnant by him and was going to have twins. Then she told him she had given birth to two boys, whom she named Moises and David. But there had been complications about their birth, and the hospital would not release them. The twins had to stay in the hospital for prolonged and expensive care.

Six months passed before he ever saw the twin boys. During that time he paid out as much as $80,000 in hospital bills.

Then Mayra told him she was pregnant again. In April 1981 she presented him with another child, a daughter.

Mayra had brought this child home within a few days after the murder of Yudelka Maldonado and the disappearance of her baby. Hugo Roman accepted the baby as his daughter, and they named her Barbarita. He had read of the murder and disappearance, though, and he could not help but wonder if Barbarita might not be Jessica Maldonado.

That was in fact what he was hearing on the street: that Mayra had never been pregnant this last time, that none of the children were his, and that he had paid out a tremendous amount of money as victim of an elaborate ruse.

None of this made any sense. Roman was saying he had

not really known if his wife was pregnant, that he had not gone to the hospital when she went to have the children, and that he had never gone to the hospital to see his sons during a whole six months that they were there. I could only figure that the man was a complete liar or the stupidest man I had ever met—or both.

With Hugo Roman's statement before us, we spent about three days checking background information. I was ready to believe the little girl they called Barbarita might actually be Jessica Maldonado. That being the case, how could we have done anything but give the case a full-court press?

On September 23, 1982, we went to her apartment and interviewed Hugo Roman's common-law wife, Mayra Roman, a fat woman who looked about the same age as Hugo. I asked her for identification for herself and the children. She produced birth certificates. Here was a problem. She had told Hugo the children were born in a hospital, but the birth certificates showed they had been delivered by a midwife.

We took Mayra Roman and the three children to the station house. She understood she was in trouble, but she also understood the trouble might not be serious if she cooperated. After about three hours she admitted that the children were not hers.

We immediately called the Latent Print Unit. One detective in that unit was a specialist in pediatric footprints. He took the footprints of the baby girl and compared them to the footprints taken at Columbia Presbyterian Hospital when Jessica Maldonado was born.

Barbarita Roman was Jessica Maldonado.

But who were the other two children? And where had they come from?

During further interviews, Mayra Roman told us that in the spring of 1979, she had approached a friend of hers named

Mercedes Arzuaga and asked for help with a serious problem. She had told her common-law husband Hugo she was pregnant with twins, when in fact she was not pregnant. She had told Hugo this because she knew he was seeing other women. She was getting old, and Hugo was losing interest in her. If Hugo found out she had lied about her pregnancy, it would be even worse. She asked Mercedes if she could help her locate a baby. Since Mercedes was a singer and traveled in show business, she might know how to do that.

Mercedes said it should be no problem, because there were always pregnant young girls looking for homes for their babies. She also told Mayra it would cost money. The girl would have to be paid; and she, Mercedes, would need money for expenses.

Mayra gave Mercedes a thousand dollars. From time to time after that she gave her more money.

Not long after her talk with Mercedes, Mayra confided in another friend, Angelita Rybin, and asked her too if she knew where to find a male infant. Angelita said unwanted infants were constantly being born in the Dominican Republic. Angelita offered to fly down there and get one. It would cost about $4,000. Mayra gave her the money. Angelita spent three or four months in the Dominican Republic and came back without a baby.

In September of 1979, Mercedes Arzuaga called Mayra from Puerto Rico and said she had located a family whose fifteen-year-old daughter had given birth to an unwanted child. Mayra sent Mercedes the money to bring the child to New York, and soon Mercedes arrived with the baby.

This was the little boy Mayra named David.

Mayra paid Mercedes $2,000 for her help in getting David. Then, a couple of months later, Mercedes came to Mayra's apartment accompanied by a young girl. Mercedes took Mayra aside and told her the girl was David's mother. She told Mayra not to talk to the girl about the baby, because the girl didn't know Mayra had the child. She said the girl and her family were very poor and were asking for more money. Mayra didn't have any more money, but she gave Mercedes her jewelry, worth probably $4,000.

At about this time, Hugo began to press Mayra about the other twin, Moises. Where was he? Mayra told Hugo that Moises was still in the hospital. The baby had a serious heart ailment and needed an expensive operation. Hugo gave her money for the operation.

In the spring of 1980, Gladys Villar, who was a cousin of Mayra's housekeeper, came to work for Mayra, doing ironing and other small chores. Eventually Mayra confided in this woman too. She told Gladys she needed a baby about the same age as baby David and asked if Gladys knew anybody willing to sell one. Gladys said she would ask around.

Gladys was a grim-looking woman, not really bad looking, just sharp-faced and obviously on the lookout. You could see she was a player of the main chance. I think she would have done anything if she saw an advantage for herself in it.

Between December 12 and 17, 1980, Mayra received a call from Gladys at about five in the morning. Gladys told Mayra that she had a baby boy available. Mayra went to the Villar apartment, carrying $2,000 in cash. Gladys had told the truth. In the apartment she had a little boy about the same age as David.

Loreto Villar, Gladys's husband, was also there. Mayra had met Loreto before. He had once come to her apartment to ask Hugo to lend him money to buy a garage. Hugo had not made the loan.

Gladys would not give Mayra the child for the $2,000, but

a day or two later Mayra was able to deliver another $2,000, and Gladys then let Mayra take the baby home. It was understood that Mayra would pay still another $2,000, making $6,000 in all.

Now Mayra decided she needed another child. Her motive in all this, we must remember, was to keep Hugo. Hugo was a real moneymaker, who had supported Mayra in style and given her expensive gifts. Besides, he was something of a stud. Mayra had been very happy with him. In fact, she had been proud to be known in the neighborhood as Hugo Roman's woman. But younger women were hustling him— maybe only for the big tips he left on bars, but hustling him just the same. Mayra could see herself losing Hugo. So she told him she was pregnant again.

On April 7 or 8, 1981, Gladys Villar brought a little girl to Mayra. Mayra paid for that child too—for Jessica Maldonado.

Mayra admitted to these facts—which left us with an odd situation. Under New York law as it was at that time, we had no charge against Mayra Roman. Buying a child was not a crime. It was crazy, but that was the way it was.

I have to admit something about Mayra Roman. She had bought these three babies like property, for money. But so far as we could determine, she loved them. They were deprived of nothing. They were not abused. They were well dressed, well fed, had nice little toys, and lived in comfortable rooms. She'd had a photographer in to take baby pictures of them. She was rearing those children to the best of her ability. We had to take them away from her, of course, we had no choice about that. But when we took them from her, we could see the children were not happy to be separated from Mayra Roman.

On the other hand, she had to suspect how they had come to be in her custody. Of course, she didn't want to think about it, but she had to suspect.

Mayra told us that Gladys Villar was in Jacksonville, Florida. She gave us the address and telephone number. Two detectives went down to get her: my partner Bill Kelly and Luis Gonzalez, a detective from Brooklyn.

Bill Kelly went because he already knew Gladys. He had once arrested her for the murder of her boyfriend. She had admitted that but had offered the battered-woman defense, plus the defense that the boyfriend had been trying to turn her daughter out as a prostitute. The grand jury had not indicted her.

Luis Gonzalez went because he spoke Spanish.

Luis Gonzalez, incidentally, is an amazing guy. He speaks and understands both English and Spanish fluently. His command of English is superlative. He does the *New York Times* crossword puzzle in ink. But he has never been able to get rid of his Puerto Rican Spanish accent. I used to kid him by saying "I need an interpreter to understand *you*." He was a great and pleasant man to work with, but you had to listen very carefully to understand what he was saying. He is retired now. He did his twenty years and left.

In Florida Bill and Luis met with Gladys and convinced her it would be in her best interest to come back to New York. She understood, of course, that if she didn't come back voluntarily, they would get an arrest warrant and have her locked up in Jacksonville.

She asked that she be allowed to go home and explain to her family why she had to go back to New York. The family included teenage children who had been born in Cuba. Their father was Loreto Villar. Bill and Luis waited outside her house while she talked to her family, and eventually she came outside and went with them to the airport.

When they arrived back in New York, Gladys was arrested. She was taken from the airport in handcuffs and directly to the precinct station for questioning.

Luis Gonzalez conducted the interview. It soon became apparent that Gladys Villar wanted to cooperate. We never knew why, exactly. Maybe it was her mother instinct. Maybe it was because she knew she was in deep trouble and just wanted to get it over with.

The man we wanted to talk to was Loreto Villar. We had concluded he had almost certainly murdered Yudelka Maldonado to steal her child.

Gladys never admitted she knew anyone was dead. She said she saw a resemblance between the little girl whose picture she had seen in the newspapers—Jessica Maldonado—and the child she sold to Mayra Roman. But when she had asked Loreto where he got the baby, he told her to mind her own business.

Or so she insisted.

She said he came home one night with blood on his sleeves. She asked him what had happened. He said it was none of her business, that he had done what he had to do to get the baby she'd said she needed—so shut up.

Personally, I never believed a word of this, not for a minute. I believe that Gladys Villar knew perfectly well how Loreto got the babies she sold.

Anyway, Gladys admitted she had sold two babies to Mayra Roman. She also said that within weeks after she sold Mayra the second baby, Loreto disappeared. She insisted she never saw him again. Both of them were Cubans and didn't like New York. It was too cold for them. That, said Gladys, was why she had moved to Florida. Loreto, she said, had told her he was going to Texas.

Gladys Villar pleaded guilty to kidnapping and spent seven and a half years in prison.

Seventeen months before, we had seen Ramon Maldonado cry—when he looked at the body of his wife in the morgue. Now, on September 23, 1982, we saw him cry again—when his baby daughter was handed back to him. This time he didn't cry alone. Three hard-boiled New York City detectives—Bill Kelly, Luis Gonzales, and Tom McKenna—cried with him.

That didn't close the case, not by any means. Who were David and Moises?

Finding out would be no easy job. It would take hard work, perseverance, and plain old-fashioned smarts. But of course we were motivated, both to identify the children and return them to their rightful families and to find and bring to justice a man who would kill mothers so he could sell their babies. There's not an animal in the jungle vicious enough to do that. If you needed motivation to work on this case, you had to be dead.

Gladys and Loreto Villar had sold Moises to Mayra Roman early in December of 1980. Our job, then, was to check the records of the New York Police Department, looking for young mothers who had been reported missing in the last quarter of 1980.

No easy job. Missing Persons had no open cases from the period. We had to look at closed cases. We had to look for a report of a missing woman who'd had a boy baby with her when she disappeared.

Procedures followed at that time made the job more difficult than it would be now. Then, when a woman disappeared and had a child with her, only one file was established: for the woman. The report would note that she had a child with her, but no separate file was established for the child. Only if the woman was found and the child remained missing did the child become the subject of a separate file.

All we could do was call the complainants in all the closed cases. We set to work on the telephones. For example, "This is Detective McKenna, Three-four Squad. We're checking out all missing-persons reports from the last months of 1980. You reported So-and-so missing and then reported she returned a few days later. Is this information correct?"

We called, probably, a thousand people. Some of the complainants didn't have telephones, and we had to go see them personally.

Ultimately we came across the name Leonor Reyes, who had been reported missing by her mother in December 1980. The file indicated that Leonor was nineteen, about the age we were looking for, but it said she had returned home. We called her mother, who said no, her daughter had never returned. She said her son-in-law had reported that she had returned, but the mother had never seen her again and supposed she had gone to Puerto Rico.

Photographs of Leonor Reyes showed a pretty girl, maybe a little chubby, wearing maybe a little more makeup than I would like, but basically a happy-looking girl, smiling at the camera.

The son-in-law, Leonor's husband, was named Ruben Reyes. The police department knew Ruben Reyes. His rap sheet showed arrests for attempted murder, burglary, possession of a loaded firearm, possession of stolen property, and possession of a controlled substance. Some of the charges had been dismissed, but he had served a year on Rikers Island on a felony weapons-possession charge. What he was, was a street guy and a hustler.

When we located Ruben he told us that his mother-in-law had sent Leonor to Puerto Rico to keep her away from him.

Part of what he told us was tragically familiar. He said his wife had taken their baby, Ruben Reyes, to Lincoln Hospital in the Bronx because the infant was sick. He believed, he said, his mother-in-law had taken Leonor and the baby from the hospital and sent them to Puerto Rico.

The detective from Missing Persons who'd had the case of Leonor Reyes had recently retired. We interviewed her, but she did not recall the case. As I've said before, the volume of cases that Missing Persons has to handle is so great that only rarely does an officer get to give a case enough personal attention to retain any real impression of it. The unfortunate difference about this case was that it was badly handled. Within three days after Leonor Reyes was reported missing, an unidentified female body was found, and Missing Persons did not make the connection. With all due respect to the load they have to carry, that was sloppy work.

Today the match would be made by computer, in minutes. Ten years ago it was all on index cards, and making the matches was anything but easy. Even so, it should have been made—between a report of a missing female, nineteen years old, and the body of a woman about the same age.

*We* made the connection. Leonor Reyes had been the right age and reported missing at the right time. She had disappeared with a baby that was reported missing too. She had last been seen taking the baby into a hospital. The match could not have been coincidental.

The body of the young woman we finally identified as that of Leonor Reyes had been found in an abandoned building in the Bronx. Someone had smeared it heavily with tar, poured kerosene over it, and set it on fire. The flames set the building on fire, and when the fire department arrived and put out the fire, they found a corpse so badly charred that identification was all but impossible.

I didn't see the corpse, but I have seen color photographs of it. It is no wonder they couldn't make an identification. Whoever had burned it had done it so as to make identification impossible.

In fact, when the body was found the arms and legs were missing. At first it seemed the body had been cut up. It turned out, however, that the arms and legs had separated from the body as it burned and had fallen through the burning floor. Remains of the arms and legs were found below.

If this whole grisly case had any redeeming feature—which it didn't, really—at least the medical examiner was able to report that the young woman had definitely been dead before she was set afire.

Leonor's mother told us who her dentist had been, and we got a subpoena for her dental records. When we delivered those records to the medical examiner, he told us he did not have enough information to determine whether they matched the teeth of the charred body. The only way he could make a positive identification would be by disinterring and examining the corpse.

We got a court order to dig up the body. Bodies buried in Potter's Field are in wooden coffins, stacked six deep in graves. They are numbered and can be located. I don't know the numbers now, but the body listed as found in the burned building in the Bronx on December whatever, 1980 might have been in, say, grave 1256, fifth coffin down. In any case, the body was disinterred and taken in for dental examination.

The body was Leonor Reyes.

The dental examiner had no doubt about it. I myself looked at the X rays taken of the teeth of the corpse and compared them to the X rays taken by the young woman's dentist when she was still alive. Of course I am not a dentist, but even I could see that the X rays matched exactly.

We notified Leonor's mother of the painful news. She had still hoped her daughter was alive in Puerto Rico.

It was difficult to tell if Ruben Reyes, the girl's husband and the baby's father, cared or not. He was a street guy, and we couldn't be sure he even understood.

We believed now that baby Moises was in fact Ruben Reyes, the child of Leonor and Ruben Reyes. Our evidence, though, was only circumstantial.

Unfortunately, the footprint evidence that had been conclusive in identifying Barbarita Roman as Jessica Maldonado was not conclusive with respect to Ruben Reyes. He had been born in Lincoln Hospital. The hospital sent all its footprint records to a company in New Jersey to be microfilmed. Once the microfilm was made, the company destroyed the original records. That was the agreed-to procedure. The microfilm record provided to us was not adequate to establish positive identification.

In any case, because Ruben was more than two years old, it was not certain that footprint evidence would be of much value. As children grow older and bigger, it gradually becomes impossible to match the footprints.

Another technique was available. That was DNA testing—then a very new technique.

DNA stands for deoxyribonucleic acid. Every living cell contains DNA, and the pattern of nucleides determines whether a cell is from a plant, a fish, a cat, a dog, or a human—and, what is more, from *which* human. DNA is the cell's genetic code. Only identical twins have identical DNA. Properly prepared, a sample can be viewed under a test instrument and compared to another sample. It is not entirely wrong to think of the DNA code as looking something like the bar code on merchandise.

The DNA from a sample of sperm found on a rape victim can be matched to a sample of blood from the accused—or even from fingernail cuttings or hair—and a positive determination can be made as to whether the sperm and the blood or whatever came from the same person.

(In the Jogger case, remember, DNA tests proved that some of the semen stains found on her clothing were from the friend with whom she admitted she'd had intercourse—but other stains were *not* from him.)

Using the test another way, the parentage of a child can be determined.

The test was done by Dr. Robert Shaler, a pioneer expert in the field of DNA testing. A blood specimen had been taken from the charred body of Leonor Reyes. Blood was also taken from Ruben Reyes and from the baby still called Moises. The samples were compared.

The test indicated that the baby could not be the child of Leonor and Ruben Reyes.

That result upset us, and we couldn't accept it. A group of detectives and Inspector Dan McMahon challenged the test. Dan McMahon had been the chief of Brooklyn North Homicide when the body of Yudelka Maldonado was found. Later he had been transferred to Manhattan North and so was present as the information developed. He knew the whole case backward and forward.

When Inspector McMahon and the rest of us confronted Dr. Shaler with the accumulated evidence that we believed proved the baby was the child of Ruben and Leonor Reyes,

Dr. Shaler said he had not done the test. It had been done by an assistant, and he himself would do it over.

Two days later Dr. Shaler called to say the child called Moises Roman *was* a child of Ruben and Leonor Reyes.

We were now able to take baby Ruben Reyes from a foster home and turn him over to his father, who in turn handed him over to Leonor's parents, the baby's grandparents. It was almost as emotional a scene as when we returned Jessica Maldonado to her father and grandparents.

That left the third baby, David. Who was he?

David was the baby Mercedes Arzuaga had brought from Puerto Rico. Fortunately, his mother had not been murdered.

Baby David's family in Puerto Rico had allowed Mercedes to take the baby to New York, where, she told them, he would get better medical attention. Later she sent word to the family that the baby had died in a hospital—when in fact it was alive and well and living in the apartment of Mayra Roman in Washington Heights.

This baby was returned to its family in Puerto Rico. Mercedes was not prosecuted. She had not actually kidnapped the baby but had brought it to New York with its parents' consent.

We felt good about returning these children to their parents. Our satisfaction was incomplete because we did not have Loreto Villar in custody. It remains incomplete because we still haven't found him.

We believed that Loreto Villar had killed the two young mothers and kidnapped their babies. He was the one who had brought the babies to his wife, Gladys. She had said he came home with blood on his clothes. On at least one occasion when Mayra gave money to Gladys, Loreto was there and grabbed the cash. We could have convicted him of kidnapping.

During his short time in New York he accumulated fourteen unpaid parking tickets. He acquired a reputation as a man with a 'tude—street talk for a bad, aggressive attitude. He'd also made it plain that he didn't like New York and meant to leave as soon as he could.

I am not absolutely certain we could have convicted him of homicide, because the evidence was mostly circumstantial.

We did not believe a woman had killed the two young mothers. It must have taken a man's strength to lift the two bodies, put them in a car, and move them—the one to be dumped on a street, the other to be carried inside an abandoned building to be set afire. Also, whoever did it had to have access to a car. Loreto had a car and worked for a gypsy-cab service.

We could not be sure, but apparently he had loitered around hospitals, watching for young women with babies. We doubt that he went after a specific mother; rather, he just watched for the opportunity to overpower a woman, kill her, and snatch her child.

On the other hand, no witness came forward to testify he had seen Loreto Villar at either hospital.

In any event, Loreto Villar disappeared. So did his car. We supposed he left New York in it. Remember, sixteen months passed between the murder of Yudelka Maldonado and the time when Hugo Roman came to the police to suggest the babies in Mayra's house might not be hers. In other words, Loreto Villar had been gone well over a year before he was identified to us as a possible suspect in the two murders.

He could have gone anywhere.

We did get some information about him. Loreto Villar had

entered the United States on April 22, 1980, approximately six months before the murder of Leonor Reyes. He was a Cuban who had come to the States from Spain, where he had been living on a tourist visa. His full name was Loreto Melquidoes Villar Bencomo. He told the Immigration and Naturalization Service that he had been in jail as a political prisoner in Cuba—his political offense being an attempt to escape from Cuba—and he said that even after his release from jail, he was still persecuted by the Cuban government. Villar said he had the equivalent of an American high school education and was an electrician. Because he claimed he was a political refugee, the International Rescue Committee had sponsored his entry into the United States. He had also been sponsored by his wife, Gladys Villar who had been in the United States for years.

There was an odd circumstance about his entry into the United States. He had applied for permanent alien resident status, and such applicants are invariably photographed and fingerprinted. The Immigration Service was able to supply photographs but no fingerprints. The Service had no explanation as to why Villar was not fingerprinted—or, if he was, where those fingerprints were.

I have absolutely no reason to believe one explanation for the fingerprint puzzle, but I will give it, for what it is worth. Someone suggested, maybe as a joke, that Villar had performed some service for the Central Intelligence Agency in Cuba, in return for which the CIA arranged his escape to Spain, then his entry into the States, and finally his disappearance and establishment of a new identity. As I said, I don't believe that explanation.

Other questions—If Villar had been jailed in Cuba for trying to escape, how did he get a Spanish tourist visa and simply fly out of the country? If he had been, as he said he was, an electrician in a poor country, where did he get the money to fly to Spain as a tourist, live there for a time, and then fly to New York?

It is strange too that the Cuban government, which ordinarily extends no cooperation to American law-enforcement agencies, supplied a set of fingerprints they say are Loreto Villar's.

The biggest question is: how could a man who had allegedly committed two murders have disappeared so completely? We checked every available resource looking for him—Social Security, Unemployment Compensation, a driver's license in any state, the FBI, and so on. He disappeared so completely that the best law-enforcement agencies in the nation have failed to find him.

Almost invariably, a man who commits crimes as serious as two murders commits some other crime sooner or later. It is all but impossible to believe this man wouldn't at least get a speeding ticket somewhere.

Three times, Loreto Villar has been featured on the *America's Most Wanted* television show. Twice an anonymous caller has telephoned from Florida, saying she knows the Villar family and is convinced Loreto himself was murdered. She goes on to say that he did not kill Leonor Reyes or Yudelka Maldonado and did not steal and sell their babies. He was murdered, she insists, by the man who did. She will not identify herself, so we have no way to check her story.

Loreto Villar, if you think you might have seen him, is a husky dark-colored man, African-American, not Latino, in appearance. He would be in his forties. Spanish is of course the language he prefers to speak. He said he was an electrician, and maybe he is. He drives and probably has some facility for working on cars. I would also say he is extremely dangerous.

\* \* \*

In telling this story, I have mentioned myself and a number of other detectives. I have mentioned certain bureaus and departments. I want to make it clear, though, that the people I have mentioned are by no means the only ones who were involved in the case and who contributed to the result. The Baby Maldonado case, as I think of it, was typical of the way our department works. Many men and women, with many different skills, all willing to work hard and go the extra mile, played important parts. While I may not have mentioned many by name, I don't mean to ignore the efforts of the others.

To survive in my line of work, you have to remain objective and not allow yourself to become personally involved in cases. And usually I don't. But I will never forget the Maldonado and Reyes families. My own daughter Danielle was born not many months after Jessica and Ruben were born, and I couldn't help but reflect that my family and I had the privilege of watching our daughter grow, as we learned to love her more and more, and she learned to love us. The mothers of Jessica and Ruben had been brutally murdered and their families were deprived not only of the young mothers but of their children during important years of their lives. It *was* personal. I couldn't help it. It was.

I won't forget Loreto Villar Bencomo either. I still look forward to the elation I'll feel when I snap the cuffs on him and give him his rights.

That's nothing personal. That's business.

bar. He insisted he had seen nothing. His bartender and other employees insisted they had seen and heard nothing. None of them had any idea what had happened.

The following day the Klagsbrun family's attorney, Nicholas Scoppetta, held a news conference in which he announced that the family was offering at $25,000 reward for information leading to the arrest and conviction of their son's murderer. The news conference was broadcast on all the major New York television stations. As a result of statements Scoppetta made, the tabloid newspapers branded the young man who had killed Klagsbrun as "the Karate killer," or "the Karate Kid."

One of the newspapers quoted one of Klagsbrun's friends as saying the killer was "a walking machine who doesn't need a weapon to kill." A headline called the killer A MURDER MACHINE.

Daniel Klagsbrun, on the other hand, was described as "a peacemaker, a conciliator" who had tried to prevent a fight.

The media coverage was not just wrong; it was wild. The newspapers and broadcast stations had a circus.

The extensive media coverage meant that the case of "the Karate Kid" was no longer just a case for Chris Heimgartner, Bobby Clark, and me; it was a case for the whole police department. The "walking machine," the "murder machine," had to be caught.

This was the only case I ever worked on where a district attorney was assigned to prosecute the case even before we had identified a suspect. Not only that. The man assigned was Gregory Waples, one of the most meticulous and effective prosecutors in New York.

As a result of the publicity a young man who was a student at All Hallows High School in the Bronx talked to a religious, a Christian Brother, and told the brother he had information about the Karate Kid case. He said that he in fact knew who the Karate Kid was. The Kid, he said, was not a criminal but was just a young man who had been out drinking with his friends and got in a fight in which unfortunately another young man had been killed.

We will call the religious brother by the name Brother Jeremy. That is not his name, and I will not violate his confidence by revealing his name. Brother Jeremy called the Two-oh and told us he had information.

Four of us went up to All Hallows High School. Though I was not the most senior man in the group, I thought Chris Heimgartner should go in and interview Brother Jeremy. It was my judgment that the senior detective in the car was too aggressive. Anyway, Chris had a way of getting information out of people without their realizing they were giving it. He always asked the right questions. This was a delicate situation because the brother didn't want to betray the student's confidence, yet at the same time he had a moral obligation to give us as much information as he could without betraying that trust.

Bob Clark went in also. It was his case. The other man, though he didn't like it, sat in the car with me.

We waited for an hour and a half. Sitting in that car with that man was the longest hour and a half I ever spent. In detective work, waiting is a big part of the job. You wait on stakeouts. You wait for witnesses. Nothing ever runs on time. But sitting there with that egotistical bum was maybe the worst time I ever spent in the police department.

When Chris and Bob came out, they said Brother Jeremy's informant, whom he would not identify, had told a very different story of what had happened outside the Dublin House. He said he believed the death of Klagsbrun was not the Kid's fault.

According to the Brother's informant, the young man everyone was calling the Karate Kid had been bullied unmercifully by Daniel Klagsbrun's friends, if not by Klagsbrun himself. The Kid had long blond hair and had worn a silly-looking beret, an unstylish overcoat, and combat boots. They had called him a freak and had made fun of him. When he left the Dublin House, they confronted him on the street and continued taunting and bullying him. There were six boys in Klagsbrun's crowd, and the Kid, though he had two or three friends inside the bar, was essentially alone outside.

The truth is, none of this crowd would have taken on the Kid—or anyone else—alone. But since there were six of them, all drinking if not drunk, they decided to have some fun at the Kid's expense. What they failed to realize was that the Kid, being something of a fighter, was not going to back down.

After the crowd had enjoyed themselves taunting this young man, they walked off. He went back into the bar and said to his friends, "Come with me, I'm gonna have a fight." The two friends had no interest in a fight. They had just met two girls and had focused their attention on them.

So the Kid left the bar again. He ran west on 79th Street. One of his friends from the bar came out and followed him, walking, not running.

Brother Jeremy felt he could not tell us who the Kid was, but he did say he was from Washington Heights. He also told us that the Kid sometimes hung out in a park on Fort Washington Avenue and drank beer there.

From what Brother Jeremy told us, it was obvious we were not talking about a mad-dog killer. Supposing the Kid was a karate expert, we had inquired at maybe fifteen karate schools. We had visited about every karate school in Manhattan, plus other schools of martial arts. Not only had the instructors never seen the young man in the sketch; they insisted what they taught was not an offensive weapon but a defensive weapon.

I had been in the Three-four Squad for seventeen years and knew exactly what park Brother Jeremy had told us about. I asked Chris Heimgartner what he wanted to do. He said we should go up to Washington Heights and see if we could find the Kid. The other detective from the Two-oh insisted on going back to the precinct to tell the bosses what we'd found out. He pressured Bobby Clark to go with him. Chris and I went up to Washington Heights alone.

Having grown up in New York and drunk beer in schoolyards and parks, Chris and I knew the kids who drank in that park had to get their beer somewhere. Great detective work! Circling the park in our car, we saw there was only one grocery store in the immediate area where a kid could buy beer.

We went into that grocery store, carrying a sketch of this silly-looking kid with the long blond hair and funny hat. The owner looked at the picture and said, sure, he'd seen that young man. The Kid bought beer there. We gave the man a card and asked him to call us if he saw this young man again.

Which direction did he come from? South. This meant that we had approximately a ten-block area to cover. We called the Two-oh and spoke to Lieutenant Jack Doyle, commanding officer of Manhattan North Homicide. He was working out of Two-oh temporarily as this case was pursued. Doyle said he would send up the night team, which was about to come on duty, and have them meet us at 192nd Street and Fort Washington Avenue.

We wanted to check maybe eighty apartment buildings that surrounded the park. Of course, we couldn't check every apartment. Our strategy was to check with the supers in every building, asking if any of them knew this kid.

It was important that this work be done by detectives of the homicide squad. We could be confident our guys would do it right. If later we needed to be sure a certain building had been checked, there would be a report we could refer to. It's our job as detectives to be thorough and make a report about canvasses and interviews.

We got the night team together and told them what we had and what we wanted to do. Then we broke up into groups and went to work.

We had been working for an hour or so when we got a call from the boss, Jack Doyle. The grocery store owner wanted to see us.

Chris and I went there immediately. The owner told us that two girls, teenagers, had just been in the store. He sold newspapers, and they had been looking at the sketch of the Karate Kid on a front page and discussing the case. The girls had been incensed by the story as the paper presented it. They knew the Kid and said the picture didn't look much like him. Besides, they said, the story was wrong.

Okay, great. But where did these two girls go? He said he didn't know but they had called a car service to pick them up. What car service? The one that had a sign beside his telephone.

This was Audubon Car Service. We called and told the dispatcher we wanted to talk to her and would be there in a few minutes. The dispatcher said yes, she had sent a car to the address of the grocery store, and the car had taken the two girls to an address on Fort George Hill. They had told the driver they would call later and would want to be picked up and brought back. That would be in an hour or so.

We were on a roll! Everything was working out right. The adrenaline was pumping!

We waited. Sure enough, about an hour and a half later

the expected call came to the dispatcher. We followed the car dispatched to pick up the two girls. When they came out to get into the car, we approached them and identified ourselves and said we wanted to talk to them. We told them we would save them cab fare; we would drive them home. We gave the cab driver $2, so his run would not be a total loss.

The two girls in the back of the car knew they were riding with detectives and knew why we had picked them up. They were reluctant to give us information. On Fort Washington Avenue, just at the park, we stopped to talk. They started out by telling us they had no idea what we were talking about. But we told them what the store owner had told us. We told them we could hold them as accessories after the fact, that we would take them to the station house, that we would call their parents and so forth.

I'm a bad guy. Basically, I browbeat these two girls. And they told us who the Karate Kid was.

What we had in that neighborhood, as you'd have in just about any neighborhood, was a tight-knit group of kids. They all knew each other. They hung out together. And what any of them did, they all knew.

The Karate Kid was Robert Wallace. Wallace had gotten in a fight. By the next morning the whole crowd knew Robert Wallace had gotten in a fight.

We took statements from the two girls. They gave us the names of the other young men who had been with Wallace in the Dublin House.

I had served in the Three-four Precinct a long time and knew all these kids. Not only that, I knew all their parents. I *knew* Washington Heights. I knew it as a cop, but I knew the area otherwise: socially and so on. I've got friends there, including people who were never in the police department. I had worked in that precinct so long that I had a reputation even among people I had never met.

I knew the father of one of the kids who had been with Wallace in the bar. I knew him very well. I knew Bobby Wallace's father too—just well enough to say hello. The father was a stagehand. The son worked as a stagehand too, and in the evening he worked in a butcher shop.

We made a tactical plan. We had several addresses to cover, and groups of us would cover each address.

Detectives Tommy Sullivan and Bill Kelly went to the Wallace house. They understood they were not going after a mad-dog killer. They were going to pick up a kid who'd gotten in a fight and had been unfortunate enough to kill another young man. It was perfectly obvious that the Karate Kid had never had a karate lesson. It was just one of those things that can happen when young men fight, and it can happen to anybody. When Sullivan and Kelly knocked on the door, Mr. and Mrs. Wallace invited them in and asked them to sit down and have a cup of tea. They knew why the detectives were there. Their son had told them what had happened.

With no hesitation they told the two detectives that Bobby was on a Continental flight to San Francisco that had left some three hours before.

Bobby was going to California, flying under the name of a friend of his. This friend had just been discharged from the army. That night in Dublin House they had been celebrating the friend's discharge, and the friend gave Bobby his jump boots, the steel-toe boots Bobby had been wearing when he kicked Daniel Klagsbrun. Bobby was on his way to this friend's home.

At this time Chris Heimgartner and I were in the Two-oh, taking statements from other young men who had been in the bar. By the time we got the call, the Continental flight was about forty minutes from San Francisco. We hoped San

Francisco cops could arrest Bobby Wallace as he got off the plane.

Fortunately, I knew a woman named Grace at Continental Air Lines who could help. Sometimes Grace went into a bar frequented by detectives—in fact, a bar where almost no one but cops and employees of Continental Air Lines ever went—and we had gotten acquainted with her. I called her and asked her to do the New York Police Department a big favor. Fortunately, she was happy to do it.

She ran the name of Bobby Wallace's friend through the computer and was able to confirm that our murder suspect was on the flight his parents had told us he was on. She could even tell us what seat he had. Of course, from his parents we knew what he was wearing. We had plenty of information for the San Francisco police.

Our problem was to have Bobby Wallace arrested as he got off the plane. If he got out into the airport terminal and then away from the airport, he would be very difficult to track down. We asked Grace for an even bigger favor. And she did it. She teletyped San Francisco and kept that airplane flying in circles around the city until the local police could arrive and be ready to arrest Bobby on the plane when it landed.

It worked out perfectly. When the plane landed, four San Francisco cops went aboard, went to Bobby's seat, asked him if he was So-and-so—using the name he was flying under—and arrested him.

The San Francisco police were willing to hold Bobby Wallace, but they did need an arrest warrant from New York. We obtained an arrest warrant, took it to the airport, and asked an airline pilot to carry it to San Francisco and hand it over to a San Francisco detective at the airport. Bobby indicated he would waive his rights and return voluntarily, so Chris

Heimgartner and Bob Clark flew to San Francisco to bring him back.

When they arrived at Newark Airport there was almost a media riot. Happily, our brothers of the Port Authority are very good to us. The incoming flight stopped out on the tarmac, Bobby was brought out and down a flight of stairs. We had him in a car and on his way before the plane ever reached the ramp.

In fact, we had a convoy of three cars. We ran with lights and sirens and rushed him back to Manhattan as fast as we could.

Bobby Wallace, we all discovered quickly, was nothing like the mad-dog murderer the media had made him out to be. He was a nice kid, a likable kid. On the way back on the plane he drew sketches of Chris Heimgartner and Bob Clark, and they were really good.

The indictment originally returned against Bobby Wallace was for second-degree murder. But there was no way in hell this was a murder. There had been no intent to kill anybody. In fact, Justice Rena K. Uviller shortly dismissed the murder charge and Bobby went to trial on charges of manslaughter and negligent homicide.

He was convicted of negligent homicide, sentenced to zero to three years, and was released on bond pending his appeal. Because his time in jail pending trial was counted against his sentence, he never returned to jail, even though he lost the appeal. He spent about six months on Riker's Island. Today he is again working as a stagehand.

# ■● 9

## A CASE OF MISTAKEN IDENTITY

IN THIS CASE WE DEAL with two separate homicides that occurred on the West Side Highway in 1988—one on August 21 and the other on September 5. These homicides occurred between 85th Street and 88th Street, in grassy areas just off the highway. If you look at a map of Manhattan you will see that the highway at that point runs between the Hudson River and a long narrow park. Both victims were shot in the back of the head, probably while lying facedown in the grass a few yards from the roadway.

On the night of August 20, Michael Kyriakou, a thirty-one-year-old Greek immigrant, said good night to his family and left home in Queens for his night's work. Michael was a handsome man, well put together, a loving husband and father, and a good provider. He had invested in a black Lincoln Town Car, a limousine. Driving it was his livelihood. For the next twelve hours he would drive it through the streets of New York, serving corporate accounts.

He was affiliated the 123 Car Service Group, one of the services that use radio to dispatch driver-owned cars to pick up people who want to be driven from one place to another—as distinct from taxis that get most of their business by cruising and picking up passengers on the streets. Car-service cars are sometimes called black cars, and typically the car is a black Lincoln Town Car, although some are Cadillacs, Mercedes, and so on. Almost all of them are spotlessly clean and well maintained. Most of these groups serve corporations as their regular customers, having contracts with them that guarantee twenty-four-hour service.

During the day, black cars take passengers to the airports or pick them up there, deliver executives to meetings, and sometimes carry documents from one office building to another. Corporations, particularly those in the financial district, often require their employees to work in the evening, sometimes even into the middle of the night, and a car-service limousine is called to take these people home. Usually the passenger does not pay the driver; the company gets a bill.

One of the companies that had a contract with 123 was Salomon Brothers.

On the same evening, August 20, Kenneth Harris sat in his bedroom in his family's apartment at 250 West 63rd Street. Harris was a twenty-two-year-old black man, something of an oddball, a loner. He lived with his parents. His room at the rear of the apartment was always locked with a padlock. Because his room was kept locked, his parents did not know that Kenneth's room was jammed with two-way radio sets. As he sat in his room staring at his collection of radios, Harris fantasized about what he would do that night to add to his collection. As he left the house, he did not say good night to his parents. He usually didn't. They supposed he worked at night, but they did not know what he did.

On that evening, too, another young black man, this one a nice-looking fellow, articulate and in other circumstances sociable, sat in his cell in an upstate prison, pondering the fate that had put him there. He'd had a good job, had been going with a nice girl, and was now locked up, doing time for armed robbery. We will call him Kevin Donaldson, which is not his name. He had no one to say good night to, and when they turned out the lights he lay on his cot and cried himself to sleep. He was serving a long sentence for a crime he had not committed.

On the morning of August 21, 1988, Michael Kyriakou was found lying facedown at 86th Street and the West Side Highway. It was a case for the Two-four Squad, meaning detectives of the Twenty-fourth Precinct. Because it was a homicide, Manhattan North Homicide was called to assist. My partner in this case was Chris Heimgartner, and we arrived at the Two-four about nine-thirty that morning.

I should say something about Chris Heimgartner. He's a lieutenant now and back in uniform, but he and I worked together for four years, and he's a fabulous guy. Before he joined the police department he was a licensed electrician. He has a German mind—by which I mean he is always methodical, always the planner.

He has what I call a typical Bronx approach to police work—he's seen it all, heard it all, and won't take any crap. I remember a line he used to take in interviews:

"Whatta you think? You think I fell off a turnip truck? You think out of eight million people in the City of New York, we just *happened* pick *you* up? You think we fell out of the sky and just *happened* to land on you? Don't shit me, fella. I've been there. You don't have something straight to tell me, then don't tell me anything. Either tell me straight or shut up."

The fact is, most of them want to tell you something. The guy you're questioning hopes he can get away with telling you something that will make you believe he's not the bad guy. There is no end to the lines they will try to put over on you.

Anyway, at the Two-four the investigation was already under way. Detective Billy Gillings had been assigned to the case. Though a twelve-year veteran, Billy is a young detective, in his thirties—though he is already showing a touch or two of gray. He's about five foot ten and weighs about 180, all muscle. He's a bodybuilder. He pumps iron, and I guess he'd rather pump iron than pump a beer like the older, more traditional detectives of the New York City Police Department.

The victim was a nicely dressed young man, but there was no indication on or about him as to who or what he was. His driver's license was on him, so we knew his name and address, but that wasn't enough; we needed to know more. We didn't know *who* he was. It looked like a dump job—that is, a case where someone is killed in one part of town and the body is dumped in another part of town. Very often dump jobs are homicides resulting from dealings in narcotics, and that is what this looked like.

Detectives were sent to notify his family and interview them. This is one of the hardest things we have to do. The two detectives faced a young mother and had to tell her that her husband was dead. It was painful for her to talk, but she did tell the detectives that her husband had been driving his car the night before. She told them he owned the car and got his passengers by radio calls from 123 Car Service. His Lincoln Continental was missing.

Detectives went to 123 Car Service Group to check the records of where Michael Kyriakou had been dispatched the night before. We learned from 123 that he had been dispatched about midnight to the World Trade Center, for the Salomon Brothers account. The call to the dispatcher indicated that the service would not be charged to the corporate account but would be a cash transaction.

We learned that the murder of Michael Kyriakou was the first murder in a long series of armed robberies, twenty or more of them, going back more than a year.

The detectives at the Two-four RIP—meaning Robbery Identification Program—told us Central Robbery had established that there had been a pattern of black-car robberies, beginning a year or so before. Central Robbery has the duty of establishing these patterns, which often cross precinct lines. In other words, Central Robbery had matched reports from the Two-oh, the Two-four, and the Two-six and had seen a pattern.

The central point of these cases was that almost all of them had been of cars that had been dispatched to the vicinity of the World Trade Center. Also, in almost all cases the robbery had happened on the Upper West Side, from as far south as 68th Street to as far north as 125th Street. Some of them had occurred just off the West Side Highway, some just off Riverside Drive, which runs parallel to the West Side Highway and also is bordered by a grassy strip.

Until the murder of Michael Kyriakou, none of the drivers had been killed. The MO had been that a passenger in the backseat put a gun to the head of the driver, told him not to look in the rearview mirror, to stop the car and get out, then to lie facedown on the pavement or on the grass. The robber would demand the driver's money and his keys, and the passenger would drive away with the car. Some of the cars were recovered eventually—always stripped, particularly of their radios.

Because the pattern was obvious, the car services recognized that they had a big problem. Consequently, a call to the World Trade Center late at night generated a certain nervousness. One night in April 1987 a call came for a car using the Salomon Brothers account number. It happened that one of the drivers for 123 was a retired New York City police officer named O'Neil, and when this call came in the dispatcher sent O'Neil to pick up the passenger. As a retired cop he was still carrying his gun, and he felt he could handle the situation if a situation should arise. He drove to the address given and found his passenger waiting.

The passenger turned out to be a young black man named Kevin Donaldson, and he wanted to be taken to Brooklyn.

On prior occasions Donaldson had met his girlfriend when she came out from her job with Salomon Brothers and had accompanied her in the limousine that took her home. We will call her Lucy Carter, which is not her name. She was a very attractive, very well spoken, very well dressed young woman. Kevin had watched Lucy write the Salomon Brothers account number on the driver's voucher and had memorized that number. Several times he found himself downtown late at night and thought it would be convenient to be driven home in a limousine. He would ask to be picked up outside Salomon Brothers, which has its corporate headquarters in a building just across the street from the twin Trade Towers. When he reached his home in Brooklyn he would write the Salomon Brothers account number on the voucher and scribble some kind of signature. He knew it was wrong, but he didn't think it was any big deal. He suspected something that turned out to be true: that big companies don't check these vouchers very carefully; they just glance at them and pay them.

With Donaldson in the car, O'Neil questioned him about his employment with Salomon Brothers. He learned that Donaldson did not actually work there. What's more, he seemed to fit the description of the man who had been committing the pattern robberies on the West Side Highway. Not satisfied with Donaldson's answers, he drove him directly to the First Precinct station house, where he placed him under arrest for theft of services. They took his picture and fingerprints and released him with a summons to appear and answer the charge.

RIP detectives now began to look into the whole deal. They established a photo array—that is, a series of six pictures, one of which was Kevin Donaldson—and began to show the photo array to drivers who had been robbed. One of the drivers identified Kevin Donaldson as the man who had robbed him. Based on that identification, Donaldson was picked up by Central Robbery, placed in a lineup, and again identified by the driver.

No other driver recognized Donaldson. The reason was, they had obeyed the order not to look in the rearview mirror. Nearly all of the drivers were foreign-born, all of them had been badly frightened, and they honestly could not or would not identify the man who had robbed them.

Central Robbery charged Donaldson with armed robbery and locked him up. He went to trial, was convicted, and was sent to prison for three and a half to seven years. Everyone supposed Donaldson had committed all the car-service robberies, though Central Robbery could get the identification and convict him of one only. The fact is, Donaldson was not guilty of robbery. He got three and a half to seven for being stupid, and that's a heavy rap for stupidity.

Detectives thought the imprisonment of Donaldson would put an end to the West Side Highway limousine robberies. The robberies did not stop, though, and before long they realized that either there had been more than one criminal committing these pattern robberies or there was a copycat robber out there. Then Michael Kyriakou was killed. That brought Manhattan North Homicide into this case for the first time. Before that it had been strictly a series of robberies, in which no one had been killed.

Sitting over lunch, Chris Heimgartner, Billy Gillings, and I decided to visit Kevin Donaldson in prison. Obviously he had not killed Kyriakou; he was in prison when it happened. What we wanted to know was if he had given the Salomon Brothers account number to anyone else or if he had described his MO, maybe to somebody in jail or prison—somebody who was later released and began to commit robberies the same way.

We visited Donaldson and asked him some questions. We explained to him that his cooperation would help him get an early parole.

Donaldson insisted he had not robbed anyone. He admitted he had used the Salomon Brothers account number to steal car service, but he said he was doing somebody's else's hard time. It was during this interview that he mentioned crying himself to sleep.

After interviewing Donaldson, Chris Heimgartner developed a gut feeling that Donaldson was serving time for a robbery he had not committed. Before he left him, Chris promised Donaldson he would try to help him. On the other hand, Gillings didn't believe Donaldson. Gillings was skeptical. He was what we might call a Missouri detective; he had to be shown.

The next day we contacted Central Robbery and asked for an update of information. We wanted to know about any robberies similar to the Kyriakou murder—that is, cases where Town Cars were taken. They told us about the pattern robberies. Except for Kevin Donaldson, no one had been arrested for any of them. This was of course the first Manhattan North Homicide really knew about these robberies. Until the death of Michael Kyriakou, the robberies had been a problem for precinct detectives and Central Robbery.

Among the things we found out was that not long ago, three men had been arrested in a stolen Lincoln Town Car. One of those men was Kenneth Harris, who had been driving. The car had been identified as one that had been stolen in an armed robbery, not just taken off the street, but the driver could not identify any of the three men as the one who had robbed him. Harris was charged with grand larceny, auto, which is not a terribly serious crime in the City of New York.

He didn't do any time for it. But he had learned a lesson. He had been caught driving a car taken in an armed robbery. When he was placed in a lineup, he knew exactly why he was in that lineup—because he was a suspect in a robbery. He was not charged with robbery because no one identified him. But if somebody had identified him, he would have gone up for at least three and a half to seven. If he had been convicted of multiple robberies, he might have gotten consecutive sentences and might have spent most of the rest of his life in prison. In my opinion, that was when he made up his mind he would kill his robbery victims.

Robbery is far more serious than larceny. Larceny is just theft. Robbery is theft committed by confronting someone and stealing by threat of violence. Armed robbery involves threatening with a weapon. Sometimes people come home, find their house has been entered and property stolen, and they say they've been robbed. They haven't. What has happened there is burglary. Robbery requires confrontation.

Harris had been caught in the Twentieth Precinct, which is a precinct bordering the West Side Highway, the next precinct south of the Two-four. Chris and I wanted to know more about Harris, and we went to interview the arresting officers. They gave us the information we wanted, but they also told us that within their patrol sector, on a vacant lot on 58th Street between 11th and 12th avenues, four Lincoln Town Cars sat abandoned and stripped. We called the Auto Crime Unit to check out these cars.

The VIN numbers—vehicle identification numbers—had been popped off the dashboards of these cars. But there are two other places on a car where the VIN number is to be found. The guys from Auto Crimes found them, and a computer check of the numbers established that all four of these cars had been stolen, not from the street but during gunpoint robberies. All four of them were cars from the pattern robberies.

Kenneth Harris's address, at 250 West 63rd Street, was very close to the West Side Highway. It was also close to the lot where the four cars had been dumped and ideal for the kind of operation we were looking at. Putting the facts together, we decided Harris was not just a suspect but a prime suspect in our homicide.

On September 4, 1988, Ahmad Shamin, a male Pakistani, twenty-eight, said good night to his wife and children and left his home in Brooklyn to work the next twelve hours driving his Lincoln Town Car for a car service. His radio dispatcher sent him to the World Trade Center. The next morning his body was found lying faceup beside the West Side Highway at 88th Street.

Chris Heimgartner and I didn't know about this case because it happened on our day off. The team that worked this case was the B Team, under command of Sergeant Terrence Quinn. Mike Sheehan was in that team, and Jack Freck. They put out a bulletin for the missing vehicle.

When I came in to work at four o'clock on the next day, the boss asked how our investigation of the Kyriakou murder was going. We told him we thought Kenneth Harris had committed the murder. Things about him fit. He lived very near the area where all the robberies occurred. He had been caught in a limousine that had been stolen in a gunpoint robbery. We said we were going slow on Harris but we were convinced he was our man. It was important to accumulate enough evidence against him to make a tight case. We were working to build the case.

Actually, we had reported earlier that we thought Harris had murdered Kyriakou. When the Shamin case broke, they should have called us. But they didn't.

Two days later Shamin's car was stopped on Park Avenue and 123rd Street, only four blocks from our office. Kenneth Harris's brother was driving. He was stopped, I have to say, because he was a young black man driving a Lincoln Town Car, and by the way he was dressed and so on he obviously didn't fit the car.

Chris and I went to interview the brother. Then we decided we were ready to present the case to a district attorney. The prosecutor in this case was Bill Hoyt, a former Marine Corps officer, a tank commander. He was a little fellow, but he was a marine officer every inch. He never talked. He bellowed.

We needed a D.A. at this stage in the case because we had to get an arrest warrant and a search warrant. We had to show reasonable cause for issuance of the warrants. Considerable legal paperwork was involved.

About one-thirty in the afternoon of September 8, Kenneth Harris came out of his apartment. We were waiting for him, and we grabbed him. Harris was sent to the Two-four.

We took the search warrants and went to his apartment. Since no one was inside, we broke the door down. In Kenneth Harris's room at the rear of the apartment we found twenty transmitter-receivers of the kind used in car-service cars. Each radio was clearly marked with the name of the car service that owned it. In addition, we found personal property that had belonged to the victims of the murders and robberies—their billfolds, driver's licenses, and things like maps of New York with the drivers' names written on them—"Property of So-and-so."

It took a truck to haul away all the loot we found in Kenneth Harris's room.

Harris had sold none of the cars he had stolen. He had fenced none of the radios. He would drive around in a stolen limousine for a while, then strip it and abandon it. He took the radios to his room and kept them. He was obsessed with two-way radios. They were valuable, and he might have fenced them for a lot of money. But he never had. The only money he got from his many robberies was what he got from selling batteries and other parts stripped from cars, plus what he took from the victims' billfolds.

Before Harris was arrested for car theft he had never killed anyone; after he was arrested, he decided he would not allow any future victims to live to identify him. We found in his room the evidence that convicted him of two murders. The stupidity of the man in keeping personal papers—worthless to him—taken from his victims is typical of thieves and murderers. But why he committed repeated robberies and ultimately murdered two men just to steal radios—which he then kept in his room—is something I will never understand.

Kenneth Harris was tried and convicted of both murders. The judge imposed *consecutive* sentences of twenty-five years to life. He will remain in prison for a minimum of fifty years.

One of the radios found in Harris's room was from the car Kevin Donaldson was serving time for robbing. Also, the driver's license of the man who had identified Kevin was found in Harris's room. This was a complete vindication of Kevin Donaldson.

When we arrested Kenneth Harris, we called Lucy Carter,

Kevin's girlfriend, immediately and told her to call Kevin and tell him. She had remained loyal to him throughout his imprisonment, visited him when she could, and never believed he was guilty.

It took two months to get Kevin Donaldson out of prison. Chris and I had to press the D.A. about it almost every day of that two months. If I recall correctly, I don't think the Legal Aid Society filed the papers that resulted in Kevin's release. I think it was done by the office of the district attorney, in the interest of justice. When the case came before a judge, he released Kevin Donaldson without bail, and when review of the case was completed, the conviction was thrown out and the charged dropped.

On Thanksgiving day that year, Chris Heimgartner and I worked in the morning. Kevin Donaldson and Lucy Carter, a very happy couple, came to the office to see us, to thank us. Kevin said he'd found it hard to believe that white detectives would go to bat to correct an injustice done a black man. But that's part of our job: exonerating the innocent as well as convicting the guilty.

# ■● 10

## OVERSELL, OVERKILL

NOT EVERY INVESTIGATION IN WHICH Manhattan North Homicide is called on to participate involves murder. We were, for example, called on to take part in the investigation of the rap-concert tragedy that occurred on the campus of the City College of New York on the evening of December 28, 1991.

Orders to report to the CCNY campus interrupted an investigation in which Bill Kelly and I were assisting Mid-Town North detectives into the death of Sergeant Keith Levine, who had been shot down while off duty, when he interrupted the robbery of a man withdrawing money from an ATM machine. We had set up a likely arrest. A surveillance van was watching the street, looking for the suspect, the man an informer had identified as Sergeant Levine's killer. An arrest team was waiting nearby. We were ready to move in and take the suspect very efficiently and quietly.

Suddenly the radio message came through that all Manhattan North Homicide personnel were to report forthwith to the gymnasium on the campus of City College of New York. We asked that the message be repeated, and it was repeated. We were to report to CCNY immediately. All available personnel were being sent there.

Sitting where we were, at the corner of 116th Street and Eighth Avenue, we had noticed a lot of emergency equipment going north. We had noticed a lot of police units going in the same direction. We hadn't thought much of it, because in that part of the city ambulances racing along the streets and police cars in a hurry with flashing lights are not unusual.

On our way to the CCNY campus, we switched our radio to the Fifth Zone frequency. What we heard was very confusing. The reports on the air indicated that shots had been fired in the Nat Holman Gymnasium during a rap concert and that there were multiple deaths and multiple injuries. The reports said that as many as six people had been shot and killed.

We switched on a light and the siren. When we got to Convent Avenue, we could not get close to the campus. The streets were blocked with police cars, medical emergency vehicles, and fire equipment. We parked two blocks away.

People on the street were screaming about shooting and deaths, and we didn't have a clue about what was going on. So we hurried as fast as we could to the campus and to the gym.

As it turned out, there had been no shooting. What had happened was that nine people had been crushed to death and thirty-four others had been seriously injured, in a stairwell and the small hall just outside the gymnasium.

When we reached the floor of the gymnasium, we confronted a shocking scene. I am a homicide detective and see death all the time, but what we confronted in that gym that night was appalling. It was sickening.

People clustered in groups were crying. EMS people knelt beside lifeless forms on the gym floor, trying to revive people who were dead or dying. Police radios were blaring. Young people were lying all around, obviously in pain from severe injuries, and other young people were trying to administer what they supposed was CPR, though they had not been trained to do it.

I remember seeing a young man kneeling over an unconscious young man and pulling him by the feet until his legs almost touched his chest, then pushing them back and pulling again—as if he were trying to pump him up. It was the wrong thing to do, and yet obviously the young man was sincerely, desperately trying to help.

The chaos was so great that arriving EMS people were having great difficulty getting to the victims who most needed their help. Some teams had to be led in through the men's locker room. It was impossible even to get a count of how many were dead and how many injured. The situation was horrifying.

Bill Kelly and I, and other detectives, were shocked. Even so, the scene when we arrived was not total chaos. Teams of men and women—police, EMS crews, firemen—were doing their jobs, doing what they had been trained to do. There was at least a little order, a little organization.

It was the job of the detectives to identify the dead and injured and notify next of kin. It was our job also to conduct interviews and try to find out exactly what had happened. Detectives from almost every squad in Manhattan North were there.

One of the first detectives I remember seeing on the scene was Maria Bertini from our own office. She was walking around with a pad and pencil and was trying to find how many people were dead and who they were.

Bodies were being pulled under the bleachers, where they were laid out in line, tagged and covered. I remember seeing at least six at that time.

Looking at this many tragic deaths, we knew the possibility existed that a criminal offense had been committed. It would be our job to find out. We also knew that huge problems of civil liability also would arise from the situation, though that was none of our business.

On the whole, the crowd had been just a lot of exuberant young people who had come to have a good time. Some had come without tickets, hoping somehow to find a way in—which makes them hooligans maybe but not criminals. Unfortunately, some people stole money and jewelry off the dead and injured. *They* were criminals.

We could not determine just how many had been killed. As EMS ambulances arrived, people were carried out and put in them, to get them to hospitals as quickly as possible. People with broken arms and broken legs, people with chest pains, people with head injuries, all were put in the ambulances and taken to hospitals. Some were unconscious and may in fact have been dead. Some may have died on the way to the hospitals or even at the hospitals. We would not know the death toll until detectives had finished the work of visiting every area hospital and identifying the people who had been brought in.

The bottom line of what had happened was this: At CCNY, an organization called Evening Student Government had sponsored an exhibition basketball game between two teams of rap stars. It was billed as The Heavy D & Puff Daddy First Annual Celebrity Basketball Game. The following were among the promised players:

| Heavy D's Team | Puff Daddy's Team |
| --- | --- |
| Mike Bivins | Jodeci |
| Boyz II Men | Brand Nubian |
| Run-D.M.C. | Ed Lover |
| Phife Dog | Jeff Redd |

| | |
|---|---|
| G-Wiz | Guy |
| Heavy D & the Boyz | Bubba |
| Big Daddy Kane | Smiley |
| Todd I | Nice-n-Smooth |
| The Afros | Funkmaster Flex |
| Red Head Kingpin | On the I & II |

Puff Daddy, whose real name is Sean Combs, was an organizer of shows of this kind. The event was billed as a fund raiser for an organization called AIDS Education Outreach Program, a division of the New York City Health Department not authorized to receive charitable funds.

The event had been heavily promoted, particularly by radio station WKRS-FM. The gymnasium could not have held more than two or three thousand spectators, but far more tickets had been sold. Besides, radio announcers continued to say that plenty of seats remained available and people could buy them at the door. They were still saying that when the crowd assembled outside the gym was obviously too big to get in and Sean Combs was asking men with bullhorns to tell people who didn't have tickets to go home. As many as five thousand young people eventually showed up.

At first the crowd was orderly. Two doors had been opened outside the gymnasium. One was for the people who had bought their tickets earlier, and the other was for the people who wanted to buy tickets. Then it became apparent that thousands of the young people outside the gym were not going to get in—those with tickets they had bought and paid for and those without tickets. Many became angry and rushed the doors.

They kicked in one of the glass doors. The security people had been letting people in single file, but when the crowd broke down the door, the campus security people panicked and ran. The people who were selling tickets grabbed the money and tickets and ran down the stairs and into the gymnasium. Behind them came a crowd, no longer single file but a pushing, shouting mob.

The witnesses described what had happened. There were of course hundreds of them. The injured were especially important witnesses because they had been where the tragedy developed, and they knew what had happened. Their stories differed about details but on the whole were consistent. Essentially the stories painted the same picture.

Bill Kelly and I were sent to Mount Sinai Hospital to interview injured people.

One of those we interviewed was a young man of eighteen, probably six foot one and maybe 155 pounds. He said he had bought his ticket to the event at Boss Emporium on 125th Street. When he got to the gymnasium, security people told him to get into a line. He followed that line to a ticket table at the top of a stairway. There he exchanged his ticket for a numbered ticket that was supposed to admit him to the gym. The people at the table told him to go down the stairs to the entrance to the gym. He said when he went down the stairs he saw that only one of the doors into the gym was open. All the rest were closed. The reason the other doors were closed was that the ticket takers had been working at the one open door, checking to see that no one got in without a ticket—a genuine concern, since many gate-crashers were expecting to shove their way in.

Our witness started down the stairs. Then he said he heard a tremendous banging noise up above. People began to yell and scream. He looked back and saw a large group muscling down the stairs and pushing toward the open door. People who didn't have tickets had decided to "bum rush"—as they called it—the door. Many young people could not escape and were carried into the stairwell by the struggling crowd. The pressure became unbearable. People could not breathe and began passing out.

The tragic fact was that the stairwell could not contain that many people. According to one estimate, 150 people were there. What was more, all these people could not enter the gym through the one open door. The result was a brutal crush. People were shoved against each other so tightly that they literally could not breathe and so suffocated. One of the dead was a man six feet five who probably weighed 285. Another was a little girl five feet three who couldn't have weighed more than 115. They had died horrifying deaths, the breath of life squeezed out of them. As big as the six-five guy was, he had been unable to save himself. So what chance had the little girl had?

Some of the young people had brought video cameras and had taped the scene. They had come to see a celebrity basketball game featuring well-known rap singers, and they had hoped to tape some of that. Instead they had taped a tragedy.

In one of these videos, the camera was located up in the bleachers, and the amateur cameraman had taped the arrival of the rap stars. He had been totally unaware that only a few yards away from him, on the other side of a wall, people were dying. When at last he did become aware of it, he swung his camera around, and the video shows people pulling people into the gymnasium through the one open door while others were being crushed to death on the other side of the door.

The video also showed the seven closed doors. They could not be opened, because all the doors in the gym opened out, as the fire laws required, and they could not be opened against the crush of people just outside.

Most of the people in the gymnasium did not learn for a long time what was going on. They couldn't see beyond the one open door, and the music in the gym was so loud that they could not hear the screams. While people were dying in the stairwell outside, guys were running around the floor innocently shooting baskets.

When Bill Kelly and I returned from Mount Sinai Hospital, we began taking statements from EMS and fire personnel who had come to the scene. I recall seeing Mayor Dinkins. Fire Commissioner Carlos Rivera was present. First Deputy Commissioner—later Police Commissioner—Ray Kelly was there.

Politicians and political wannabes were also there, all making noises to the effect that a full investigation would be conducted, that the results of the investigation would be made public, and there would be no cover-up.

Politicians and the press began to demand that guilt be placed on somebody. As always, they tried to shove part of it onto the police.

Investigation was exceptionally difficult after the first night. Everyone involved—promoters of the event, CCNY, and the victims—retained legal counsel and prepared for litigation. Naturally, their lawyers told all of them to keep quiet.

Another impediment to the investigation was that witnesses were soon tainted by the media. Too often a reporter does not just ask a witness what he or she saw; he suggests what he wants the person to say, to support the story the reporter wants to tell. After being asked half a dozen times, "This is what you saw, didn't you?" the witness begins to believe that is what he *did* see.

Fortunately, we had gotten many consistent statements on the night of the tragedy. Fortunately too, some of the injured ignored their lawyers and talked to us again.

It was not our purpose to sustain anybody's lawsuit. Our immediate purpose, that night, was to identify the victims and notify their families. After that, we looked for violations of criminal law, if there were any. No prosecutions followed.

I would like to say something about the responsibility of the police department. The department was criticized in some quarters, as if it had *let* the tragedy happen.

It is to the credit of Ray Kelly, then deputy commissioner, that he assembled the facts as quickly as he could and refused to place any blame on the uniformed police at the scene. Some tried to make a scapegoat of Captain Daniel Carlin, the uniformed captain in charge that night. Ray Kelly would have none of that.

The facts are these:

Uniformed officers of the NYPD were not on the campus but on the street. CCNY does not want police officers patrolling the campus. They say it upsets the students. The area immediately surrounding the gymnasium and the inside of the building were the responsibility of what we on the Job call "square badges"—that is, private security officers who wear square badges, not the shields of the police department. They were, in short, campus cops. In addition, CCNY had employed a contingent of Pinkerton security guards for the event.

Also on the campus that night was a group of civilians who had been hired to help keep order, a sort of private security force. They were supposed to organize people waiting outside into two lines, one for ticket holders and one for people who had to buy tickets, and to keep the lines orderly. They also had metal detectors and were looking for guns.

The department had been told about what size crowd CCNY expected that night—a fraction of the number who showed up—and ten uniformed men under the command of Sergeant Calvin Randall was assigned. That was a sufficient number of men to do the job the department was supposed to do.

Sergeant Randall soon saw that the crowd was far bigger

than he had been told to expect, so he called for help. Manhattan North Task Force sent men to augment the detail. A lieutenant, two more sergeants, and sixteen officers came. Captain Carlin also heard about it and came.

This meant that about thirty cops were present. That was a large force. An event at Madison Square Garden doesn't require that many officers.

The NYPD personnel on the street had no idea what was happening in the gymnasium. The square-badge police inside the gym communicated with each other on their own radio frequency and did not communicate with NYPD. The tragedy inside was invisible from outside the building and was, of course, invisible from the street. The uniformed cops could see the top of the stairwell but could not see what was happening inside. What was more, because of the loud music, they couldn't hear that anything was wrong.

When word came out of what was happening inside, the neat young men of the private security force turned on their heels and quickstepped off the campus.

The uniformed cops decided they had to move in. Their first job was to prevent more of the crowd outside from entering the gymnasium. It took only two men to do that. They simply took up a station in front of the door and wouldn't let any more people in.

So who was at fault? There is plenty of blame to go around. In the first place, the promoters of the event grossly oversold it. The gym could not have held half the ticket holders. The radio stations kept broadcasting that there were plenty of seats and urging people to go see the event, even while the crowd milled outside the gym and saw they could not get in. The campus cops who panicked and ran may have been right; they could have been trampled. The most immediate blame falls on the hooligans who decided to "bum rush" the door. Some of them were undoubtedly among the dead and injured.

That so many should have died and been hurt is of course an immense disaster. The damage to City College of New York has also been great. A traveler returning from Europe reported a conversation she had with an acquaintance she made there. The European asked where she had been educated. When she mentioned CCNY, the European replied, "Oh, yes, where all the young people were killed at the rap concert." The European was not aware that people like Edward G. Robinson and Dr. Jonas Salk were educated there. She did not know that ten Nobel Prize winners and many winners of the Pulitzer Prize graduated from CCNY. In her mind, CCNY was identified with Heavy D, Puff Daddy, and death at a rap basketball game. Too many people identify the college that way, not with its distinguished schools of engineering, computer science, and other disciplines. That's another element of the tragedy of December 28, 1991.

A final point. When the call came to respond immediately to the CCNY campus, Bill Kelly and I had been ready to move in and arrest a suspect in the killing of Sergeant Keith Levine.

Another team of officers collared that suspect later that night.

It turned out they had arrested—*we* would have arrested if we hadn't been called away—the wrong man. We had been working on the word of an informer. Later investigation demonstrated that the informer had been wrong and that the wrong man had been arrested and charged.

## 11

# CRACKHEADS AND BROKEN HEARTS

GENERALLY I HAVE USED THE true names of the people involved in these accounts of crimes and investigations. In this chapter I am going to use none of the actual names. The people involved have suffered enough. If the people involved read this book, they will recognize themselves, because the facts of the case are so dramatic and unusual. Others need not know their names.

On Tuesday, July 14, 1987, I was doing what we call an eight-by-four tour of duty—that is to say, from 8:00 A.M. to 4:00 P.M. My partner that day was Detective Chris Heimgartner. We had been working on a case from the Two-five Precinct involving the murder of two prostitutes. About eleven forty-five we decided to stop at a deli we knew, get a sandwich and a cold drink, and take them to a place on the riverbank where we could sit and eat and watch the boats go up and down the river.

It had been hot all week. Exceptionally hot and muggy, one of those summer weeks that makes for tension in New York City. Sitting in the shade where there was a cool breeze seemed like a great idea.

The Dyckman Deli on Dyckman Street was owned by a retired detective named Burt. He had been with the Three-four Squad, the Thirty-fourth Precinct, where I had served for many years, and I knew him well. When we came in, two uniformed officers from the Three-four were there also, at the counter getting sandwiches. I knew them too.

One of the uniformed cops said to me, "Hey, Tom, you guys working?" I said we were. He said, "Well, there's a fresh homicide up at 16 Cooper Street. And I don't remember the name, but the victim is the son of a retired detective from the Three-four."

I had served from 1969 to 1987 in the Three-four, and I was sure the retired detective they were talking about was going to be someone I knew. There were very few guys in the Three-four I didn't know. Chances were, the son was going to be somebody I knew too. I had a terrible feeling.

Chris and I told Burt to hold the sandwich order, and we immediately went to the car and drove up to the address on Cooper Street, a distance of some three blocks.

As we pulled up to the scene, two things struck me. First, Detective Jack Collich was standing on the street blowing his nose. Jack Collich was an experienced hand and not the kind of man to let something get to him, but he looked a little green. Second, the doors to the apartment building were wide open. These two things told me that we had a messy situation inside; what we had was a decomposing body.

I turned to Chris and said, "This is gonna be a beauty." Just as I said that a gust of wind came, and I got a full breath of the stink right in the throat. If you experience that smell once, you never forget what it smells like. A body that has been decomposing for several days in hot, muggy weather produces a stink that is enough to make anybody vomit.

I have had experience with this kind of thing, but I was

glad I hadn't eaten lunch. If you get a real whiff of it, you simply cannot hold down whatever is in your stomach. I have seen seasoned detectives barfing on the street after walking out of a crime scene where there was a decomposing body. The guys from the coroner's office, who have to deal with this, wear gas masks. Uniformed officers arriving at a scene scatter crystals that are supposed to cut down the stink, but in this case they weren't much help.

What is more, the stench clings to your clothes and skin. You have to shower to get it off. You have to have your clothes dry-cleaned. Chris and I took off our jackets and hung them in the car, so they would not absorb the overpowering odor. I was wearing a knit golf shirt, and I poured some aftershave lotion on the right sleeve. We carry a bottle of that in the car for situations like this. We could duck our heads down and breathe through our sleeves and get some escape from the smell.

We spoke to Jack Collich, and he told us the victim was Fred Stark. (Here I begin using names that are not real.) I had met Fred many years ago, when he was a teenager. He was the son of a detective who had once worked with me as my partner, Robert Stark. Bob had served some thirty years in the Thirty-fourth Precinct and was a great guy. I had met his son Fred seventeen years ago, when he came to the office one day to meet his dad before they went to some picnic or party together. At the time of his death, Fred was a court officer in Bronx County.

Jack Collich told us that Robert Stark and his son Robert Stark, Junior, had been trying to get in touch with their son and brother for almost a week. Robert Stark, Jr., was also a policeman, a narcotics detective. They last saw Fred on July 8 when he was taking his two children to a ballgame at Yankee Stadium. Fred was living apart from his wife, who was calling herself by her maiden name, Linda Kimble. She had custody of the children, but they were living with her parents. Robert Stark contacted the grandparents, and they confirmed that Fred in fact picked up the children and took them to a game. He did not return them. Dave Trotter, their mother's boyfriend, returned them home.

The Starks were very upset. Fred was a court officer, was not on vacation, and he had not shown up for work for eight days. Robert, Jr., came to the apartment on Cooper Street, which he knew was where Linda lived with her boyfriend. He knocked on the door and got no response. Several days later—today—both Starks, father and son, came to the apartment and knocked on the door. They got no response. But they could smell the corpse.

Robert, Jr., went around to the back of the building and climbed up on the fire escape. He broke a window. The smell came out. He took a deep breath and entered the apartment. He ran to the front door, opened it, and there gagged and vomited. His father then came in, and they returned and searched the apartment.

When they got to the bedroom they found a fifty-five-gallon drum sitting in the center of the room. Robert, Sr., walked over to it and looked in. Though he didn't yet know it, what he was looking at was his son's backside. The murderer and his brother had cracked Fred's spine with a machete so they could double him over and stuff him in the drum. The father grabbed and started to pull. Then he had realized what he was pulling on. He and his son ran out of the building and called the police.

To give this thing its peculiar character, I am now going to set forth verbatim the statement given to me by one of the participants in this crime, changing only the names.

These are the names I am using for these people: The victim was Fred Stark. His estranged wife called herself Linda Kimble. The murderer was Dave Trotter, Linda's boyfriend. Dave had two brothers, Bill and Dick. Bill, who'd had a fight with his girlfriend, was living temporarily in the apartment with Dave and Linda. The following is Bill's statement, given to me on July 15 and signed by him.

Statement of William Trotter taken by Det. Thomas W. McKenna, Shield 1868, Manhattan North Homicide Squad.

On Wednesday 7-8-87 at approximately 6:00 P.M. Fred Stark returned to 16 Cooper Street with the children Kenny and Deirdre. They had been taken to the Yankee ballgame at the Stadium. Fred was yelling at Kenny about his acting up on the bus ride home from the Park. Linda and Fred started to discuss Fred yelling at the child and she finally asked him to leave, and he did. At approximately 10:00 P.M. I returned home and Dave had left the apartment to go and meet Fred. They had stated they would meet each other when Fred left the apartment earlier. At 12:00 Linda left the apartment to get some medication for a headache and around 2:00 she returned with Fred and Dave. Linda and Fred went out again and returned at about 4:00 A.M. Fred came in first and said that Linda said he could stay until morning. A short time later Linda came in and said that he couldn't stay. Dave told him to leave and he did. I fell asleep. In the morning Thursday 7-9-87 I woke at about 7:00 A.M. I showered dressed and went out to find some friends. During the course of the day I was in and out of the apartment. I didn't have keys so either Dave or Linda were present in the apartment all day. Neither one mentioned anything about any problems during the night. During the night Dave, Linda, and I were partying. At about 11:00 P.M. Linda and I went out to get some drinks. We wound up in Joel's Bar on Broadway. We stayed there until about 4:00 A.M. and walked home. When we got home, Dave and Dick were there. Dick was drunk. I left to get crack and bought 6 cracks for $50. I returned to Cooper Street and we partied. At about 5:30 A.M. Dick and Dave left the house. I left at about 6:00 A.M. to cop some more crack. At the corner of Academy and Cooper I met Dick. I asked what was up and he said Dave had killed Fred, and he is upstairs in the apartment. I said bullshit, I was there and he couldn't have. I didn't even see Fred. Dick said it's true he's there. I left him thinking he was full of shit and I went to cop. I got six cracks for $50. I went back to the apartment. Linda was there alone. I did some crack and Dave and Dick came in. We partied again. It lasted all day. About 5:00 P.M. I was in the kitchen and Dave came in. He asked me, "What did Dick tell you?" I told him that he told me you killed Fred. He left without saying anything and went out to get Dick. Five minutes later they came back to the apartment. Dave asked Dick why did you tell him (me). Dick said he would have found out anyway I had to tell him. Dave asked Linda and me to leave. Linda and I left and went to Inwood Park. We were bullshiting on the rocks and I asked Linda what happened and she said that Fred had left and come back and when she woke up she saw Dave and Fred fighting. She ran back into the bedroom and Dave said it was over. Dave told Linda that he strangled Fred. I figured the less I know about it the better; we didn't talk about it anymore.

We left the park about 9:00 P.M. and went back to the apartment. Dave and Dick were there. On the way back to the apartment I got Valium for Linda. She took one and I took two, she went to sleep and Dick was already sleeping. I watched the ballgame with Dave. After the ballgame Dave and I took the bus to 238 Street and Riverside Avenue and went to the cash machine at 238 Street and Johnson Ave in the Chemical Bank. I waited on the corner and Dave went to the bank machine which is outside. He took five hundred dollars out of the bank. [He was using Fred's bank card.] We took a bus to 231 Street and Broadway, we got off the bus and took a cab to 204 Street and Broadway. Dave gave me $100 to cop and he went to the apartment. Dave and I partied all night. Saturday morning 7-11-87 at about 8:00 A.M. Dave left and Linda and I went to cop. We got 12 cracks for $100. We came back to Cooper Street and Dave had the van. It's a white van that says John's Trucking on the side. He got the van from Billy Thompson on Vermilyen Ave. The three of us went up to the apartment. The apartment smells a little bit but they were burning incense. We smoked all the cracks. Linda and I went to the park because Dave said they was going to take care of the body. I know this because Dave told me. Dave told Linda to [call] him later and about 11:00 A.M. we called him and he said there were complications. Linda and I went to Cooper Street and Dave was at the van. I got in the van and Linda got in the van and we went to a car wash to get a barrel. [The barrel, which the Trotters called a "barr'l," was a fifty-five-gallon plastic drum.] Dave paid $5 to a kid for the barrel. We went back to Cooper Street and up to the apartment. Dave brought the barrel upstairs. Linda and I watched TV and Dick and Dave were using a handsaw on the barrel. The handsaw didn't work, so Dave went to the super to borrow a saw. He returned with an electric saw. They cut the barrel open. Dave said I need your help to lift him up. I said I'm not going to touch him. He said I don't have to all you have to do is hold the barrel. I got up and went into the bedroom with Dave and Dick. As I entered the bedroom I saw a body on a mattress covered by two black trash bags. Dick and I took the barrel and laid [it] down by his feet. Dave went to the other end by the head. Dave then got a two × four and lifted the feet and Dick and I pushed the barrel but we couldn't get him into the barrel. We got it in as far as the thighs. Dave kept trying but we told him the barrel is to small. We went outside, talked, and went back inside and stood the barrel up. We pushed the barrel to the wall and loaded him into the barrel against the wall and left the room. We talked and told Dave the barrel was too small. Dave went back into the bedroom. I didn't return to the bedroom until the next day. On Sunday afternoon I went into the room with Dave and the body was covered with a drop cloth. Dave had gotten another barrel on Sunday and it was in the room. Before he took the drop cloth off he started to take some of the lime out of the barrel and he was putting it the other barrel. [In Bill's statement he describes their putting small objects, including a plastic knife, in lime and water to see if the mixture would dissolve these things.] I got sick and left the room. I left the house to get some air. Linda went with me. We walked around and got a six-pack and went back to the apartment. The smell was real bad. I told

Linda and the others we had to leave. Linda and I left and copped 5 cracks and went to the park. It started to rain and we went to the hallway at 666 W. 207 Street. We went to McSherrys Bar on Broadway and had a beer. Linda called Dave and when she returned to the bar she said Dave told her everything was taken care of. We went back to the apartment. Dave said he had laid the top with plaster and we had to wait for it to dry and we would move the body in the barrel. Dave went into the room about 9:00 A.M. and checked to see if it was dry and then went to get the handtruck. He came back and went back into the room and said the Sakrete cracked and the body came back up. About midnight Linda and I went to the cash machine on 238 Street but it was down so we went to 167 Street and St. Nicholas Avenue and got $500. We got cracks 12 for $100 and went back to the apartment. We partied all night and Dave went to sleep. At about 10:00 A.M. I went to the [illegible] and bought some more Sakrete. I brought it back to the apartment. At about 11:00 A.M. Fred's brother started banging on the door. Nobody answered and after about five minutes he went away. I went out and copped some more crack for Dave. I returned and woke Linda and Dick. Linda and I left and went to the Van Courtland Motel Room 41. This was about 4:00 P.M.; we stayed there at about 6:00 P.M. Dave and Dick met us there. Tuesday at 12:30 P.M. Dick and I left and went to the George Washington Hotel, it was closed and we [went] to the Kenmore and checked in.

They had abandoned their effort to dispose of the body in a plastic drum. They had abandoned the apartment because no one could stay there with the stink. This was Tuesday, July 14, the day on which Fred's brother broke into the apartment and he and his father found the body.

Entering that second-floor apartment was one of the most difficult things I ever had to do. It was just sickening—apart from the fact that I knew the victim and knew his father as a friend. Even so, we went upstairs with Jack Collich and found and looked at the body. We didn't stay any longer than we had to. At that point the Crime Scene Unit had not yet arrived, so we did not even search the premises. A later search would produce the machete and other items associated with the crime.

When the coroner examined the body, he found that Fred Stark had not been strangled but had died of multiple stab wounds.

Finding the criminals was no great piece of detective work. We did the normal things we do in such cases. We interviewed many people who knew Fred and Linda. Linda's mother and father were very cooperative. So, for that matter, were the Stark family.

Linda's parents were unhappy about her having left Fred and taken up with a worthless punk like Trotter. Fred Stark had had his faults. He was a drinker. But he was a working man and a provider. The Trotters were crackhead bums, and Dave had turned Linda into a junkie. Fred was dead. But Linda was dead too, for all practical purposes. Drugs had destroyed her.

The Trotters were walking dead too—their minds and bodies ruined by crack and whatever else they used.

Bill and Dick were downtown, staying in a hotel in the area of Gramercy Park. They had made telephone calls to friends, so we had no problem locating them and picking them up. I might say that we made their friends understand very clearly that if they heard from any of these people and didn't tell us, they would be in big trouble. These people were dealers and junkies, and they knew we could make trouble for them. So when these guys called friends, the friends called us. We arrested Bill and Dick and charged them with hindering a police investigation. The brothers gave us statements.

But we had no idea where Linda and Dave had gone. Every effort to locate them failed, and we suspected they had left New York. We had, of course, notified the bank of Fred's death, and the last time Linda or Dave tried to use his bank card, the machine ate it and dispensed no money.

The facts were that Linda and Dave had fled from New York. They had worked various places and ultimately wound up in Virginia Beach, Virginia. Eventually Linda decided she'd had enough of Dave. So she called her mother and said she needed $39 for bus fare home. Her mother called us. We told her mother to tell her to go to the local police, who would put her on the bus for New York, and we would pay the bus driver when she arrived.

Linda told her mother that Dave was coming to New York too. He came to New York and went to the apartment of a friend of his. The friend called us immediately. He had arrived at the apartment at nine, and at nine twenty-five he was under arrest.

We interviewed Dave Trotter. He really had no idea why he'd killed Fred Stark. He had been so high and so drunk he didn't know exactly what had happened. He went to prison for twenty-five to life—time enough to try to figure it out. Linda cooperated and was eventually released, as were Bill and Dick.

If there is a redeeming element in all of this, it is that Linda and Fred's children wound up in her parents' custody, which gave those kids some hope of a decent life.

I have never been able to understand what people think they are doing when they start using substances like crack. Reading William Trotter's statement, you can see what it does to you. At very best the Trotters were not very bright, but as crackheads they were, as I've said, walking dead. They simply could not function.

If it were not so tragic, their efforts to dispose of the body of Fred Stark might have been comic. It makes you think of Laurel and Hardy trying to move the piano—only Laurel and Hardy were a pair of genius comics entertaining us with a show, and these characters were seriously trying to stuff Fred Stark in a drum so they could haul him out of the apartment.

I've seen too much of this. All the teaching we try to give young people about the tragedy narcotics will bring into their lives seems to be futile. I wish some of them could see the mindless, vacant, ambly-shambly derelicts intelligent and competent people become when they turn into addicts.

They think it won't happen to them. I bet Linda thought so too.

# 12

## IT'S NOT EASY

I AM OFTEN ASKED IF I have ever had to shoot anybody. The answer is yes, but having to use deadly force is an extremely rare occurrence, particularly for detectives. The reason it is rare is that when detectives go into a situation where violence might happen, we go well prepared, with a plan. We work fast, and we come with overwhelming force. Rarely do we get shot at, and rarely do we shoot.

Uniformed officers often find themselves in situations they could not have anticipated and could not have planned for. They come on crimes in progress. They face people who are emotionally disturbed. They are threatened with death.

Officer Steve Sullivan, for example, could not have anticipated the situation that resulted in the death of Mrs. Eleanor Bumpers. He could not have planned in advance how he would react and what he would do if that kind of situation came up. His partner was attacked by a woman with a butcher knife, and he reacted by shooting her. He didn't want to, but he could not have anticipated what he would face and have planned his reaction.

Two situations I've described earlier involved detectives in unplanned situations that got dangerous.

In the case of the parking garage, I was off duty. I *happened* on a robbery. I was alone. The guy in the Mercedes fired his gun.

The situation where Billy Blue Eyes Muldoon was shot, and where the shooter died of shots fired through the bathroom door, was unplanned. The suspect Muldoon had gone to arrest was not there. Instead, other people were there, wanted for serious crimes and ready to shoot to avoid arrest.

Even though guns must sometimes be used, it is a fact that 90 percent of all New York police officers serve their entire careers and never fire a shot except on the range.

However, there have been situations in which I have had to use my gun.

The case I want to describe happened in a county outside the boroughs of New York City. I had moved my family out to a small town, frankly to shelter them from the violence that had become too much a part of life in the city, also to get away from the situation, where I found myself bound to act when I was off duty. I am not going to give the names, not of the county or the town or of the people involved. My first wife and our children still live there, and I do not want to embarrass them. The names don't make any difference anyway.

This happened in 1971. At the time of the incident I am about to tell, I was assigned to the Manhattan Robbery Squad. That week I was working a four-to-midnight tour. Leaving the precinct a little after twelve, I could be home a little after one. It was roughly a sixty-mile drive.

At that time we worked a day tour for one week, a night tour the next week. Leaving the office at midnight after a four-to-twelve tour, I liked to have a couple of beers to help me unwind. I thought it was better if I drank my beers in a little bar in the small town where I lived, rather than have them before the drive.

You needed that kind of relaxation sometimes. I've mentioned pulling off the Palisades Parkway and standing for a while, looking out over the river the night Billy Blue Eyes was shot and thinking a lot of thoughts. The bar was only three or four blocks from my house; and, being an Irish guy, I enjoyed having my beers in that little pub, with somebody to talk to, rather than having them in my kitchen after my wife and kids had gone to bed.

So, on this particular night I arrived at a bar I am going to call Charlie's. It was owned by a guy named Charlie, and I'd gotten to know him pretty well. He and I played on a local softball team, which is why I went to his bar. I'll call the young bartender Johnny. He played on the same ball team. So I knew the guys who ran the place, and they knew me.

I need to describe the bar a little. It was a friendly kind of place, the kind of place where you usually found somebody you knew when you walked in. The world is full of those little bars: not too brightly lighted, many times having a neon sign in the window advertising one kind of beer or another, usually kind of quiet, usually with the smell of stale beer on the air. When you came in through the door, the bar was directly in front of you. It extended to the left and to the right; and on the right-hand end it curved around ninety degrees. It did not make a right angle; it curved.

On that night I recognized a man sitting at the left end of the bar. He was a New York state trooper that I knew very well. His name—his real name—was Dick Wright. He was off duty and out of uniform. I walked over, sat down next to Dick Wright, and we started to talk. I ordered a Budweiser, and we sat and talked, about nothing much, just what kind of day it had been.

While we were talking, two or three people left the bar. One of them was a male white in his twenties. I noticed that he left but paid no particular attention to him.

Then Johnny the bartender came over. He knew who Dick Wright was and knew that I was a New York City detective. He spoke to Dick and said, "Hey, Jesus, you know that guy had a gun here. In his waistband."

Dick Wright asked, "What guy?"

Johnny said, "The guy who just left. Larry Vogel."

Dick Wright had heard of Vogel and asked if he wasn't the guy who lived at such-and-such a place, giving the address. Then he asked what had happened.

What had happened was that Vogel had been in the bar earlier that night and had gotten into a hot dispute with a couple of young women. During the course of a violent argument, Vogel had pulled a gun, put it to the young women's heads, and demanded they give him money.

"Well, why didn't you tell me before the guy left?"

Johnny said he was afraid.

I guessed this one. It sounded to me like the girls owed Vogel money for drugs. Dick Wright asked Johnny a few more questions and came to the same conclusion.

Dick decided to obtain a warrant to arrest Vogel and search his apartment. He took Johnny's statement and made him the complainant for the affidavits to support the arrest and search warrants. He was off duty for a couple of days but said he would get and execute the warrants when he came back on duty.

That was the end of the incident.

The next day I had another four-to-midnight, and I did the same thing I'd done the day before. I left the office a little after twelve and drove upstate. A little after one I pulled into the parking lot in front of Charlie's Bar.

As I parked my car, Johnny came out. He told me that

Vogel was in there again and had the gun on him again. He said Vogel was at the right end of the bar and had the gun in his belt directly in front of his stomach—right in front of his belly button. He was making no effort to conceal it. In fact, he had pulled the gun on people in the bar that evening.

I asked Johnny if he had called the state troopers. He said he had not, because he was afraid. In fact, he said he hadn't had time to get away from the bar and use the phone. But when he saw my headlights in the parking lot, he guessed who it was and came out to talk to me.

I asked Johnny how many people were in the place. He said there were only two, besides this guy. I'd know the guy, he said, because he was sitting just at the turn of the bar, to the right. I told him to go back inside, go behind the bar, and whatever he did, not get involved. He was to stay away from me, no matter what happened. I didn't want anybody getting hurt.

I had moved sixty miles out of town so I wouldn't have to get into this kind of shit when I was off duty—but here I was. Just because I'd moved didn't mean I wouldn't get involved in something if I had to. I knew what I had in there: a young drug dealer with a gun. I couldn't guess whether this was going to be an easy go or a tough go. The point was, I didn't know whether this guy would tolerate going to jail or not. If no, he was apt to get rough.

I walked into the bar and went to the right. I saw Vogel as I went around the bar, and I saw the gun sticking out of his belt. When he noticed me, he grabbed at his dark-blue sweater and pushed it down over the grip of the gun. I passed him and stood basically next to him and to his right, except that being around the curve I was at an angle to him, and his profile was toward me. He was facing the bar, and his right arm was on the bar.

He was six feet three, a sort of ugly, smart-ass-looking

kind of guy. You could see he figured he had the whole world under control, because he had a gun in his belt.

Johnny came over and said, "Hi, how ya doin'? Long drive out here tonight."

I said, "Yeah, it's a long ride. Give me a Bud."

He poured me a Budweiser and asked if I'd had a tough night, talk like that.

Vogel paid no attention to this small talk and didn't take part in it.

I was watching for a chance to take him, to get that gun away from him and hold him for the state troopers. The chance came. From where I stood I faced the door. From where he stood his back was toward it. The door opened, and a man came in. Vogel turned to see who it was.

While he was looking the other way, I pulled my gun. When Vogel turned and saw me again, I held my gun pointed at his face and had my badge in my left hand, showing it to him.

"Okay, my friend," I said. "I'm a police officer, and what I want you to do is step back from the bar and get your hands up."

He looked down the barrel of my gun and said, "Fuck you."

I couldn't believe this. I'd been a cop for six years, a detective for two, I'd faced some pretty hairy situations, but I couldn't remember anybody ever looking straight down the barrel of anybody's gun and telling the guy with the gun to go fuck himself. I've now been a policeman for thirty years, and that's the only time I ever saw anybody do that. Vogel wasn't high on drugs either—I don't think. He'd been drinking, but he wasn't high on drugs. The fact is, he had guts. It was awesome.

At this point everything seemed to go into slow motion.

I've had that experience other times. It seems to happen; I don't know why. I guess your adrenaline is rushing. You've got all kinds of thoughts, all at once. What happened took a second or two, but it seemed like it took a whole minute. And I remember it that way. I can remember every instant.

He started pushing me. I grabbed for his gun and tried to pull it out. He punched me. He hit me hard, a glancing blow on the left temple, that stunned me but didn't do anything more than that. I was still functioning.

At that point I hit him. I didn't hit him with a fist. I hit him with my gun.

I gave Bill Harrington a close look at my gun. "See. Look at that. You ever see a Smith & Wesson revolver that looks like that?"

"No, I never saw a gun with a trigger guard bent in like that."

"Well, that's what happened to this one when I hit Vogel with it. I hit the son of a bitch one hell of a shot. You understand, I didn't want to have to use the gun the other way."

"You've carried that pistol with that trigger guard bent like that all these years?"

"Well, it's a trusty gun."

Anyway, Vogel started going down. As he was falling backward, he reached for his gun. I was yelling *"Don't move! Police! Police!"* But he pulled the gun anyway and pointed it toward me.

At that time, I fired one shot. You understand, I didn't have time to aim much; I just shoved my gun toward him and pulled off one shot.

Vogel dropped the gun and sprawled on the floor. He was bleeding from the nose and mouth and ears. I knelt over him for a moment but didn't see where I'd hit him. I'd fired to hit him in the mass of the body. That's where we are trained to shoot if we have to—where we are most likely to hit the subject, where it will do the most damage—and I supposed that's where I'd hit him. But, as I've said, I hadn't had time to aim.

I looked up at Johnny. I said to him, "Call the state troopers. Tell them there's been a man shot, and there's a New York City detective involved, and we'd like them to respond."

Johnny asked me what I was going to do. I put my gun back in my holster and said I had to go to the bathroom.

I went in the bathroom. I don't remember exactly how I felt, except that I knew I was going through a horrible experience. I remember leaning against the wall and trying to get control of my arms and hands, which were shaking violently. I do remember thinking I had moved upstate to get away from this kind of thing but I must be followed by it, like a great black cloud. Here I am. I've moved out to the country to have a different life at off-duty times, and it's no different at all.

I think I made a mistake. I'd spoken too softly. What I should have done was yell at him. I would today. Experience has taught me that the time for being gentle with a man you are going to arrest is after he is cuffed. *Then* you can be a nice guy. If you are nice sooner, the guy may mistake kindness for weakness. Then you have a problem. If he thinks you are weak, thinks you're not strong enough or mad enough to do what you have to do, he may decide to try to take you.

My mistake was in thinking that out in a suburb with trees and flowers the criminals were different from criminals in the city. This guy was carrying a gun. He had threatened people with it, last night and this night. In the city, in my own element, I would have slammed the man into the bar and grabbed that gun from him. Here I was a little easier about it, which had turned out to be the wrong thing to do. He might have just surrendered, if I'd been tougher. I blamed myself, sort of, for what had happened to him.

I returned to the bar, keeping my hands in my pockets because I didn't want people to see how they were shaking. I wasn't scared. It's just a reaction I get whenever something like this happens. My hands just shake. I stepped up to the bar again, and I told the bartender to pour me another beer—even though I hadn't had a sip out of the first one.

He poured the beer, and then I heard a moan on the floor. I looked down and saw that Vogel was moving. I told Johnny to toss me a damp towel. I wiped Vogel's face. And—

My shot had not hit him in the mass of the body. I had shot off a piece of his ear! He was alive! What had happened was, he had heard my gun go off, maybe had felt the bullet tear off part of his ear, and he had fainted dead away!

So why had he been bleeding from mouth and nose? From the whack I'd given him with my gun. The blood I had seen on his ear was of course from the slight wound to his ear.

I was glad the man was alive. Believe me, I was glad I had not killed this man, no matter how bad a guy he might be.

I wanted to talk to him. I wanted to know why he would face a gun pointed at his face and say "Fuck you." I'd never seen that before and couldn't imagine why he'd say that.

Later, when he was in jail, I interviewed Vogel. I asked him what in the world he'd had in mind. He said in the first place he'd known I was a New York City cop; but he figured this wasn't New York City and I had no right to bother him. Besides, he said, he was a lot bigger than I was, and he figured he could take me. Anyway, I'd spoken softly, and he'd figured I was afraid.

He threatened me. He said he'd find out where I lived and sooner or later he'd get me. He also threatened my family. I didn't take this too seriously. I knew he was just a jerk, blustering. Still, when somebody threatens your family, you have to be concerned. I didn't tell my wife and kids. Anyway, Vogel went directly from the bar to a hospital, from there to a justice-of-the-peace court, from there to jail, and from there to Attica. He was never again on the street, so his threat never developed into anything I really had to worry about.

Getting back to the scene in the bar, the troopers and an ambulance arrived, and Vogel was removed to a hospital. At the hospital they covered his ear with gauze and bandage, then let the troopers bring him to the local justice of the peace.

The scene in the home of the justice of the peace was amazing to me. It was totally different from the way they'd have handled the case in the city. I'm not saying it was wrong, just that it was amazingly different.

I'd lived in the town about five years, so the justice knew me. In a town that size, everybody knew everybody. His wife made a pot of coffee, and the three of us sat in their dining room and chatted over doughnuts and coffee while the trooper used the justice's typewriter to type out the complaint. Where was Vogel during this time? They locked him in a closet!

The justice of the peace fixed bond at $25,000. Vogel couldn't have made $250. He was a suburban drug pusher, who shot up all his profits. He hardly broke even as a dealer. He went to jail.

Vogel pleaded guilty to illegal possession of a firearm and to threatening the two women with the firearm. This kind of thing is handled differently upstate than it is in the city. Upstate they take crime a good deal more seriously. Crime is wrong to people upstate. There are no excuses for it. They don't look for excuses for it.

Vogel was sentenced to a term of imprisonment in Attica.

It was lucky for me that he pleaded guilty and went to prison. If he hadn't, he might well have sued me for shooting him. Sure, I'd have won the case—probably—but I'd have had to pay lawyers a fortune to defend me. The City of New York would not have paid for my defense, because the incident occurred outside the city. The state would not have paid for it. In essence, during the time a lawsuit was pending I would have had to worry if next month, next year there would be a roof over my family's head. If for no other reason, the threat of being sued, rightly or wrongly, tells a police officer not to use his gun unless he absolutely has to.

To finish the story of Vogel, he arrived in Attica just in time for the Attica prison riot. His fellow convicts killed him. Why, I don't know. He was nothing but a drug-dealing punk, and I doubt he was any kind of leader.

The point I want to make here is that the hardest thing anybody has to do in police work is to shoot somebody. It is not easy. I don't care who you are in this job, nobody comes to work expecting a gunfight. If they did, they'd take the day off. You anticipate situations where this might occur, but nobody says it's going to happen ahead of time. Again, if you knew you were going to be involved in something like that, you wouldn't want to go to work. It's a tough, tough deal.

A lot of people think cops are gun-happy, that they get some kind of thrill out of shooting people. It isn't that way. I've never known a police officer who wasn't shaken after he'd shot a person, particularly if the person died. You don't shoot somebody unless you or somebody else is being threatened, so you are scared. You know you are going to be closely questioned as to whether you really had to do it. You know some of the questioning is likely to be unfair—vengeful, in fact, by people who will try to hang all kinds of motives on you: motives you never had and never thought of.

I've had to use my gun in the course of my work. It's the last thing in the world I want to do, and I don't know any cop who feels otherwise.

# ■● 13

## THE BROOKLYN BRIDGE SET

FEBRUARY 27, 1994, WAS THE first day of what proved to be an exceptionally interesting set. A set is a four-day work chart. The first two tours of duty are nine-hour night tours, usually beginning at 4:00 P.M. and ending at 1:00 A.M. The second two are eight-hour day tours, beginning at 8:00 A.M. and ending at 4:00 P.M. After a set, we have a two-day break before another set begins.

The break between the second and third tours is just seven hours. Assuming I am able to get away at 1:00 A.M., which is often not the case, I go home and get to bed about two-thirty. I get up at six. We have a dormitory room in the precinct station, with showers and lockers and so on, but I'd rather get three hours of good sleep than five hours of bad.

This set turned out to be very busy.

Near the end of my first tour we got a call about a girl in the Bronx who said she had some information about a homicide we were working on that had occurred in the Two-five Precinct. Her life had been threatened, and she had run into a Bronx precinct house. She wanted to get out of town. A detective named Brian Speer and I went up there to interview her, and we talked with her for about three hours. It was five o'clock before we finished that tour.

Incidentally, what happened in that case was that we arranged for the girl to be put aboard an early-morning flight to Florida, which was where she wanted to go, to be out of New York and with her family. As I've said, New York does not have a witness-protection program, but she was an important witness in a developing murder case against a Latino gang, and the district attorney paid for her airfare to Florida. It was cheaper to send her there than to try to maintain protection for her in the city.

I came back to work at four the same afternoon for another night tour. I went to the Two-five and worked with Spear in developing the information the girl had given us. About eight o'clock I got a call from the Manhattan Detective Borough dispatcher. I was informed that a hostage negotiator was needed in the Nineteenth Precinct.

The information was that a woman in a seventeenth-floor apartment had fired shots at officers responding to a 911 call. She was apparently an EDP—emotionally disturbed person—and it was uncertain whether she had hostages inside her apartment. The site was a high-rise building of luxury apartments on the Upper East Side.

Because my office is in the Two-five and I was there when I got the call, I could go to my locker for my Point Blank vest and a windbreaker with HOSTAGE NEGOTIATOR printed on it. I then went to the address, and the building security officer directed me to the frozen zone—that is, an area where no one is admitted without a heavy vest.

I learned what had happened so far. The woman—we'll call her Peggy—had begun screaming, throwing things around in the apartment, and yelling she was going to kill herself. A neighbor called 911. Two officers came to her door and identified themselves as police. At that point she fired four shots at the door. None of the shots had penetrated the steel door. They had made bumps on it but none had come all the way through.

The officers sent out a radio call: "shots fired." When that call goes out on the radio, officers at a scene like this will have all the help they need within five minutes. Additional officers and a supervisor will appear, then probably a captain. The captain will evaluate the situation and determine what services are needed.

Usually in a situation like this the captain will call for negotiators and for an Emergency Services Unit, which is a tactical unit equipped with all the tools necessary to save lives or mount an assault—including jaws of life, battering rams, mirrors on long poles that enable them to look in windows, rifles, shotguns, and so on. They even have a robot equipped with a television camera and a shotgun that can search a premises without risking the life of an officer. The Emergency Services Unit also functions as a Rescue Unit—to stop people who want to jump off bridges, for example. The Technical Assistance Resources Unit (TARU)—the guys who rewire the telephones at a crime scene, drill holes and put probes through walls, and so on—will also respond.

We had learned that the apartment was the home of a man in his eighties, living with a companion who was in her seventies, and we feared that these two people were being held hostage.

The responding Emergency Services officers had established the frozen zone, ordered the doorknob tied so that the door could not be opened from inside, had ordered a ballistic shield set up in the hall, and were preparing ballistic blankets to be lowered over the windows. Ballistic blankets are made of a material that will smother bullets, so the EDP or hostage holder cannot fire out the windows at the crowd that invariably gathers. They were lowered from the windows of the apartment above. Of course they do present a problem. We can't see in either.

In this instance we did not have to evacuate the apartments above and below, because it was a relatively new building with concrete floors. We did evacuate the adjacent apartments on the same floor, because shots could have penetrated plaster walls.

Officers were able to bring to the scene a number of people who knew the woman and her father, some of them people she had called after she went bonkers and caused the 911 alarm. They were assembled on the fifteenth floor and interviewed. The information obtained from them was sent up to me, the negotiator.

The woman who had fired the shots was the daughter of the elderly man who lived in the apartment. She did not live there with him and his companion. A woman in her late thirties, she came to visit them only occasionally.

The information friends and family can give you often proves very useful. For example, I learned that I should not talk about the woman's ex-husband. That would drive her into a fury. On the other hand, I could talk about her father, saying things like "Look, you love your father, so why do you want to do a thing like this to him?"

I established initial contact with Peggy by yelling through the door. Then I told her I was going to call her on the phone and she should answer and talk to me. TARU had rewired the telephones so that I could talk to her that way. The telephones are wired into speakers so that everyone involved in the effort can hear both sides of the conversation. Also, every word is tape-recorded. We set up a "war room," so to speak, in another apartment, and the phones were wired into there.

We could, if we wanted to, let Peggy make a call and talk to someone else, but the conversation went through our speakers and would be heard by all of us.

With the assistance of TARU we control the phones in a hostage site; also the lights, the heat, the air conditioning, and whatever.

Our temporary headquarters was the home of an elderly lady who extended every possible cooperation, including offering coffee, tea, and candy to the many officers in her studio apartment. We offered to move her to a quiet, comfortable place, but she was fascinated with what we were doing and wanted to stay and watch. She sat up all night, watching and listening.

Peggy was on an emotional roller coaster. She was up, she was down, then up again, then down again. If I said one wrong word to her she would go into hysterics, saying she was going to kill herself. She also said she wanted to kill police officers. Then I'd reason with her, and she would calm down and say of course she wouldn't shoot police officers. A minute later she might be saying she wanted to kill cops.

I told her my name, and after that she called me Tom. If she spoke my name once, she spoke it a thousand times:

"Tom, where are you? Tom, why aren't you talking to me? Tom, don't let cops come through this door, or I'll kill them." The fact is, the woman was begging for understanding.

For a long time we could not ascertain whether her father and his friend were in the apartment—or if she had killed them. I asked her to put her father on the phone, and she refused. I asked her to put his friend on the phone, and she refused. Whenever I asked her about her father and his companion, she would say, "They're fine. There's no problem."

I asked her if she was in the care of a doctor, and she said yes but she would not talk to him. I pursued that. Eventually she gave me the name of a doctor, and we called him. He didn't want to talk to her, saying he hadn't seen her in two years. He was a regular medical doctor, not a psychiatrist, but he said she was not emotionally stable. So far as he knew, she had not seen a psychiatrist.

We learned that she had recently split with her husband.

Peggy was an EDP but she was a hostage taker too. She had gone off the deep end while she was in an apartment with two other people and would not let them out. *And* she had a gun. We wanted to get her out of there alive and get her to a hospital. More than that, we wanted to save the lives of the two elderly people who were in the apartment with her—assuming they were still alive.

A little after midnight, a female negotiator by the name of Rafaella Valdez arrived. Ralphie, as we call her, is a specialist in hostage negotiation. She trains other negotiators. I am a homicide detective, doing negotiations when necessary; but Ralphie does nothing else and does them anywhere in the city. She is an attractive Hispanic black woman. I don't know what kind of detective she is, but I do know she is one hell of a negotiator.

I introduced her to Peggy. I said I had to go away for a short time and that she should talk to Detective Rafaella Valdez and could call her Ralphie.

I had been talking to Peggy for almost five hours, and now Ralphie talked to her for an hour and a half. But in time it began to appear that Peggy had placed her trust in me and wanted to talk to me again.

While Ralphie was talking to Peggy, we decided we would have to enter the apartment by force. Peggy was not coming down, she was not going to sleep, and we still didn't know if her father and his friend were alive.

At one point when Ralphie was talking with Peggy, a classic exchange took place, something like this:

"Okay, I won't kill cops. I'd rather jump out the window."

"Listen to me. You're up seventeen floors. If you jump, you're going to shit your pants on the way down, and that shit is going to be spread all over Second Avenue."

"You're right. I'd rather shoot the cops."

I shook my head and said to Ralphie, "Hey, that's really great! Now she's gonna shoot cops again. How about if you be the first one through the door?" We had a good laugh.

One of Peggy's lines was that we were not the police. She said we kept telling her we were the police but she knew we had been sent by her ex-husband to kill her. We asked her to call 911 and get confirmation that we were the police. She wouldn't do it.

Having decided we would have to go in by force, the first thing we wanted was to get a better look in. We began to unscrew the peephole device from the door. She saw that immediately, went into a rage, and demanded to know what we were doing. I told her we had put tape over her peephole so she couldn't see out, and now we were trying to take it off so she could see we were the police—only somebody had put it on with Krazy Glue and we couldn't get it off, so we were unscrewing the peephole. "You said you wanted to look out, so now you can look out."

She cursed and yelled and hung up—as she had done several times before.

We got the peephole open, and we could see Peggy and she could see us—though we didn't dare put our eyes to the peephole, for fear she would shoot us.

About two in the morning, I called again. This time Peggy didn't answer. Her father's friend did. I could hear Peggy screaming in the background, "Don't answer that phone!"

The elderly woman said she was okay and that Peggy's father was okay. Then she asked, "Why are you doing this to us?" I told her we were there to bring Peggy the help she needed. The woman said Peggy didn't need help, she was just a little upset. I asked to speak to Peggy's father. I wanted him to talk her into giving up the gun and coming out. His response was that Peggy had done nothing wrong and that the whole scene was our fault.

Now I felt I understood what the situation was. Peggy was a spoiled brat who always had her father's sympathy, no matter what she did. Her husband had left her, and she had run screaming to Daddy. So far as Daddy was concerned, she had done nothing wrong when she fired four shots at the door when the first officers on the scene were just outside.

Peggy began to yell that she wanted to speak to me, and he handed her the phone. I said to her, "Your father and his friend seem like nice people. Why do you want to put them through this hell?" She screeched at me to go fuck myself and hung up again.

At this time we had to rethink the situation. We talked it over. It looked as if the two elderly people were in no great danger from Peggy. The decision to enter an apartment cannot be made by any officer or detective. That decision is made by a chief, usually the borough chief.

Around two o'clock the chief of patrol, Louis Anamone, had arrived. He had been listening to the negotiations. He asked everybody's opinion. He asked for my opinion. I told him she was not going to come out, was not going to let us in, and was not going to go to sleep. She had as many as fifty cops tied up. It was a quarter to five, and we had Second Avenue shut down. He then made the decision to enter by force. How to do it, he left to Emergency Services.

I called Peggy on the phone. I told her to come to the door.

I wanted her to look through the peephole and see the police outside. At this point Emergency Services broke her rear window by hitting the glass with long pipes from the apartment above.

When she heard the glass break, Peggy ran to the rear of the apartment.

We were ready to force the door. A machine for that purpose was in place. It works by applying extreme air pressure to the door. With Peggy in the rear of the apartment, the machine was activated, the lock popped, and the door swung open.

Emergency Services officers entered, tackled Peggy, and subdued her.

She was strapped to a gurney. She asked to talk to me. I spoke to her, told her I was Tom, and assured her that she was going to be all right. "Tom, don't let them hurt me," she pleaded.

She was taken to a hospital. So were the two elderly people, for a checkup.

Peggy's father's apartment was a mess. She had broken it up.

When we were finished and left, TARU replaced everything in the apartment we had used as temporary headquarters, so that things were the way they had been when we first entered—except that we had eaten all the woman's candy.

On March 1, 1994, I was doing the 8:00 A.M. to 4:00 P.M. tour. Other detectives were out working on various cases, and I was in the office catching whatever might come in. About eight-thirty I got a call that a dead woman had been found in Central Park at 76th Street. I drove over there. The corpse was that of a black female who appeared to have been dead about two days. Her pants were down. She had no apparent wounds—no gunshot wounds, no stab wounds, no apparent sign of strangulation. I surmised that she had simply gone into the park to relieve herself. It is not unusual for a person with a weak heart to suffer a heart attack during a bowel movement. We found no identification on her and tentatively concluded she was a homeless person.

On the other hand, we could not come to any conclusion until the medical examiner had seen her.

While I was doing some paperwork on this matter, I got a page on my beeper. I called in and was told to go immediately to the Seventh Precinct in Manhattan. I asked what the situation was. It was this.

The Lubavitcher Rebbe, Menachem Mendel Schneerson, had undergone eye surgery at Manhattan Ear and Eye Hospital. Many Hasidic Jews had gone to the hospital to pray for the recovery of their religious leader. Among these was a group of Hasidic rabbinical students, who had traveled from Lubavitcher headquarters in Brooklyn to Manhattan. These students had traveled in a van. As they crossed the Brooklyn Bridge, their van was suddenly attacked by a gunman, armed with automatic weapons, who fired volleys of shots into it. Two of the students were critically injured, and one later died.

Detectives from all over Manhattan were called to the scene. At the Seventh, which I reached about eleven o'clock, I waited for my partners Bill Kelly and Tom Sullivan and the rest of the team from Manhattan North Homicide to arrive.

I don't have to say that this was a major investigation.

Many calls came in, from all kinds of people, ranging from honest citizens to nuts, saying they could identify the shooter. Of course, we had to check all these out. In cases like this you have to face the fact, however, that well-meaning people think they see things they didn't really see.

At one point Sullivan and I went to Newark Airport to talk to a man who was booked on a flight to Jordan. He was entirely innocent, but we had to check.

Eventually, the supervisors recommended that we be divided into two groups, that some of us stay on the case as the night went on and some of us go home and rest, to pick it up in the morning. This recommendation was acted on, and our group from Manhattan North Homicide was told to stay on until eight o'clock the next morning. We expected to be working twelve-hour tours for a while.

For us, this became a twenty-four-hour tour. It happens.

About eleven o'clock Lieutenant Frank Rahill told us that an informant had identified the vehicle used in the shooting as a car belonging to Pioneer Car Service on Van Brunt Street in Brooklyn. The informant was Amir Abudaif, an Egyptian immigrant who worked as a garage mechanic in a shop in Red Hook, Brooklyn. He had not only identified the car but also the shooter, who was a longtime customer. The shooter had brought the car to the shop and demanded that Abudaif fix the brakes. He told the mechanic he had just "killed four Jews on the Brooklyn Bridge." When Abudaif told him there was nothing wrong with the brakes, the shooter pulled a gun on him and threatened to kill him if he didn't fix the brakes. Abudaif had tried to give this information to the FBI, but they had brushed him off, apparently not taking him seriously. He had then walked into the Six-two precinct station in Bensonhurst to give his information. There a civilian employee treated him the same way the FBI had. Fortunately, a young officer overhead, intervened, and took the man upstairs to see detectives.

Abudaif actually had found a bullet in the car door and turned it over to the detectives.

We were given the name and address of the car service but

not the name of the shooter identified by Abudaif. We don't communicate the names of suspects by radio. Our assignment was to set up surveillance of the Pioneer Car Service.

We went in two cars, Tommy Sullivan and I in one, Tom McCabe and Bill Kelly in the other.

First we set up surveillance of Pioneer Car Service. Kelly and McCabe parked two and a half blocks south of it, and Sullivan and I set up the same distance north. Once Kelly and McCabe confirmed that they had the location under observation, Sullivan and I did a grid search of the area. We knew we were looking for a blue Chevrolet, and we had the plate numbers. We searched all the nearby streets—except those within one block of the car service, because we didn't want to be conspicuous. The industrial character of the neighborhood was such that we *would* have been conspicuous if we had not been careful. That is, it was quiet at that time of night with minimal pedestrian and vehicle traffic.

Sullivan and I returned to our surveillance point two and a half blocks north of the car service. There was unusual pedestrian traffic in and out of the place. Fifteen or twenty people went in or came out in the two hours or so that we watched. If we hadn't known it was a car service, we might have thought this amount of activity indicated a drug location.

It was a chilly morning, and our job for the moment was to wait and watch. We talked. A lot of thoughts were going through our minds. Our primary thought was that we were involved in a major investigation that could go on for a long, long time. Another thought: We might be ordered to work on St. Patrick's Day—and Tommy Sullivan is head of the New York City Emerald Society Pipe Band. (He is the soloist bagpiper who plays "Amazing Grace" at all police funerals.) I've been in major investigations—the Jogger case, the Penn Station sniper case, and the Yeshiva University shootings—

and, believe me, I've had enough of them. I'd rather do my
regular tours of duty and handle the routine homicides. We
had another thought—that we were looking for a man who
had sprayed gunfire into a van on the Brooklyn Bridge, who
may have acted alone or with others.

As we sat there we observed a male with a dark complex-
ion, maybe Hispanic, maybe Arab, leaving the car service.
He walked up Van Brunt and passed us. A little later he return to the car service, again walking by us. After twenty
minutes or so, he did the same thing. Each time he passed us
he gave us a long, hard look. I don't know if he realized we
were cops. God knows what he thought. Two men sitting in a
car on the street in that neighborhood at two in the morning
is very unusual.

Then we received a radio call: "Empire base to empire
units. Enter and secure the premises you have under observation." The code-word "empire" referred to various teams
watching several places in Brooklyn. My immediate thought
was "Holy shit, I don't have my vest." When we entered the
car service, we had to go in fast and take control of the situation immediately—and we didn't know who might be in
there. What's more, we didn't have a floor plan. It was an
unnerving situation.

The steadying factor was that Sullivan, Kelly, McCabe,
and I had over a hundred years of police experience among
us, and we had worked together for eight years. We didn't
have a plan for entering this place, but we could be confident
that each man knew what he had to do.

I drove the two and a half blocks to Pioneer Car Service,
where we met Kelly and McCabe in the other car. We left the
cars, with our guns drawn, and ran into the storefront, yelling "Police! Don't move!" Kelly went in first, then McCabe,
then Sullivan, and I was the fourth one in.

There was a dispatcher's desk to the right, equipped with the radio used to send cars to pick up passengers. A female sat behind that desk. To the left was a couch where three males sat. Another male stood to the right, in front of the dispatcher's desk. To the rear was a long, dark hallway. Kelly immediately started down that hallway. McCabe went halfway down the hallway and stopped where he could see Kelly and Sullivan in the rear and me in the front, ready to offer support to any of us. Sullivan passed him to join Kelly. I stopped and ordered the three young men on the couch to move to the dispatcher's desk—all the while yelling at them to keep their hands where I could see them.

The situation was a little hairy, not heavy hairy, just a little hairy. We had seen so many people going in and out that we had expected ten or more people to be in the storefront. It turned out there were just five.

I asked the girl behind the desk who she was, and she said she was the dispatcher. I asked her who the others were, and she pointed to one of the young men and identified him as her boyfriend. She identified two others as his friends. She said the fourth man was one of the car-service drivers.

I asked the driver for identification. He gave me his driver's license, which told me he was Rashid Baz, who lived in Brooklyn. I told him to sit down, and he did. He asked me to return his license because he had to go pick up a car. I told him to relax, we'd have everything under control in about ten minutes.

We waited for a backup to come. We had gone in there blind, not knowing exactly what we would find. We had the situation under control, but we needed more information. In about ten minutes a Brooklyn detective named Brown arrived. He asked what we had here, and I identified the various individuals for him.

The owner was not on the premises. The dispatcher said she did not know his address by number but could take us there.

At this point I told Brown that the dispatcher had been calling Rashid Baz by the nickname Ray. Immediately he grabbed the man, put him against the wall, and began to search him. I asked what was going on, and he said, "Ray is the shooter!" Ray was the name by which Abudaif had known Baz and the name he had given to Brooklyn detectives.

That we had caught Baz in the car-service storefront was the luck of the Irish. If we had arrived five minutes sooner, he would not have been there. If we had arrived five minutes later, he would not have been there. What's more, if he had been a religious zealot and still had a gun on him, he would almost certainly have pulled it and fired, rather than submit to arrest.

Brown took Baz out and put him in a car driven by another Brooklyn detective. At that point a car pulled up and out got the man who had walked past Sullivan and me and given us the hard looks. One of the Brooklyn detectives identified him. He was the owner of the car service, Bassan. We took him in our car.

The first thing we asked him was where was the car Baz had been driving. Right around the corner, he said. And, sure enough, there it was. It was parked on one of the blocks we had not done in the grid search because it was too near the car service. There it sat, the blue Chevy we were looking for—shot-out windows and all. It also had bullet holes in the doors. Shots had been fired from inside the car, right through the sheet metal. We called for a uniformed unit to come and take charge of it, and then we called for a Crime Scene Unit to come and take pictures of it, take fingerprints off it, and so on.

We took Bassan to the Seventh Precinct in Manhattan, in through the basement because there was a tremendous amount of press outside. For an hour or so we let him sit in a room, watched by a detective, and didn't say anything to him. We didn't want to question him until we knew more than we did. We knew he owned the car used in the shooting, but we didn't know if he had anything to do with it. You don't interrogate in the dark, bumbling around. The person you are questioning will pick up on that. It is better to wait until you know something concrete.

We got a rundown on him, and two of us went in to talk to him. I started in the usual way, something like this:

"I'm Detective Tom McKenna. This is Detective Tommy O'Sullivan. We're trying to figure out what happened with your car today. We know it was used in the shooting on the Brooklyn Bridge. Two young men are probably going to die. Is this your shit or somebody else's shit? If it's not yours, why do you want to make it yours? Think about it. We'll be back in five minutes to talk some more."

This is a common ploy. We let them think about it. A negative statement or a positive statement will lock them in, so that if facts prove different it works against them.

We let him have more like forty-five minutes, then went back in. At first he said that Ray had told him he'd had a fight with some guys who'd broken his windshield. We said, "C'mon, don't feed us that. We saw the car. You saw the car. It's got bullet holes in it." He said he didn't know anything about the bullet holes. We asked him who had taken the car to the garage to have the bullet holes covered and the glass replaced. He said Ray had done that. Anyway, the man at the garage said he couldn't do that kind of work.

Bassan then said he'd driven Ray home. Ray was carrying a heavy blue bag. We would later learn that the contents of that bag were two 9 mm pistols and a street sweeper—a semiautomatic shotgun capable of firing a dozen or more shotgun shells in rapid succession, which sweeps the street where it is fired, one way or another.

We questioned him for several hours. He kept changing his story. Eventually he committed his statement to writing.

Within twenty-four hours after the shooting on the Brooklyn Bridge we had a suspect in custody. I testified at his trial and he was convicted.

The arrest of Rashid Baz was good police work but not brilliant. We had amazing luck, first in the informant Amir Abudaif, who not only heard the suspect say he had killed Jews on the bridge but then persisted in trying to get his information to law-enforcement people even after being rebuffed. He was given credit at the time of the arrest, but he should have more. We were lucky also to have found Rashid Baz in the Pioneer Car Service office.

I have to think of the case this way: Rashid Baz is Lebanese. The victims of his crime were Hasidic Jews. The informant who brought the case to quick justice is Egyptian. The new mayor who laid so much emphasis on law and order and a better quality of life in the city is Italian. The four detectives who laid hands on Baz are all Irish. That's what the Irish do in New York, isn't it? Enforce the law. We are lucky we are not as nearly alone in that as we once were. Hispanics, blacks, and others have joined forces to fight the good fight in the streets of the city.

So ended a set. I got twenty hours of overtime. It was not a typical set, still it wasn't terribly unusual either. Now I could go home and be with my family and get some sleep. Two days later, another set.

# ◗ 14

## YOU THINK WE FELL OFF A TURNIP TRUCK?

THE INVESTIGATION INTO THE DEATH of Mrs. Kim Stapleton illustrates about as well as any case I've ever taken part in just how the New York Police Department really works.

At about 12:40 P.M. on Wednesday, January 10, 1990, Mrs. Kim Stapleton was standing on the northwest corner of Park Avenue and 92nd Street, waiting to cross the street. Mrs. Stapleton was sixty years old. She was a sister-in-law of the actress Jean Stapleton, who was probably best known for her role as Edith in *All in the Family*. As Mrs. Stapleton stood on the corner, a dark-colored van came along. As it pulled up near her, a hand reached out from the passenger side and made a grab for her shoulder bag. She did not or could not let go of her bag, and the man in the van did not let go. As the van sped away, Mrs. Stapleton was dragged some fifty feet along the street. When the bag finally came loose from her, Mrs. Stapleton fell under the van and was run over by the rear right wheel. She died of her injuries.

This was a case for Manhattan North Homicide, and our B Team responded, under the supervision of Sergeant T. J. O'Connor. Jack Freck and Mike Sheehan were included in that team. These detectives did the preliminary investigation, which included interview of witnesses and canvass of the neighborhood. The duty of notifying Mrs. Stapleton's next of kin also fell on that team—which is always a tough thing to do.

One of the problems you always have is that different witnesses see different things. A number of people had seen what happened, but they didn't even agree on the color of the van.

Even so, there was one good witness.

Our guys interviewed a man who had been in a car behind and had seen the van run over Mrs. Stapleton. The driver of the van had turned right on 91st Street, and the man had kept up behind him in his car. When the van stopped for a light at Madison Avenue, the witness pulled up alongside, rolled down his window, and yelled at the driver of the van that he had hit a lady. The man didn't know exactly what had happened, but he knew the van had hit a lady. He saw that the driver was a young Hispanic.

When the light changed, the van turned right and proceeded north on Madison Avenue. The witness followed, but the van blew a traffic light and got away.

The witness would prove an important part of the case when we had identified the man he had seen and had him in custody.

I had been off duty when the homicide occurred and became involved in the case two days later, when in early evening I received a telephone call from the commanding officer of the Nineteenth Precinct Detective Squad, Lieutenant Pat Barry. Pat Barry had been a homicide detective and a hostage negotiator, and I've described how he and I worked together in a laundromat hostage situation.

Lieutenant Barry told me that a young woman in custody in Brooklyn said she had information about the Kim Stapleton homicide and wanted to talk to someone. Her name was Mildred Salas. He was going to Brooklyn to interview her and wanted someone from Homicide to go with him.

I suggested to Lieutenant Barry that he get on the phone to Brooklyn and see if he couldn't stop the processing of this young woman until we could interview her. Once she got into court a lawyer would be appointed for her, and the lawyer undoubtedly would tell her to say nothing. The lawyer would want to make a deal for her, contingent on her giving the police her information, and it might be hours or even days before we could interview her.

I remember arriving at the courthouse about eight o'clock. Lieutenant Barry's call had succeeded in delaying Millie's processing. Her case was being held up until we could interview her. I found her waiting in a hall outside a courtroom.

Millie Salas was a young Hispanic woman in her early twenties. It was easy to see she had been—and maybe could be again—an attractive girl, but she was obviously addicted. She had all the marks of a person whose life is being destroyed by crack. She was cuffed behind her back. She wore filthy clothes, and you could tell from the smell off her that she hadn't had a bath in weeks. She was about as forlorn a person as I have ever seen.

She told me she had been in the Central Booking holding pen most of the day, and there she had encountered a man she knew. His street name was Cano, and he had told her he was involved in the Stapleton homicide. It isn't unusual for someone involved in a case that has been covered on television and in the newspapers to brag to someone he thinks he can trust that he was involved in that crime.

She knew Cano only as a dealer and user. They had done drugs together. He was being held on a minor charge and was released.

Millie was about as down and out as a person can get, and you may wonder where she got the money to buy crack. I don't know where she got it, or how, but I know how many young women get their drugs. They give sex for it. Any kind of sex. Not always to dealers. A user who has been lucky enough to get his hands on fifteen cracks will give five of them, or ten, to an addicted girl who absolutely degrades herself to pay him. It is worse than prostitution, because every transaction brings the girl closer to death.

Millie knew Cano lived in the Brooklyn neighborhood where she lived. She thought he probably lived on Jefferson Street. That was in the Eight-three Precinct, basically in the heart of Brooklyn.

Millie was being held on a bench warrant, which is a warrant issued for the arrest of a person who has skipped bail or otherwise failed to appear in court. The charge against her was that she had been found riding in a stolen car—which, frankly, is a way of life in the part of town where she came from, and the charge was no big deal. We wanted the warrant vacated. What we wanted to do was flush Millie out of the system so we could use her as a witness. Ideally, we wanted her arraigned on the charge against her and released without bail. Then we could get her cleaned up, put her in a hotel room in the custody of a couple of female detectives, get her clean so far as crack in her system was concerned, interview her more, get her statement, ride her around through the streets looking for Cano, and so on. Unfortunately, the young assistant district attorney working the case felt she had no authority to ask the court to vacate the warrant. So Millie wound up on Riker's Island.

Getting ahead here a little bit, the next day the Manhattan district attorney talked to the Brooklyn district attorney, and we were able to get Millie out, put her in a hotel, and all the rest of it.

Lieutenant Barry and I went to the Eight-three to talk to the precinct detectives. We went directly upstairs to the squad room and found it empty. All the detectives were at that time out on investigations.

We sat down to wait. We made some calls to Manhattan to report where we were and that we had identified a suspect in the Stapleton case, at least by his street name. The lieutenant called the Nineteen. I called Manhattan North Homicide.

Sometimes important things break on stupid, silly things. I was sitting at a desk, just waiting, looking around, seeing everything and nothing. Suddenly my eye is caught by a notice with the picture of a guy and saying "Wanted for Attempted Murder of a Police Officer." It gave the name of the wanted man as Angel Hernandez, 180 Jefferson Street, Brooklyn. He was wanted for attempting to murder a police officer the night before. At the end of the notice were the words, "AKA Cano." Holy . . . !

Could I believe this? According to Millie Salas, the man who killed Kim Stapleton was called Cano, and she thought he lived on Jefferson Street in Brooklyn. The man we wanted to question for murder was wanted by Queens Central Robbery for attempting to murder one of their detectives! The murder of Mrs. Stapleton had happened on Wednesday afternoon; the attempted murder of a detective had happened Thursday of the following week; and this was only Friday. In that period of time, several more drive-by purse-snatchings had occurred. If this all worked out to be true, Cano really got around!

I got on the phone and called Queens Central Robbery. I got a detective on the line and asked what was the deal with Cano. They said he was a car thief. He stole cars, then drove around snatching women's purses. They had him positively identified in one such robbery.

At this point I started licking my chops. This was too good

to be true! We had a street name and an address that matched what Millie had told us. We had an MO that matched what had happened in the Stapleton case. And besides that, the suspect was also wanted for trying to kill a cop!

Queens Central Robbery said that detectives had confronted Cano in a stolen car on the night of Thursday, January 11. They had a warrant for him, and they approached the car. The detectives had no idea they were approaching the man who had been driving the van that killed Mrs. Stapleton. But Cano knew he had driven the van, and he supposed they might want him for homicide.

So he decided to lock the doors. He locked the doors, and they couldn't get in. They pulled their guns and began yelling at him to get out, but he is very street-smart, and he knew these cops were not going to shoot him. It is strictly against department policy to fire a gun in these circumstances. In the first place, we're not supposed to shoot cars. Too much danger of ricochet. Besides, Cano hadn't shown a gun. He might be unarmed.

It has been suggested that in a situation like that one of the detectives could simply have knelt down, put his gun to one of the car's tires, and BOOM—car's disabled. But that also is against policy. It really would make a risk of somebody innocent getting hurt.

So anyway, one of the detectives cracked the window. He was going to break out that window and reach in and pull this guy out of the car.

But Cano realized these cops hadn't pulled a car across in front of him to block him. So he decided to hell with this, I'll scram. He jammed the car into gear and took off. But in doing that, he hit the detective and knocked him up on the hood.

Now he's barreling along the street with the cop on the

hood of the car. He flipped the steering wheel back and forth, trying to shake him off; and when that didn't work, he jammed on the brakes.

The detective was injured. He had broken bones. And Cano was flying.

Queens Central Robbery wanted Cano—Angel Hernandez—for sure. But they worked a Monday-through-Friday week and had weekends off. I advised Queens Robbery that detectives from Manhattan North Homicide and the Nineteen Squad would be coming over in force to look for Cano. Queens Robbery called six or eight of its guys and told them to work the weekend—on overtime.

This was a high-profile case. There had been a series of purse-snatchings from cars and vans, and the news media were full of it. In fact, Cano and his accomplice had done most of them. Besides, this case involved an injury to a cop. It was never going to go on the back burner.

For a month our squad spent every tour looking for Cano. One of the first things we did was take Millie Salas around in a van with tinted windows. We drove around with her for a week, and she pointed out drug dealers and drug spots and people she thought were friends of Cano. Sometimes we let her out on the street. When we did, we had to follow her closely. She had been free of crack since her arrest, but she had an overpowering hunger for it. No matter what risk she had to take, she would take it for a lump of crack. We did not lose her, and she proved to be a helpful witness. In fact, I should say she was entirely cooperative.

We checked Cano's arrest record and got the names of people who had been arrested with him. We put together a good list of all the people who'd been associated with him. Then we began to go see those people.

The day team went out to Brooklyn; then the night team

went out. We went to his home, to the homes of his friends, to drug spots—anywhere he might be found. We made repeated visits, many of them in the small hours of the morning. We'd knock on the door at 4:00 A.M. and ask for Cano. They'd say he wasn't there. We'd say sorry to bother you, and we'd leave. A night or so later we'd knock on the door again. We made these people miserable. The idea was that sooner or later one of them would tell us where Cano was to get us off their backs.

In this respect, we were lucky to be working with Central Robbery. Each borough has a Central Robbery, and most precinct commands have a unit called RIP—Robbery Identification Program. Central Robbery in Queens and in Brooklyn constituted a tremendous manpower pool for this search. If we had a tip on Cano, we could call Central Robbery for that borough, they could send an order to the RIP unit in the precinct, and a team could go to look into it and maybe make an arrest. Homicide, in contrast, is not a big manpower pool. If you call Homicide, usually nobody is in, because all the detectives are out working on cases.

On February 14 at about three in the afternoon we got a call from Queens Central Robbery, which is located in the One-oh-nine in Flushing, that they had good reason to believe that our guy, Cano, was going to show up in Brooklyn at a fleabag hotel that afternoon. They asked that Bill Kelly and I come out to meet them in their office in the One-oh-nine.

It took us about forty minutes to get there, and when we arrived at the One-oh-nine we were told that a team had already gone to this hotel in the Eight-three Precinct, in fact exactly on the boundary between the Eight-three and the Eight-one. The Eight-one RIP was responding.

Cano, they had been told, was in a room in the hotel. Bill

Kelly and I set out for the hotel. On the way we listened to the radio band used by Queens Robbery, and they were telling their units converging on the hotel not to move in until the guys from Manhattan North Homicide arrived. We got on their frequency and advised that we were on our way.

We found the location. As we pulled into the block, the radio advised that detectives were knocking on the door of the room where Cano was supposed to be.

We could get no closer than half a block. So many police cars surrounded the hotel that we couldn't get any closer. Bill Kelly and I got out and ran toward the hotel.

The hotel sat on a triangular lot where two streets met, and one of the narrow points faced us as we ran toward it.

Suddenly we saw a second-floor window open and legs come out the window.

Cops on the street started yelling at the guy, things like "Get back in! We're down here, and you can't get away! You're going to hurt yourself." And so on.

I remember one detective yelling at him "Hands up! Get your hands up!" If the guy had put his hands up, he'd have fallen to the pavement.

At that point hands came out the window, grabbed the guy, and pulled him back in.

Bill Kelly and I went upstairs. Sure enough, the guy was Cano—Angel Hernandez.

For a month we had made it rough for Cano's friends in Brooklyn, and it had paid off. One of them had called Queens Robbery with the tip that Cano would be in this hotel on the afternoon of February 14. What was he doing there? Well, the way it's usually said, he was shacking up. What was more, he had some crack in the room. He had gone there to relax, as you might say.

Queens Robbery took him to the One-oh-nine. They

wanted to put him in a lineup. They wanted him for drive-by purse-snatchings. We had to impress on Queens Robbery that the homicide charge took priority over everything else.

We called Lieutenant Barry at the Nineteenth and Lieutenant Jack Doyle, our boss, to tell him we had Cano at the One-oh-nine.

Kelly and I went into an interview room to talk to Cano. I was happier than I can tell you to find out that he spoke English. Trying to interview a suspect through an interpreter is worse than difficult.

Angel Hernandez, street name Cano, was a good-looking young Hispanic, not cocky but self-confident. As we would soon find out, he was sure he could not be charged with homicide and was in custody for what he figured were relatively minor crimes: auto theft and purse-snatching.

We expected an interview that might last five, six, seven, or eight hours and decided at first just to sit down and talk generally with Cano and not to press him until detectives arrived from the Nineteenth. We sat down with him and gave him his Miranda warnings. At this time I gave him our regular litany:

"Hey, man, you don't think all those cars surrounded the hotel because they knew you were in there with a woman who's not your wife? You didn't think all those cops came after you because you had a little crack in there? You think we fell off a turnip truck?"

I told him I wanted to talk to him about a drive-by purse-snatching that had occurred at 92nd Street and Park Avenue back in January. I told him we had people who had identified him as the man involved. He looked at Bill Kelly and me and said, "Yeah, I was there."

The way he saw it, he'd had nothing to do with killing Mrs. Stapleton. He admitted he had stolen the van. He'd felt the bump, he said, but he thought he'd hit the curb. He admitted he snatched purses. But the guy who had been with him was the one who had grabbed Mrs. Stapleton's shoulder bag and wouldn't let go, and *he* was responsible for her death.

Five minutes into the interview, he had told us what we wanted to know. Once more, we decided to hold things up until the detectives from the Nineteenth arrived.

While we talked, Cano told us some things about himself. First, he was a professional car thief. What was more, he was good at it. He told me there was only one make of car he couldn't break into and drive away within five seconds. He never took public transportation. He never walked any-where. If he wanted to go a block or two, he stole a car, drove it to where he wanted to go, and abandoned it. He stole two or three cars a day! I mean, this guy stole cars like I eat po-tato chips.

He was the consummate car thief. Whenever he saw a car he wanted, he stole it. If he didn't simply abandon it, he would drive it down to where he lived on Gates Avenue and sell parts off it. If a guy with a dented bumper came by, Cano would unscrew the bumper and sell it to him. If a guy wanted a tape deck, sold; Cano would take it out and sell it. He sold tail lights, headlights, engine parts, anything. He literally stripped cars on the street.

I asked him which car was most difficult to steal. He said Fords. He could steal a Ford okay, no problem. But it took twenty or thirty seconds to get into a Ford and get it on the road—which wasn't worth doing when he could steal an-other good-looking car sitting right behind it in five seconds.

"Ford builds good cars," he said—which made me tre-mendously happy, because I'd just bought a Ford. Cano made my day.

Another thing that came up was that I told him we knew of crimes he'd committed in Manhattan and Queens, so what had he done in Brooklyn? He looked at me as if I was completely crazy and said, "I never do anything in Brooklyn. I've never stolen a car in Brooklyn." I asked, "Why? Are the cars better quality in Queens?" Again he stared at me as if I couldn't understand anything and said, "Man, I *live* in Brooklyn."

When everybody got together, we decided to take Cano back to the Nineteenth Precinct for booking. He would be held there on the murder charge, and the Queens robbery cases would have to wait.

Back at the Nineteenth, Cano—Angel Hernandez—gave us a statement. He named the man who had grabbed Mrs. Stapleton's shoulder bag and caused her death. As we write this, the case of that individual remains in the courts. We will not mention his name. It took a long time to find him, so he is still awaiting trial.

Cano said that he and his friend had stolen the van the night before and had driven it to Manhattan the next day to use it for some drive-by purse-snatchings. He said he did not know they had killed Mrs. Stapleton. They had split up the money from her bag and had used much of it to buy crack. Only that night when they were high on crack did they see the story on television and realize they had killed the woman whose bag they had stolen.

Cano pleaded guilty to a reduced charge and was sentenced to fifteen years instead of the twenty-five he would have gotten on the murder charge.

His accomplice will go to trial, probably before this is published.

Millie Salas returned to the street, returned to her crack habit, and is a sorry case: a young woman whose life has been over for some years, because all she cares about is getting her next crack.

It was a sad case too. I never met Mr. or Mrs. Stapleton, but they were people who had led productive lives and were looking forward to a contented retirement. Mrs. Stapleton was the victim of sudden, senseless violence—of which we see far too much today, not just in New York but all over the country.

I tell the story of this case because it illustrates so effectively how criminal cases are resolved in the New York City system. The Stapleton case involved:

- The break: the crackhead young woman who was not particularly upset by the crime but figured she could possibly get an easier resolution with her own problem by cooperating with us. In fact, she did get help by cooperating with us. In the end it didn't do her any good, but that was her fault, not ours.

- Another break: Cano had run down a cop and was the subject of a flyer on the wall in the Eight-three. That was a stroke of luck. If we had come to the Eight-three the night before and his picture hadn't been there, who knows how long it might have taken us to identify him?

  Luck? Yes, luck. But, as the old saying goes, we make our own luck. Without the other elements, our luck would not have happened.

- Teamwork: the way the several forces in the three boroughs worked together. This is an absolutely essential element of police work, as I have emphasized before. That we found Millie was only partly luck. If Brooklyn hadn't called Lieutenant Barry to report what Millie was saying, we wouldn't have known about her.

- Hard work: the month-long, day-and-night search for Cano in Brooklyn. The pressure we applied to his associates ultimately resulted in the tip that located him in the hotel.

- Professionalism: the fact that our people know what they are doing and use the most effective methods.

I am deeply sorry we could not have *prevented* this crime and saved Mrs. Stapleton's life. Given the tragedy, we did, I believe, an effective job of police work—and I am proud to have been a part of it.